The Gunner Wore Petticoats

By

S.J. SCHINLEBER

Fideli
Publishing

For Nikki

who didn't make it into the last book
and was promised a place
in this one.

Thanks and Acknowledgements

As anyone who knows us will tell you, us will tell you, my husband and I are frequent public speakers, making presentations to schools and civic groups about the Civil War. Usually we dress up in the costumes of the time and act out the life story of one or other of our distant relatives or their friends, trying to show ordinary people living today how it might have felt to ordinary people living then to experience such cataclysmic events.

I wrote this story from that same perspective. Although the events and characters depicted here are as true to life as I could make them, and the details of uniform, equipment, and battle positions are as accurate as my readings have informed me, what follows is historical fiction. I am not trying to recreate any particular battle; rather, I want my readers to experience what it might have been like to have lived through such a battle, wearing those uniforms and carrying that weaponry. I strive in all my writing to be as historically accurate as possible; in the end, though, I am a novelist and what I write is fiction, no matter how realistic it purports to be.

This book could not have been written without the support, guidance and knowledge of my gun-wielding, tent-building companion on the battlefield, my husband, Ron, who introduced me to the reenacting world and to the American Civil War. You have changed my life forever and my appreciation of your love and concern for me grows every day. Without your support and guidance, this book would never have happened.

I would like to thank the reference librarians at the Northbrook Public Library for their unfailing support and generosity. David Nagle, Assistant Professor of German at Oklahoma Baptist University, was instrumental in researching the names of German settlers in the North Chicago area in the 1800s. Our dear friend, Northbrook paramedic/firefighter, Jim Richards, was very patient and exact in describing the wounds and likely consequences of various mishaps, mutilations and calamities visited upon the characters' all-too-human flesh. He was also far too complimentary about the efforts and abilities of yours truly, but I was energized by every word of encouragement and friendship. Similarly, Northbrook firefighter/paramedic, Hal Sanger, was alternately amused and horrified by the depredations visited upon the heroine's mother by this writer, but he gamely described the deterioration of her poor flesh as a result of having a very heavy object dropped upon her early in the novel. For his medical knowledge, sense of humor and faith in the writer, I am very grateful. For details on the Lutheran Ministry and of life on the northern plains at that time, I thank our dear friends ("mum and dad") Bernie and Jeannie Schmidt. With you in my lives, I am assured that many relatives and friends will read my book. Bernie will insist upon it! And I am very appreciative. For expert historical information, hugs and general support, I thank our friend, my fellow author, Judy Hughes, Chair of the Northbrook Historical Society.

For details of contemporaneous men's headgear and shirts, I turned to Dirty Billy's of Gettysburg, PA, from whom Ron and

I have purchased much of our civil war head gear and to whom I direct anyone who needs accurate information on these and other matters of costume.

In terms of source material, I have read widely in the area of civil war studies, but I am not aware of any particular source for anything that appears in my novel. In checking for technical accuracy, I turned to *Field Artillery Tactics 1864*, printed by New Market Battlefield Military Museum, copyright 1994. I also consulted *The Illustrated Directory of Uniforms, Weapons, and Equipment of The Civil War*, edited by David Miller and published by Salamander Books, London, copyright 2001. As a Civil War re-enactor, I am a proud member of Taylor's Battery, 1st Illinois Light Artillery, Company B. As you can read on our website, Taylor's Battery was organized early in the Civil War by Ezra Taylor as Company B, Chicago Light Artillery. The unit was accepted into Federal service in July 1861 and discharged in July of 1864. Along with our friends and fellow battery members, my husband Ron and I spend a lot of our free time pretending to be characters from that era. I have absorbed much of the atmosphere of camp and battlefield life from my experiences alongside my fellow battery members. Although the character and events in this story are purely fictional, I believe they grew from my own experiences out in the field. Throughout the novel, I tried to verify any technical information used, however, the mistakes and inaccuracies are entirely my own.

To my editor, Stacy Vailas, thank you for your on-going and enthusiastic support of my work and for being the first "stranger" to read and love my book. To my friend, the writer and historian, Jack Coombe, how can I ever thank you and Peg for the love and support you have shown a fellow writer. I only hope my efforts fulfill your confidence in me. And to my son-in-law, graphic designer Jason Grandt: this is my second book and the second book whose cover you have designed. How can I express my thanks for your talent and generosity? Finally, to my children, the ones I live with and the ones who live a ways away: thank you for believing in me, for tolerating my endless hours at the computer, and for understanding that to a writer, the characters in her head are as real, or more real, than the people in the outside world. Thanks for making room for all the others!

As a child growing up in England, I always imagined that I would lead a very different life from my mother and from my female peers. And indeed, I did just that. Looking back today, I see that reading English at university, spending a lifetime researching and teaching, and finally marrying and raising four wonderful children describes choices that are far more conventional than I might have imagined. But the world has changed so much and the possibilities set before *our* daughters are so much greater than those I imagined for myself and those are so much greater than those seized by my heroine. And yet, notwithstanding that the choices before them are greater, the fact remains that spunky women of all ages– and the men who support them– change our world every time they grasp or use the opportunities before them. This book is dedicated to their irrepressible drive

April 1861-March 1862

Chapter One

As I look back now on Rebekkah Reinhardt of Northfield Township, Illinois, I want to scream out a warning to that young girl I was so long ago. I want to warn about youthful arrogance and haste and blind faith that Providence will always shield the innocent. But life allows for no such second guessing. Full of pride and vitality, I strode forward that fateful March in 1861, convinced that I knew best and that no man, living or dead, could get the better of me.

We lived, my mother, two brothers and I, on the 160 acres my father, Ludwig, had purchased in 1835 when he arrived in this country aged 23. He had left Philadelphia with little more than $200 in his pocket and the fervent hope of a better life. Like many third sons before him, my father had left Germany determined to make his fortune in America. Over there, he thought, a young man with dreams and a strong back could make a life for himself and his family. During the dangerous Atlantic crossing, he became smitten by Anna Koch, a young Schwabian beauty traveling to America with her parents. By the time they docked in Philadelphia, they were man and wife.

A young German preacher, tired of the restrictions of the old country, married them on board ship. Once they docked, Anna said goodbye to her parents, and bravely set forth with the young stranger who became my father, to search for a farm and a few acres they could call their own. On the flat land Northwest of Chicago they found everything they dreamed of for $1.25 an acre. They staked everything they owned on that land, but their dreams of happiness were cut short.

The plot they bought was rich in trees and poor in top soil. Ludwig spent long days that first summer felling trees to build a one room cabin to shelter our mother, who was, by now, heavy with child. Eli, my older brother, was born in the spring of 1839. Two years later Nate followed him, and two years after that, myself. Despite the harsh conditions, we were, by all accounts, a happy young family. While mother attended to her growing family and to the increasing number of livestock, father busied himself planting and raising corn. First they bought Oscar, the plough horse. Next came our cow, Hedwig and then hens for fresh eggs. When it transpired I could not tolerate cow's milk, we acquired Grim, our goat.

At first, we had but the one room. Mother and father would sleep downstairs in the family room. And, as soon as we were able, the three of would climb the wooden ladder to the attic where we would talk and play and fight and finally lie down on the hay that for years was our only bedding.

In time father began adding rooms. First, he built a small room to the side of the kitchen where he said mother could tend to her weaving and sewing. Then, he added a larger room for the boys to sleep in. He said, as a girl, I needed to have my own room- although I never did figure out why. Next he built a small space for churning butter and storing milk jugs way from the summer heat. It had a floor lower than the rest of the house, so the milk would stay cool, even on days that would melt the butter right off your bread. Finally, he built a bedroom for me on the ground floor, next to my brothers' room. He always said the attic space would be for more children. But, the other children never came. And every year, my father seemed to age and grow more despondent about the future.

For me, though, it was a fine life. Every day I helped on the farm, preferring the plough and the saw to the butter churn and the hen coop. Every night after supper my brothers and I would practice our letters, while ma sewed a curtain for the windows, or a shirt for pa or a dress or a new apron for me. But to her eternal despair, I would never keep those fancy dresses on for long. Inevitably, I would quickly change into a pair of Nate's old workpants and set off for the fields chewing a straw, as happy as I could be.

"Rebekkah, how are you going to get yourself a young man dressed like that," mother would yell as I ran out the door. And I would always yell back, "Soon as I find one who can shoot as well as I can!" Truth be told, young men held no interest for me. I considered myself the equal of any of them, except perhaps my brothers. And, even so, I was taller than Nathan and fast catching up on Eli. I had been shooting since I was four years old, ever since the day Eli balanced a stock on a tree stump and showed me how to load a rifle. I hadn't practiced more than a week or two when my brothers saw I had a knack for it. Since then, most of the deer and rabbit that ended up on our table came from my shot, as did the duck and wild goose. As for cooking, I could skin a rabbit faster than most and cook it too. And it wasn't that I couldn't sew. I could do it well enough. It's just, I saw no need for it. Ma sewed anything we had a need for and any clothes I wanted, I got from Eli or Nate.

Our closest neighbor lived half a day's ride away and I didn't trouble to spend my time riding over there on account of a fancy ribbon or a fine piece of muslin. Women's talk was all about dresses and what they were wearing in Philadelphia and New York. Such talk made no sense to me since dresses didn't much belong on a farm and a new piece of ribbon was less useful than a bridle for the horse.

A few times every year, the neighbors came together to celebrate the harvest or to welcome Christmas. Sometimes, I tried to mingle with the other girls, but I found them foolish and lacking in purpose. I quickly tired of their talk about men and what they liked in this one, or that one. I told them I could not care less what a man liked, or didn't, and that few of them seemed to use the sense they were born with. None of the women liked me much after that- which was fine by me. I amused myself better without them and I preferred my own company, or that of a fine musket, any day.

One day during spring planting pa said he had to go into town and get some seed. I remember Ma gave him a strange look, but she stayed quiet and he just stared at her for a while and then off he went. He came back three days later, smelling of drink, and with nothing to show for the money he took. I heard him and ma arguing about it out back, but she never said anything in front of my brothers and me. Things continued pretty much as they had all those years. A few weeks later, he disappeared again. This time, he was gone for two weeks. He looked sickly when he came back and two of his teeth were gone. After that he started disappearing pretty consistently. Mother's face started getting

4

lines around the mouth, but she never said anything. She just pulled back her shoulders and got on with running the farm. In June of my fourteenth year, pa left again and, this time, he never came back. "Good riddance," is all I heard ma say when Eli asked her about it. After that, no one mentioned pa's name around the farm. It was like he was never there. Ma ran the house just like before, only now she ran the farm too. That's when I knew a woman, could do anything a man did, and more.

Our lives followed a routine on the farm. In the spring, as soon as the snow had melted, we went out and cleared the land to get it ready for planting. Then, when we were sure the sun was staying out for good, we planted the first of the corn. We had to water everything really well in early summer. By the time late summer rolled around, we had started in on the harvest and that pretty much lasted until fall. Like most small holdings thereabouts, we did our own repairs and there was *always* something that needed fixing. If the horse didn't need new shoes, then the plough needed a new blade, and if not that, then a window on the hen house would blow out, or a tree would need to be chopped down before it fell and caused more damage. By the time I entered my seventeenth year, the barn was getting pretty old and had probably been patched once too often. That's when the boys decided that some of the profit from that year's harvest should go to building a new one. But there's a long period of time between planting a crop and making a profit. Even if ma agreed, in her mind we needed a new plough before we needed a new barn. There was a lot of arguing, back and forth, between ma and the boys and I about whose plan was the better one. The boys said they would have the plough repaired in town, then they could put the money they saved on a new plough towards building a new barn, once we cut down the wood. Ma said we couldn't afford to lose any more trees and that the few we had left were necessary to shelter the house and the fields from the wind. And I said there was truth to all of it and we had better compare costs instead of arguing against one another. At this, everyone turned to me and stared. And Eli said, it was a fine thing when a little girl had more sense in her than anyone else on the farm. This made me madder than a rooster in a rainstorm, and I went after him with a broom. I chased him round the hen house until he begged for mercy. At least, that is the way I remember it!

And that is why, on a Tuesday morning, after the chores had been done and the horse was hitched up, Nate and Eli loaded the plough blade onto the wagon and rode down to the city to see whether it could indeed be fixed or if it had to be replaced. On the way back, they planned to drive over to the Claus's farm and see if the old fellah was ready to sell us his spare plough. A lot of the neighbors thought he had at least one, maybe two, spare ploughs that he kept as a kind of insurance in case something happened to the first one. That was his insurance against catastrophe, for a farmer without a plough is no good to anyone, least of all to his family.

When ma and I waved goodbye that brisk morning, we though we would not see the boys again until Friday. The trip into Chicago took an entire day back then, and they needed another day to haggle over the blade and a third to get back. That left a fourth day for the detour to Claus's farm out west. Meanwhile, I had a fence to mend and ma needed to dig out the vegetable garden next to the barn.

The hammer was pretty heavy and from time to time I stopped to catch my breath and looked over to where ma was digging. She was 47 years old and she had started to stoop, as if her back couldn't hold her quite as straight as it used to. Her face had the worn look of a person who spent too many days worrying and I fretted about her shouldering so much of the heavy work around the farm, even though the boys and I were old enough to take it on ourselves. Accordingly, I was fixing up the heavily damaged north fence, which left her to the digging. I watched for a moment as she moved the shovel rhythmically up and down, the black soil rising and falling with every stroke. Then I turned back to my own task. Several of the fence posts had been completely worn away or been disturbed by wild animals looking to eat our corn. The day passed quickly as I sawed and hammered the new logs into place. Over the years, we had pretty much cleared the land around the farm of usable trees and we had to walk quite far now in order to get fresh wood. By the time I finally stood upright, the light was fading rapidly. My neck and back ached from the long day of bending over and a twinge in my arms and shoulders told me I would pay for the day's exertions for several days to come. My belly was complaining too. I had long since eaten the loaf of bread and chunk of cheese I brought with me for my lunch. Even my water jug was almost empty now.

A glance at the sky told me my labors were about to end and not a moment too soon. A storm was blowing in quickly from the Southwest and the sky was already darkening for rain. I picked up my tools and started back for the barn. Ma must have seen the change in the weather too. In the distance I could see her brown work dress moving towards the door and I stopped to laugh as an old hen scurried across the field and was buffeted back by the wind, which was now picking up quickly.

The dark clouds, which moments before had seemed so far in the distance, were rapidly approaching. Almost at once, the sky turned completely black. As I started to run, the first rain drops hit me and the long shaft of the hammer caught between my legs, causing me to stumble and fall forwards. As I pulled myself up, a lightning bolt struck suddenly and violently on the ground in front of me. Startled, I clutched the tools tightly to my chest, then started running, faster now, hoping to make it to the safety of the barn before lightning flashed again. No such luck. The thunder crashed and rolled above me, followed moments later by fierce jabs of lightning that seemed to want to strike me down. I raced forwards as a crack of lightning jabbed across the field, bathing the barn and the area around it in a strange, vibrant light. I watched with horror as the lightning struck the tall oak tree alongside the barn, and split it almost cleanly in two. For a few seconds the tree seemed to hover, like a feather suspended in air. Then it groaned and the larger of the halves fell swiftly and directly onto the barn roof, which collapsed in an instant. I felt my mouth opening as the first the roof and then the sides of the barn collapsed in on themselves and a great ball of dirt and dust rose up in the air where moments before the barn had stood. In seconds it was over, the barn and all its contents had disappeared, leaving in their place a cloud of dust and a gaggle of squawking, terrified birds.

There are moments in life when time seems to stand still, and everything you ever have known and thought until that time, is suddenly and inexorably called into question. This was one of those moments. I stood there, staring numbly at the spot where the barn should have been, refusing to believe the evidence before my own eyes. The building was no longer there. It had been replaced by a pile of wood and a plum of dust twisting and swirling its way to the heavens. Suddenly, I heard a scream and someone yelling, "Ma! Ma!" The scream was coming from me. Then I was running again, running faster than I ever ran in my life, stumbling and falling across the uneven terrain, scrapping my knee and standing and running again, wiping the rain from my eyes so I could see and keep running on.

When I reached the pile of dust and debris that had been our barn only moments before, I stopped, unsure what to do. Through the silence I could hear the terrified squawking of trapped chicks and the unnatural screams of Hedwig, our poor milk cow. "Ma! Ma!" I screamed over and over. Nothing came back to me, but the pitiful cries of animals. At some point the storm must have passed over and I realized that it was no longer raining. Brilliant sunshine was streaming into my eyes and burning into my back. I remember throwing myself to my knees and clawing wildly at the wood, tearing at it with my hands, until I became aware of blood oozing down my arms from the scores of cuts and tears made when loose nails clawed at my flesh. The woodpile wasn't any lower for my frantic efforts. Gradually, I calmed myself and began looking around me for some tool, some THING, that would help me lift the pile of debris up from the spot where I guessed the barn door used to be. By some miracle, I found the shovel ma had been using moments before she entered the barn. She must have rested it against the outside wall when she went inside. Thanking God for my good fortune, I began prying it under the heaviest log, hoping to inch it high enough so I could pivot it to the side and get at the beams beneath. It must have been back-breaking, exhausting work. But I felt no aches nor pains nor any hunger, as I went about my task. All I remember of that night was the prying and pulling and pushing of logs aside and starting in on the ones below.

I slowly worked through the pile, hoping to find a glimpse of brown cloth underneath it all. After many hours, the screaming and squealing animals fell silent. I could hear nothing but the cry of a lone bird, circling the sky overhead, or a wolf howling in the forest.

A long while later, it grew dark again, only this time it was the natural darkness of a late summer evening. I ran into the house, fetched the kerosene lamp, and set it down next to the woodpile once it was lit. The sky was full of stars when I finally cleared away enough beams to catch a glimpse of my mother's dress. I thrust my hand down through the wood until I felt something warm and limp beneath me. "Hold on, ma," I yelled, as quick tears ran burning down my cheek. "I'm going to get you out."

It was dawn when I finally had her body clear enough to drag her away from the debris and onto a blanket. I prayed that my gentle pulling would not do her any further harm. I bent my face close to her mouth and I could feel her breath, labored and slow, warming my cheek. Her face was ashen, and she was barely breathing, but she was still alive. As carefully as I could, I dragged the blanket back to the house, over the porch step and inside. As careful as I was, mama still cried out with every movement. Once inside the house, I pulled her mattress off the bed and heaved her, blanket and all, on top of it. I was exhausted by this time, and I must have passed out, because when I came to it was morning and I was lying next to her on the floor. It distressed me so much that I had collapsed into sleep when my mother needed me. But my body had defied me. It was worn down with fear and fatigue. Feeling ashamed, I sat up quickly and put out my hand, dreading to feel her cold and still beneath my fingers. To my relief and surprise, she was still alive. Her color seemed worse in the harsh light of morning, and I busied myself boiling water over the hearth and trying to not see the shrunken figure over by the door. While the water was warming, I took out a hunting knife and cut the filthy clothing away from her body. I started when I found the blanket, and the mattress, soaked in blood. She was bleeding heavily from somewhere and there was a faint odor about her person. I guessed this was from the blood and grime soaked in her clothes. I gagged when I saw what lay underneath. Her body was broken in dozens of places. Small bones protruded through her skin, bruises and lacerations were everywhere. Blood oozed or congealed over gaping wounds. I cleaned her up as best I could, but I could not do anything about the broken and protruding bones. Finally, she was as clean as I could make her. I managed to slide most of the blanket out from under her and threw it into the fire, where it spluttered and filled the room with the odor of blood.

I do not remember much about the next three days. I was aware that three days had passed, but what I did and when I did it, I could not say for sure. At one point, I made a thin gruel and tried to get some into her. At another, I made sweet tea with honey. At yet another, I soaked some bread in water and made a paste, which I tried to feed her. She drooled most of it onto the pillow. I do not recall her eating much of anything. When I wasn't feeding or bathing her, I ripped up sheets and made them into bandages that I used to try and stop the oozing wounds. By this time, the smell was getting pretty bad. It was the smell of meat left out in the sun too long. Pretty soon I was gagging and retching most of the time and the person on the mattress seemed less and less like my mother. Her skin was almost totally gray and damp to the touch. The wounds were tinged green around the edges and the smell came from them, as far as I could tell. I took to burning strips of wood on the hearth and when they had cooled enough, I wrapped them in cloth and wore them like a necklace around my throat. It helped to cover the smell, a little. Day turned into night and back into day. I slept fitfully on a blanket next to ma. She never opened her eyes, nor uttered a human word. All I remember is a rattle that came from her throat, sometimes, as she struggled to breath. By this time, I knew her lungs were filling with water, the way Hugo Henning's had when his wagon ran over him last summer.

I heard somewhere there is a silence before death. I heard that the living slip out of this world and into the next, knowing in their hearts that the Lord is waiting and will meet them. For me there was no comfort in such thoughts. All those hours, I sat next to our mother, watching her die. I was hoping for a sign, any sign, she knew I was there. None was given. Her body by now was bloated and smelly. Green pus was oozing from wounds that would not heal and her face was grayer than I ever thought flesh could be. Whatever was lying on the mattress next to me, it was no longer my mother.

In the morning, I woke up and she was gone.

I slept on the porch wrapped in a blanket until the boys came home. I had no more stomach for the sights and smells of death.

Chapter Two

By the time my brothers saw ma's body, the rot had set in pretty badly. We decided to bury her then on account of the smell, even though the pastor wasn't due to come up from the city until Sunday. Back then, Runningbrook was too small to sustain a pastor seven days a week, and like many surrounding communities, the pastor traveled in on holidays or when needed.

I had always loved the front of our farm with its wide front porch stretching from the front door half way round to the back on either side. To the right, there was a copse of trees overlooking the creek by the edge of the front field. That is where we buried her. She now dwells under the shade of the oak, where she and I had spent so many happy hours talking after supper, when all the day's chores had been done.

Mother's memorial was well attended, even though it took place when everyone was readying fields for planting. All of our neighbors came, including Rosina and Karl Claus, Annamarie and Konrad Bischoff, Hannah and Klaus Kaltenbach and the widow Hennig. All of the children came too, most of them awkward in their Sunday clothes. It was a large group of sixteen people, who stood around the graveside bidding ma goodbye. She had been buried for three days now, and it made my heart glad that the pastor was there to say the right words so she could finally rest in peace.

A lot of people were crying as the pastor spoke. I felt very calm, almost serene, as if it were someone else's ma we were praying for. I looked over at my brothers. Eli looked stiff and uncomfortable, standing bolt upright in his Sunday jacket. Next to him, Nate looked serious, but very becoming. His dark jacket accentuated his tanned face and dark eyes. There was no doubt that face was going to break a few hearts before he settled down.

I didn't cry through any of the service. I still remember how the sun danced through the branches of the trees overhead. And how Eli looked over at Magdalena Kaltenbach and how she looked back at him with great compassion. I remember the women around us, snuffling and holding their kerchiefs to their eyes. And I can still picture how the three of us were asked by the pastor to throw handfuls of earth down on the grave, even though it was dug three days before.

Afterwards, most people stood around. I walked back to the house with Nate.

"You think Eli is going to call on Lena Kaltenbach?"

"I reckon he might, if he can build up the nerve! It's a shame he hasn't asked before now. I think the girl is as sweet on him as he is on her."

"Do you!"

"I'd have swept her off her feet by now!"

"Indeed you would, brother. But you'd have broken her heart just as fast!"

"Reckon I would have too! I don't know what she sees in him!"

It was true, certainly true that Eli's body was thin on his six foot one inch frame, but his deep blue eyes shone bright in his sun-bronzed face and the frame of sandy colored hair set his eyes off in a most pleasing way. I thought him quite becoming next to his darker skinned, darker eyed brother, even if Nate were the more robust. As for me, I was tall for a woman, five feet ten inches tall. I shared Eli's bright blue eyes, although my skin and hair were lighter than both of them. In my one concession to the weather, I wore a mechanic's cap in the field, to shield my face from burning.

Impulsively, I slipped my arm through my brother's.

"Oh Nate! I can't believe ma's really gone!"

He squeezed my arm.

"Neither can I, sis. Neither can I!"

When we reached the porch, we pulled the flaps down over the benches, turning them from high-backed chairs into sturdy tables. Then we spread a few blankets over the steps, making a handy seating for the children and the younger guests. As they wandered back towards the house, I could see people visibly relaxing. They weren't standing so stiffly then and folks who had known us all these years, stopped looking at the three of us like we were strangers who had just arrived from the town. Nate talked and laughed a little with the guests out on the porch. I busied myself indoors, pulling out the plates and the cloth for company. Through the window I could see Eli standing off by himself, looking out over the fields. He was joined presently by

Lena Kaltenbach. It did not surprise me that the dark- haired, serious young woman, was of interest to him. Her devotion and serious demeanor were clearly part of the attraction for our equally serious older brother. I thought them very well-matched. I trusted her attentiveness and elevated color indicated a mutual attraction between them. Their prolonged conversation, and the fact they stayed to themselves much of the time, did not escape the notice of our neighbors. Many of them remarked that, as head of household, Eli should have been a better host. But I had everything in hand. Indeed, it was a relief to have something to occupy myself and I was not displeased when Ludwig Kaltenbach begged Nate to join him and Gottfried down by the creek.

"Yes, go ahead. I can help your sister well enough." I hadn't noticed Otto Bischoff so close to my elbow, but I was glad enough for the company. So, I chased Nate off and Otto followed me inside and helped carry out the assortment of breads, cheeses and pies our dear friends had brought along to aide in the day's commemoration. I bade everyone to help themselves to the stew pot standing on the kitchen table.

"My, you have wonderful helper there!," Ida Hennig remarked with a knowing glance.

Something in her manner alerted me and I turned around in time to catch a look of satisfaction pass between them. It disturbed me to imagine Otto's helpfulness representing anything other than neighborliness. But when I stood to take my plate back to the kitchen, he grabbed it from me, with such concern, that his feelings for me became quite plain.

"Oh, do not trouble yourself my dear Miss Reinhardt," he said.

"It's no trouble at all!" I said firmly. And, pulling it back out of his hand, I marched into the house with my heart pounding.

Once inside, I leaned back against the door, aghast. Why had I not seen this before! Why Otto was …my NEIGHBOR, for goodness sake. In that moment, all thoughts of the relationship between my brother and Miss Kaltenbach flew out of my mind. All I could think of was the fact that Otto was a child, a CHILD! He stood an inch or two shorter than me. He was short and stocky with a round, earnest face and curly blond hair. He was strong of body with thick legs and a strong back. He was a kind hearted boy, a good solid farmer, but he was not the sort of man I would choose should I want a husband. Not Otto! I had known the boy since I was knee high to a grasshopper. In romantic terms, his attentions were about as appealing to me as the attentions of my BROTHER would have been! What had I done to make him think otherwise? Hurriedly, I reviewed my attitude towards him over the past three or four times we had met. I had smiled. I had said hello. I had done nothing above the minimal required. I had willingly accepted his offers of help that afternoon, but only in the interest of being neighborly. I was appalled that he would consider my actions anything more. I resolved from that moment on to refuse any and all offers of help from him or from any other male, except only my brothers.

What a strange day this was! Eli was romancing Lena Kaltenbach. I was serving food and being romanced. Nate was making jokes. It was as if everything was normal and fine, when not a hundred paces away, ma was lying under fresh turned earth.

I was pulled away from my reveries when Otto Bischoff came inside. He was standing a mite too close for my comfort and inquiring as to my health.

17

"I feel perfectly fine, thank you Otto. Why? Do I look pale?"

"No, ma'am."

I took a pace back.

"Then I can assure you everything is perfectly fine, Otto, though I thank you for inquiring."

I turned to leave, but Otto grabbed my arm.

"My dear Miss Reinhardt…" he began in a low voice.

Alarmed now, I pulled my arm away. "If you don't mind Otto, I have to see to everyone's comfort," I said. And with that, I rushed outside. I felt the color creeping up my face and prayed our guests would think it the heat of the stove. Who did he think he was, standing that close to me and touching my person! I was outraged. Thank goodness he lived four miles away and I wouldn't have to deal with him.

By now, most of our guests were enjoying a slice of rhubarb pie and a mug of beer. It had been a fine service. Pastor Weinlaeder had said some moving words about ma. He described how brave she was, coming here as a young girl from overseas, setting up house in a whole new country and making it home for all of us. I had just finished cutting the good man a second serving of pie, when Hannah Claus saw a cloud of dust down the road, signaling the arrival of another guest. No one could think who else would have known ma and wanted to attend her funeral. At that moment, Nate came running up with Gottfried and Ludwig.

"There's someone coming," he panted.

"Hannah Kaltenbach said the same!"

Then Ludwig cried, "It's Georg Kessler! What does he want?"

Kessler was universally despised for his habit of lending money at high interest rates and calling in the debt when a person was least able to pay. No one ever wanted a visit from the likes of him.

"He can turn around and leave!" Nate almost spat out the words. "No one here owes him money!"

We sat in silence as Kessler came closer, his huge body dwarfing the buggy. His poor horse was panting heavily as it made its way down the road towards us. When Kessler climbed down from his seat and threw the reins over the porch rail, twenty-three pairs of eyes glared at him. No one bade him good day.

"Afternoon, people," he said smoothly, raising his hat and inclining his head, exposing his bald glistening pate. Pulling a white kerchief from his pocket, he wiped the pools of sweat off his face and glistening head. "I'm very sorry for your loss," he nodded to Eli, and more ostentatiously, to me. Nate was standing with his back to the man, a fact not lost on Kessler. "Looks like a nice piece of pie." He eyed the food hungrily. No one stepped forward to offer him any, not even the pastor.

"Much obliged," he raised his hat again, although with less enthusiasm.

"What do you want?" Nate turned to face him. "You're interrupting a funeral."

"As I said, I'm sorry for your loss."

"We don't want your pity," Nate goaded. "Why don't you get on out of here? I don't recall inviting you."

"Well I reckon you didn't, exactly," Kessler answered evenly. "But there's some business we have to attend to and now is as good a time as any."

"What business? We don't have no business with the likes of you."

"Nate, there's no call to be rude to the man," Eli interrupted. "Let's listen to what he has to say."

"Reckon you should listen to your brother, young un," Kessler said smoothly. Nate balled his hands and stepped forward. Eli motioned him to calm down.

"Why don't we step inside?" Eli said, indicating the house.

Hearing that, Kessler removed his hat and strode up the steps past everyone, his bald head glistening in the sunlight. Eli and Nate followed quickly. I glanced at our guests, who were murmuring and shaking their heads, as I followed them inside. The four of us stood awkwardly facing one another. All the chairs were out on the porch, but the room felt suddenly crowded. I saw the stewpot was still on the table. Two flies were buzzing around it.

"What's this all about?" asked Eli.

Kessler reached inside his coat pocket and pulled out a document. Wordlessly he handed it to Eli, who unfolded it and read it slowly. Nate looked about ready to explode.

"What does it say?" I asked.

Eli just kept on reading, the color slowly draining from his face.

"What is it Eli? What does it say?"

"Yes, come on Eli, tell us what it says," Nate demanded.

"There's a lien on the farm." Eli looked back and forth from my brother's face to mine.

"A lien? What's a lien?"

"A lien's another word for loan," I said. "How bad is it?"

"Bad," said Eli.

"How bad? How bad, Eli?"

"It means Mr. Kessler here owns our farm."

"But he can't! I mean, pa bought it outright, years ago. What are you talking about?"

"Enlighten your sister," Kessler said.

We all ignored him.

"Eli, how can this man own the farm when pa bought it fair and square?"

"Pa took out a loan on the property." Eli's eyes never left Kessler's face.

"What do you mean pa took out a loan? A loan for what? We never had any need for a loan. We never bought nothing!"

"Doesn't mean pa never spent nothing," Eli said bitterly. "For all we know, he was squirreling away money until the day he left us."

"But why would he do that?"

"Who the deuce knows, Beck. Maybe he had plans to build himself a farm somewhere else."

"Maybe he drank it all!"

"This doesn't make any sense!"

"But a loan!" Nate blustered. "A loan is something you pay back! Didn't pa pay it back?"

"Oh, yes," Kessler said pleasantly. "He paid it back every year, a little at a time and after he…your mother continued to pay it back. But I'm afraid she fell behind in her payments and this year's payment wasn't made at all."

"We need a little more time," said Nate. "When the barn collapsed we lost all of our crop…"

"Along with the animals and your means of earning a living," Kessler finished. "I'm afraid that puts you at a great disadvantage."

"But as long as we pay it back, what difference would it make?"

"There's a clause, Beck."

"What kind of a clause?"

"What's a clause?"

"A clause, young man, is a rider to an agreement."

"Meaning what?"

"Which means, in this case, if we fall more than three months behind in our payments, Mr. Kessler here has the right to take over our farm."

"How far behind are we?"

"Seven months and three weeks."

It was Kessler who answered. I stared at the rolls of fat cascading from his chin onto his thick neck.

"I have been more than fair."

"More than fair, you godawful bloodsucker! Our mother is freshly buried and you come here to turn us out of our home!" And before any one could stop him, Nate leapt across the table, grabbed Kessler by the jacket and started shaking him. Before Eli and I could pull him off, Kessler's knife was out. He started slashing at Nate, who screamed and clutched his face. Blood started streaming between Nate's fingers. By now, I was yelling and slapping Kessler over Nate's back and Eli was pulling at Nate's arm. Kessler's hat flew across the room. He started after it, as if his hat were the only thing that mattered.

"Get out! Get out of here!" Eli was red in the face, his fists clenched at his side. That was the first time I ever heard Eli yell.

I was pulling at Nate's fingers, trying to get at the wound. Kessler went to the door.

"Be gone by Saturday or you'll regret it!" he was yelling. And when I take possession, I will get the furniture too!"

"We'll be taking our muskets," Nate declared.

"You'll be leaving your muskets…and your tools. The amount that your parents owe will scarce be covered as it is." He seemed to collect himself, shaking his shoulders and dusting himself off, as if brawling were a regular fact of life. He stopped and retrieved his hat, setting it firmly upon his head. Then, looking directly at Nate, he added, "A pity the young man hasn't better manners. Inclining his head towards me and then towards Eli, but clearly avoiding Nate, he tipped his hat and said, "Good day to you all," as if nothing much had transpired.

I would have gone after him, but Eli held me back.

"Don't, Beck, for pity's sake, don't."

Then he started pacing round the room, while sweeping his hands through his hair, over and over. He was muttering, "What's to be done? What's to be done?"

Nate was no calmer. Every time I tried to see to the cut on his face, he would become agitated and scream at the door, "I'll burn it down afore I let you have it!"

"Boys, for heaven's sake!" Finally I forced Nate back into his seat and pulled his hand off the gaping wound. "It's a clean cut. It'll mend."

I poured hot water over a cloth and held it to Nate's cheek, pressing hard. "We better come up with a plan of what we're going to do come Saturday morning."

"Oh I have a plan!" Nate hissed.

"And it cannot include killing Kessler! I will not watch them hang you for killing a man like THAT. I will not."

"It's pa who needs killing," Eli said. "If he borrowed that money, then he's more to blame than Kessler. Kessler's just a leech. It was pa who made the wound."

"Easy for you to say, when it's my face bleeding." Nate tried a smile. "He's scum, Eli, scum."

"Lower than that!"

"And I'll spend my life getting back at him, but for now we have to think fast."

Just then the door opened and the pastor stuck his head inside the room.

"Is everything all right? Oh my goodness! You're bleeding!"

"I'll step out with you and tell everyone what has transpired."

"We'll be out in a minute," I said. "Soon as Nate stops bleeding."

The mood outside was bleak when Nate and I joined the little group on the porch a while later. The artificial humor, that sometimes accompanies a funeral, had been replaced by the sober realization of life's endless cruelties. In the space of a few days, our whole world had been turned upside down. Ma was gone, all of our animals, save the pony and a few chickens, had perished. Most of the harvest had been lost when the barn collapsed. Now everything that was left to us had been stripped away, even the roof over our heads. We were destitute.

"You can come and live with us. All of you," Annamarie Bischoff said quickly. Each one of us can take one of you and raise you like our own."

I looked at each of my brothers in turn. The heaviness in my heart threatened to overwhelm me.

"That's very kind of you," Eli said quietly. "Very kind, of all of ye."

"It's settled then," said Anna. "You'll come and live with us, Rebekkah."

"I'm grateful," I said quietly. I looked over at the Bischoffs. They were kind and well-meaning people, who doted on their two boys and tended to overlook any shortcomings. Behind his mother's back, Karl gave me an insolent stare and stuck out his tongue. Meanwhile, Otto was grinning from ear to ear. My heart froze in my body. I could scarcely breathe. Hannah Kaltenbach looked at her husband, Klaus, who nodded and said, "Eli always has a home with us." Eli glanced at Lena, who blushed and looked down. "Thank you," he said simply, "Thank you both very kindly."

"And Nate has always been like a brother to my boys," Rosina Claus smiled.

"You mean, Nate's going to live with us?" Gottfried beamed. "Now HE can clean out the hen house!"

"Ludwig! Mind your manners."

"I'm afraid he has none," Nate offered.

"Says who?" Ludwig swatted at Nate, who swatted him back. Soon the two of them were chasing one another round the yard, causing us all to yell and laugh and break the tension everyone felt at this precipitous turn of events.

It was late when the last wagon pulled away. The three of us gathered together on the porch.

"The sounds of life, as we know it, fading away?" Nate offered cheerfully.

"Gee, thanks for making it easier on us!" I turned and gave him a hard whack on the arm.

"Ooow! Welcome, I'm sure! You didn't have to hit me!"

"You didn't have to depress us even more!"

"Let's go inside," Eli said, putting his arm around the pair of us. But none of us moved. We just stood there with Eli's arms around us, listening to the sounds of the departing wagons fade into the night.

Chapter Three

Every night, between ma's funeral and the day we left the farm, I was awake. The routine was always the same. Every night around dusk I fell into an exhausted sleep, only to abruptly wake up a few hours later, replaying in my mind the sights and sounds and smells of the past twelve days. Then, I sat up in bed, struggling for air, desperate to feel some semblance of normalcy, to find some tangible proof that life was the same. My eyes searched this familiar space that had been my home since the day pa built it. I was too agitated to stay in bed. At first, I paced round and round the room, but the boys took to banging on the wall and shouting that I was keeping them up. The following day, I slipped into my coat to walk around the farm, round and round, until daylight finally came and I could wake up for good.

My thoughts were crazed: sitting proudly by pa, him driving the wagon to market, images of the barn collapsing, the screams of dying animals, ma's bloated, broken body, the smell of rotting flesh, our friends gathered round for the funeral, the silence that night as I sat with ma's body, the look on Eli's face when he knew ma was gone, the way the two boys clung to me in their grief, Kessler's fat and ugly body, packing up our things… How could life have changed so quickly? How could we loose ma and the farm and each other? How long would we live apart?

By the time Saturday came, it was almost a relief. The three of us sat at the kitchen table, our bags and porte-manteau were by the door. A loaf of bread and a hunk of cheese sat, uneaten, on the table. I was nursing a mug of water.

"Reckon you'd call this the last super," Nate blurted. His face was drawn and gray-looking.

"That was seven days ago. No one's eaten anything since."

"Aren't you two the funny ones."

"Aren't you going to miss us!"

I took a gulp of water. I didn't dare look. Emptiness hung in the air.

"I don't want us to live apart." I said stiffly. "I don't think ma would want that either."

"She would not," Eli said slowly. "Right now, I can't think what else to do. But I will think of something."

"Good. I hope it involves Kessler and a lot of blood! " Nate's eyes looked awfully tired, like he hadn't slept in a week. I wasn't sure if he was joking, or serious, about the blood.

"We lost the farm for now, no matter what we do," Eli said slowly," but Kessler's a businessman. He likes the color of money. There's nothing to say we can't buy it back."

"Nothing but a lack of funds!"

"I'm coming to that, Beck. Land in these parts is running a dollar fifty an acre."

"Pa paid $1.25!"

"I know, Nate, but prices go up. Point is, at $1.50 an acre, a farm this size would cost us $300. Throw in a horse, a wagon, seed, some hens…"

"Not to mention a house to live in…"

"We'd build it."

"We'd still need tools. Kessler's taking everything."

"Another $300 would cover all of it with cash to spare."

"Eli, this is a fine idea!" Nate lent over and slapped his brother's back. "I like the plan. Only trouble is," he made a show of reaching in his pocket and coming up with a couple of coins, "I seem to have left my money somewhere!" He sat down again heavily.

"Look, you two, I'm not saying we can do this now," Eli continued.

"Then, what are you saying?"

"What I'm saying, Beck, is that I know what we have to do. All that remains is to figure a way we can achieve it."

Nate nodded his agreement.

"Becky?"

The very idea that we could come up with this kind of money…the absurdity of it all, took my breath away. Eli looked so sincere, so eager for my approval. I didn't have the heart to disappoint him.

"You're right, brother! Now we know what we have to do."

I could feel the weight of life just pressing on me. I could scarcely breathe.

No one said anything much after that. We left the bread and cheese for Kessler to clean up. With any luck, it would rot on the table. Then we picked up our bags and went outside. It was hard to walk with mine, but I wouldn't have anyone help me. I had the large porte- manteau ma had brought with her from Germany. It was a wooden case, with black leather straps and a black buckle that fastened in front. The boys both knew I had always loved that case. The smell of leather had long since gone and the leather was faded and worn. But inside, the wood was smooth and dark. From my earliest days, I had loved to run my hands over its smooth interior and stare in the corner where ma's initials, A.K. were stenciled in black.

"This was a wedding gift from my parents," ma had explained. "It is from Wuertemburg, Germany, where we came from."

Now it was mine. I moved awkwardly to the porch and set it down and waited for the Bischoff's wagon. It wasn't heavy; just a few clothes and a prayer book. Eli had the candlesticks, the pewter jug and the family bible. Nate had chosen two rugs hand- woven by our mother and the quilt she had kept over her bed. Luckily, I hadn't used it when she fell ill.

"I wish that schwein wasn't getting the loom," Nate said. "It makes me mad to think of him touching ma's loom."

"It's far too heavy to move," Eli said, lost in thought. "It probably counts as furniture anyway. He probably thinks he owns it."

"I hope he gets what's coming to him," Nate spat. "That and oh so much more!"

We had no time to answer, for at that moment, dust was rising at the end of the road signaling the arrival of several of our neighbors. Within moments, the Bischoffs and the Claus brothers came into view. Eli turned to where our own horse and wagon stood waiting for him.

"Rebekkah? Ma would have wanted you to have these." He reached under his jacket and pulled out ma's small silver hairbrush and the locket she always wore around her neck, where she kept pictures of the three of us. I was near speechless.

"Eli, as the oldest, these are yours by right."

"No, Rebekkah, yours."

He dropped them into my hand and closed my fingers round them.

"We're going to work on this right away," he nodded at Nate. "In no time, we'll be together again."

I could scarcely see through my tears. Any words I could have said were drowned under the cries and whoops of the Nate's friends as they whipped the wagon to a sudden stop in front of the porch.

Chapter Four

Annamarie Bischoff was tiny, well-meaning and intense. Her husband, Konrad, was kind, hard-working and devout. Between them, they did everything in their power to make me feel welcome in their home. If I shivered, someone fetched my cloak. If I yawned, everyone was ready for bed. If I looked hungry, it was time to eat. The reasons for this solicitousness were not hard to fathom. For many years, it was rumored, Annamarie had longed for a daughter. Time brought her two sons, but after that, there were only still- born sons followed by a still- born daughter. Hope faded with the passing of time and was replaced by a quiet acceptance of blessings given. Bringing me to live in their home was a dream come true for Annamarie. She wasted no time starting a quilt for my bed and a rug for my floor. The boys were moved from their room to the attic, which endeared me to Karl, I'm sure. I was to sit between them at the dinner table, the honored guest. Despite my protests, I was welcomed, fussed over and attended to every minute. This did not sit well with me.

As head of the household, ma did not have time to fuss over us. And as the only girl, in a family of boys, I was used to taking care of myself. This over- attentiveness and fussy concern was all the more constricting for its kindly intention. Along with the aching loss of ma, my brothers and the farm, I longed for the rigors of hard work and the discipline of familiar routine. Alas, it was not to be.

Like every farm family, the Bischoffs had a very busy work day. Every morning before daybreak, the boys would milk the cows while their father hitched up the plough and their mother prepared breakfast. Then Annamarie would churn the milk into butter after setting some aside for drinking. The men of the house would plough the fields or plant the corn or harvest, depending upon the time of year. My first morning there after I awoke, I put on Nate's old work pants, pulled my hair under an old cap and set out for the barn to help with the milking. But the boys laughingly told me this was "men's work" and suggested I help their mother set the table for breakfast. By the time I got back to the house, the bread and cheese were already out and Annamarie was unenthusiastic when I suggested I help her with the churning.

"Lord, no!" she said.

To every suggestion that I plough, or plant, or fix fences, I was told with increasing firmness that, "women did not do such things." When I replied that I had been working on a farm all of my life, they all but suggested I had been poorly raised and treated harshly.

At every opportunity, Karl took pains to vex me. When no one was looking, he threw stones or tugged my hair. Other times, he would hide behind a tree and jump out to scare me, or lay a branch across the path and raise it as I passed to trip or scratch me. I warned him many times, but he persisted. Until one day, when I grabbed his arm and threw him to the ground. I seized a pitchfork- the only weapon at my disposal- and held it to his throat. I told him I would run him through if he *ever* dared touch my person again! He just laid there, paralyzed with fear.

"Not so brave now, are ye, you pipsqueak!" I hissed in my fiercest voice. Releasing him all at once, I pulled him to his feet and sent him on his way. That was the last of his minor harassments. And though he continued to scowl, he never again approached me without trepidation.

Worse than Karl's spite, however, was Otto's infatuation. He followed me around at every opportunity. One minute he was inquiring after my well-being and the next he was describing the "big farm" and "large harvests" he planned to have in his future. It did not take brains to suppose he was angling for a little woman to take her place, in the kitchen of his future abode. But I was not that woman, nor did I take any pleasure in imagining myself to be such. One night, I found myself praying for Sunday church, not out of any particular reverence for the weekly service, but for the chance of seeing my brothers and figuring how to get myself out of this place. How delighted I was then, when Sunday finally came and the Bischoffs, dressed in their Sunday best, drove me to the church. There I was thrilled to see Nate, who was pacing back and forth in his Sunday jacket and playing with the brim of his hat. With a cry of pleasure, I jumped down from the wagon, before Mr. Bischoff pulled it to a stop. I then threw myself into Nate's arms, much to his astonishment and obvious delight.

"Whoa, now! My heavens! Rebekkah! I have never known you so pleased to see me!" Nate was grinning from ear to ear. "Finally learned to appreciate my charms, have ye!"

"Oh, my goodness! Yes!" I said with feeling.

"There not mistreating ye, are they," he said, looking fiercely in their direction. "Because if they are...

"No brother, it's nothing like that. At least not the way you imagine it," I started to explain, but was interrupted by Eli, who had just ridden up with the Kaltenbachs. He received a hug, just as forceful, as the one I had given his brother.

"You all right, Becky?" he asked quietly. "Is something going wrong for you out there?"

"Why yes, yes it is!" I replied with feeling. I proceeded to explain to both of them how I had been treated. How I was never to do any real work, excepting in the kitchen and the yard.

"That's it?" Eli said, leaning back in obvious relief and letting out a sigh. "Beck, don't do that! You had me worried silly for a moment."

"That's it? What do you mean, is that it? Haven't you been listening to what I said?"

"Sure I've been listening. But all I hear is they've welcomed you into their home and treated you like a lady."

"And you think this is okay?" I was incredulous. "Are you crazy, Eli?"

"No, I'm not crazy," he said, getting agitated. "Look Becky, I'm trying to make things right so we can be a family again. And all you can do, is to whine because things aren't quite to your liking."

"Aren't quite to my liking!" I could feel the heat rising in my face. "That's incredibly unkind of you!"

"And it's incredibly unkind of *you* to cause a fuss when there's nothing to fuss about," Eli replied with feeling.

"What's gotten into you?" I yelled. "I can't believe you are acting this way!"

"Is everything all right?" Lena Kaltenbach's sudden arrival was so wholly unexpected, that I jumped a little.

"I didn't mean to startle you, "she said sweetly, touching my arm. "It's just that I heard raised voices and I…"

"Everything's fine, Lena," Eli said firmly while taking her arm and walking towards church. "We'll see you later, Becky."

"See you later, Becky! What on earth's gotten into him, Nate?"

"Well, you are being a bit difficult," Nate started. "After all, they have offered you a home and you could try being a little grateful."

"Grateful! I'm supposed to be grateful that that simpleton Otto follows me around everywhere and the whole family treats me like I'm a woman or something!"

At this, Nate threw his head back and roared with laughter, causing many of our neighbors, who were walking past us into church, to look over and smile or wave a greeting.

"Beck, honestly, you are hilarious!"

Before I could open my mouth to reply, Nate had his hands on my shoulders and was staring down at me in an affectionate and brotherly way.

"Becky, dear little Becky, I well know you can ride and till a field like man and God knows, you are a better shot than I…"

"Than either of you!"

"Okay, than either of us! But look at you!"

Then I looked down at my plain, blue, Sunday dress that had a stain on the front, from when I had changed a wagon wheel, several weeks past.

"What's wrong with me?"

"Nothing, dear sister. Absolutely nothing!"

"Then wha…"

"Except that you're a woman and a darn pretty one at that-even if I am your brother!"

"I AM NOT!"

"Of course you are, Beck! No wonder Otto follows you around! He may be the first, but he will not be the last, I warrant!"

"Come along, you two! You'll be late for singing!"

We both acknowledged the cheery voice of the pastor, as he waved the last of his flock, through the gate, into the church yard.

"We'll be right there! " Nate called out.

"Don't be talking like this again!" I hissed at Nate. "It's silly and I don't appreciate it."

"Why not, Beck?" Nate asked kindly. "What's wrong with being a woman and being pretty?"

"It gets you nowhere, that's what's wrong with it!" I replied with feeling.

"Ma was pretty. Look what good it did her! I don't want that kind of life, pretty and married and basically owning nothing but the clothes on my back! I want to make my own path. I want to own land! I don't want to act pretty and be beholden to a man!"

"Beck, this is crazy talk!" Nate was genuinely puzzled. "I am sure you'll grow out of it, just as soon as you meet a man who catches your eye! Come along now, don't fret so. We 'll be late for service!"

He offered me his arm, but I scowled, so he thought better of it. We walked side by side, into the church, and took our usual seats. Eli was sitting across from us next to Lena and the rest of the Kaltenbachs. Although he gave me a warm smile, I stared at him coldly. As for Nate, he was my brother and I loved him, but his ideas were way too conventional for my taste. After a lifetime of lickin' the boys in every contest, I had no intention of sitting back and playing the little woman to some oaf of a man! I had bigger plans than that for myself.

Chapter Five

Despite the strain that had developed between us the previous Sunday, it was with a glad heart that I awoke the next church day, eager to see my kin again after seven long days without them. After we arrived at church, I excused myself from the Bischoffs, and ran over to see my brothers. They were standing to one side of the path, awaiting my arrival.

"Eli, I'm sorry about last…"

"Never you mind about that sis," he said, scooping me into his arms and giving me a hug.

"Eli! This is so unlike you, but I appreciate it!" Eli was beaming from ear to ear.

"Wait till you hear Eli's plan!" Nate kissed me on both cheeks. You will scarce believe it! We are saved, sis!

After assuring the Bischoffs that we would see them inside, the three of us turned from the path and came to rest under the shade of a tall silver pine. I looked at their eager faces and felt a fierce rush of love for them.

"You have a plan? Well? What is it, Eli?"

Eli inhaled deeply. I had never seen him so excited.

"You know the threats of war between the states are heating up?"

"The pastor said as much in his sermon last week, but what…"

"Wait a while. Just listen."

I bit my lip.

Eli looked at Nate.

"It won't last long. A few rebellious Southern states are no match for the rest of us."

"And…?" I looked between the two eager faces.

"My plan is this. The President is callin' for volunteers…"

"Volunteers? What, to fight! You want to join the army?"

"Just listen, Beck. Eli has it all worked out. And when…"

"If you two will be quiet for a minute and let me finish!"

Nate and I stopped talking. I took a step back and folded my arms.

Eli shook his head. "As I was saying, the president is calling for volunteers to fight the rebellion. I heard he's paying $300…"

"300 hundred dollars, Beck!" A look from Eli and Nate was quiet again.

A bird skittered in the tree behind us. The sun was higher in the sky now and the day was getting warmer. A breeze moved through the silver branches. Eli's quiet voice kept talking.

"He's offering $300 to every man who serves. $300! That's more money than we could make after years of farming! And not only that, there's a monthly stipend, as much as thirteen dollars! With Nate and I both signing up, we can collect almost $700 between us, in a matter of months!"

"Then we can buy back the farm and live together again!"

"Exactly. Our farm, or one just like it."

"Isn't this great, Beck! Isn't this a great plan?"

I remember staring at the two of them. Eli was smiling and quietly proud of himself. Nate was grinning from ear to ear, like cat with a big fat mouse in its claws. For a moment, neither of them saw how I was feeling, as they slapped one another on the back.

"We're saved! We're saved sis!" Nate grabbed me and would have danced me round and round the tree, but I pulled back. I clutched my arms across my chest while a rising fury grew inside of me.

"What's the matter, sis! This is a great, great plan!"

"You two are too stupid to breathe! There isn't an ounce of brain between the both of you!" I was so angry, I believe I stomped my foot up on the ground. My brothers stared at me in amazement.

"Becky? We're going to be rich!"

I shook my head. "God help the North if this is the kind of men we're recruiting!"

"What!"

"What makes you think you're going to LIVE long enough to collect the money?"

The boys looked at me stupidly, as if the thought of dying had never occurred to them. Then Eli smiled.

"Becky," he took my hands between his own. "In the first place, a few rebellious states are no match for the rest of the country! Second, everyone says the war's going to be short, no more than a month or two! We'll collect our money and be home before you know it!"

"You're crazy, both of you! There's no saying how long this thing will last! "

"Becky, they can't win!"

"Says who, Nate? Look, when it started, the President called for a few thousand men to enlist for three months, 'til this was over. That was in February. Here we are in July and he wants another forty regiments to serve for three years! What's next? Five years? Ten?"

"Becky, you're a smart woman. Look, it's all politics! The President said three months in February, because that was what the law allowed. Now they changed it, to allow longer terms."

"Because they need more troops!"

"Well, they *think* they might."

"My point exactly."

"But that doesn't mean they will."

"And it doesn't mean they won't, either!"

"Okay, well don't be stubborn, Beck. The President isn't any more clairvoyant than the rest of us. He's taking precautions, that's all."

"Because he knows the war won't be ending any time soon."

Nate got between us.

"Why do women have to worry so?" Nate laughed. "There are more of us and fewer of them. What can go wrong?"

I made a face. "Look around you, Nate. Plenty can go wrong! And what do you mean by saying women don't have to worrry?"

"It ain't gonna be much of a fight," Eli continued. "We have to get in while there's still money to be made. I know things have been tough lately, but now we have a plan and everythin's gonna to be fine."

"And where'm I, while you're off playin' soldier?"

"You'll be staying with the Bishoffs."

"How nice," I said bitterly.

"Besides, Otto likes you!" Nate teased.

"Even better! Why don't you marry me off while you're about it? Don't give *me* any say in anything!"

"Rebekkah," Eli said softly. "It isn't that we want to fight."

"Oh, I wouldn't say…," Nate began. Eli shot him a look and Nate shut up.

"It's just that we don't have a lot of options."

"I know that. I know that, Eli. But why do you have to come with an option that leaves me behind?"

He looked at me strangely. "Because you're a girl, Becky," he said simply. "What else could it be?"

I sat through church that day numb with fear. The feeling of gloom and despondency stayed with me, all though the week, until the evening Eli rode over to the Bischoffs to let me know how things were proceeding. He had wasted no time. Northern recruiters would be in nearby Deerfield Township in two weeks and he arranged for Nate and himself to be there. Nate's friends, Gottfried and Ludwig, would drive them over and would take the buggy back to the Kaltenbach's, where it would stay until the brothers came home. Eli would give them $3 towards the upkeep of the horse, the rest to be paid later. It was understood that if both he and Nate failed to return, the Kaltenbachs would take possession of both horse and wagon.

Eli had heard that new recruits were generally whisked away as soon as they signed their papers. The army, no doubt, was afraid of changed hearts and minds. This being the case, Eli and I persuaded the Bischoffs to let me have the wagon to go and see them off. The Bischoffs seemed mighty pleased and proud of my brothers.

"You'll get to wear a uniform and march with the colors!" Karl declared solemnly.

"And all the women will think you're special!" Otto said pointedly, looking at me.

"It's a great thing to be fighting for your country!" Mr. Bischoff declared, "I would be proud of any lad signed up to do the same."

Annamarie shot him a look that would have felled the enemy, then and there. "Some of us can ill afford to lose the lads we have!" she declared angrily. "Not that anything will happen to the two of you, but some of us can't afford to take any chances!"

And with this leap of illogic and poor judgment, she busied herself by the hearth, banging pots and pans around to cover her embarrassment. The rest of us talked of the weather and the harvest and the like, until she had calmed herself and came bustling over again.

"Well, dears, we will take good care of your sister while you're away fighting for us all," Annamarie said, setting mugs of beer on the table. "This calls for a celebration! You'll each take a slice of my best fruit pie and we'll eat and drink to a swift victory and your safe and speedy return!"

It was generally supposed that I was proud of my brothers, and happy to be staying behind. With only a small family of her own, and both her children male, Annamarie was in need of a daughter. And since I was clearly in need of a mother, my staying with the Bischoffs was seen to be ideal. Of course, no one thought to consult me on the matter. Far from feeling gratitude, I felt only frustration and resentment. In the space of two weeks, I had lost my only surviving parent, since father was already lost to us. I had lost my home, my sense of security and now I was losing my brothers. Everything I held dear had been stripped away. I considered myself the most unfortunate young woman in all of Illinois. There seemed to be no limits to my suffering, unless I were to discover one of my beloved brothers missing, or God forbid, dead, in this terrible outbreak of fighting between our government and a group of rebellious Southerners. I was restless with anxiety and paralyzed with fear- all at the same time. And I was surrounded by neighbors, cheering and congratulating my brothers on their sense of patriotism and their bravery in face of Southern defiance! I thought I should run crazy!

The dreaded morning finally arrived. While the Bischoffs generally whooped and hollered their approval of this patriotic event, I, who had lost so much in so short a time, could only feel dread, horror and numbness at the thought of my brothers' imminent departure. Thankfully, neither Otto nor Karl could be spared from their duties that day. So reluctantly, and with many admonitions, the Bischoffs let me drive myself into town to say goodbye.

As I set off, the sun broke through the clouds. I was finally, thankfully, alone for the first time since I had kept my vigil with ma, during all those long days before.

The land around the Bischoff farm was about as flat as the land around ours had been. But while we had the blessing of the creek and the shaded trees that lined its banks, the Bischoff farm sat on slightly elevated ground, with flat land on all four sides, stretching as far as the eye could see. I recalled many hot summer days, when I would sit alongside the water after my chores were done, thinking that heaven could not feel much better than that shade did.

As I drove along, the sun rose higher in the sky, warming my skin. A gentle breeze blew around me and gradually a feeling of well- being arose in my heart. I was no stranger to wagons and on the easy road to Deerfield Township, my thoughts turned to the life stretching out before me. What was to become of me once my brothers left? I couldn't spend the rest of my life with the Bischoffs, nor for that matter with my brothers, whose safe return was by no means guaranteed.

The road stretched out before me, all was calm when suddenly, the image of a general store came into my mind. I could see it all. There would be rows of shelves lining the walls on either side, filled with all manner of goods from New York and Philadelphia. In the back of the store, there would be bins and bins of coffee and tea and all manner of grains. A corner would be devoted to patterns and fabrics from all across the east coast, and women from all the neighboring towns would flock to the place to see the latest fashions. Meanwhile, their men folk would supply themselves with grain and beans and all the essentials that a working family needs. I would call my store *Rebekkah's Emporium*. It would be the most up to date store in the town. I might even make it somewhere other than Northfield. Maybe I would establish myself in Wheeling. Or maybe in Chicago itself! I would make money! I would support myself and would need help from no man, not father and not my brothers! I would be independent!

Preoccupied with these marvelous reveries of a life dramatically different from my own, at length I approached Deerfield and saw, at once, all manner of congestion. I left the wagon, tied to a post, well away from the main square. By the time I had walked to the meeting hall where the recruiting was to begin, a sizeable crowd had formed.

A platform had been built outside the meeting hall. It stood some four feet off the ground and on it were seated the township supervisor, along with several elected officials and two men in splendid blue uniforms with red trim. Posters everywhere boldly proclaimed, "JOIN NOW! JOIN NOW! **CAPT. EZRA PAGASCZ'S BATTERY J, ATTACHED TO COL. MIKE MILLETTE'S PROUD NINTH REGIMENT**!" I knew from reading the paper that the red trim stood for artillery, whereas yellow stood for cavalry and blue for infantry. Eli had already told me they were going for artillery for each prized his skill with a musket. But truth be told, I thought them only average shots.

The older of the soldiers looked to be in his fifties. He wore a four button sack coat with three red inverted v stripes and a rectangle design set at an angle above them. On his head sat a fine-looking Hardee hat with the insignia of his company, the Third Illinois volunteers, and a bold red band. A man in front of me said the stripes denoted a first sergeant; whereupon, his companion exclaimed, "Then the other is the captain." I wondered how a man got to be an officer when the war had just begun. He was some ten years younger than the sergeant, a very imposing fellow, dressed in a much finer frock coat with gold insignia on the shoulder, a sash, a pistol and a saber. Unlike the sergeant, who slouched in his seat exchanging pleasantries with several of the men around him, the captain sat bolt upright and wore his hat at all times placed squarely atop his head, two gold-crossed cannon glinting boldly in the sunlight. I thought him a very cold-looking man.

It was clear from the murmuring of the crowd around me that the proceedings were scheduled to begin any moment. I scanned the crowd anxiously, hoping to catch a glimpse of my brothers. But in the crush of people pushing their way towards the flag-covered platform, it was hard to know for sure where they were. None of us had reckoned on such a crowd of volunteers, and I began to fear they would disappear into the army without so much as a goodbye. Then, out of nowhere, Nate was upon me. He pulled my arm and dragged me back through the crowd to where Eli stood patiently.

"Why did you give up such a prime spot near the platform?" I asked them, once our initial greetings and pleasantries had been exchanged. They determined that my journey had been uneventful, and that the horse and wagon were indeed secured. Then they looked over at the throng of people.

"All this," Eli assured me, "is just for show. And most of these people...," indicating the crowd, " are here for the speeches and the hoopla. The real action takes place over here." He pointed to a tent set a few hundred yards away. "While they are listening to preening politicians ..."

"And two splendid looking soldiers," Nate gushed.

"...and two splendid looking soldiers, the recruiting goes on over here, which is where we are going!"

No sooner were the words out of his mouth, than a wagon rolled into the square behind us and a band struck up a healthy rendition of "Glory, glory hallelujah," to the roaring approval of the crowd.

"Oh, that is LOUD!" I exclaimed, covering my ears.

"It sure is!" Nate yelled back. "Let's move over here a ways so we can hear ourselves think."

A large white tent was set off to one side of the square. Several military men were milling around in front of it, and a rope had been strung between two poles a few feet from the entrance. Three men dressed in an assortment of work clothes were already standing in line behind the rope. Two of the three had brought along their own muskets and were leaning against them as they waited. The day reckoned to get very hot, and several ladies from the town were setting up a drinking station for the men, in case the wait grew too long. They had a large barrel filled with water, and a table covered with drinking mugs and what looked to be plates of bread and cake on them. Two of the women, in plain bonnets, were stringing a sign over the table. Once it was pulled tight enough, I could read the words, WATER AND VICTUALS FOR OUR BRAVE FIGHTING BOYS!!! and DEERFIELD IS BEHIND YOU!!! written in bold black letters across the white cloth.

Behind us, the township supervisor was on his feet shouting exhortations to the crowd. We turned around to listen, but his speech was punctuated every few minutes by roars and whoops, and the band kept interrupting with a few bars of a patriotic song. It was hard to hear what was actually said above the ruckus. Alls I could make out were a few phrases, such as, "time of pressing need," "cowardly acts of a few," "call to duty," "strength of arms," and so on. My brothers seemed to be taking it all in. Indeed, the general atmosphere was one of merriment and optimism. I was alone with my misgivings and hesitation.

The crowd paid little mind to the sergeant, whose speech was as broken up as the mayor's had been. But when the captain rose to speak, a general air of expectancy and respect settled on the crowd, and everyone grew quiet. Even the band set their instruments down, and settled back to listen. For a moment or two, the captain surveyed them. Then he began speaking. When he spoke, his voice was strong and unwavering. Unlike the sergeant, he seemed familiar with public address and his manner was direct and forceful.

"Ladies and gentleman, I am honored to address you this morning. I wish to thank," he turned to his left, "the town of Deerfield for inviting me here this morning. I bring with me the greetings and salutations of none other than our President, the honorable Abraham Lincoln!" At this, he swept off his hat and made a low bow. The crowd went wild, cheering and whooping and crying, "*God save the Union!*"

"I come to you at a moment of extreme importance in our nation's history. We are a young country, scarcely a hundred years old. Our forefathers came to these shores seeking a better life for themselves and their children. They found it here, in the generous land of America, where we are privileged to make our living and prosper by the sweat of our brows and the strength of our hands and minds."

My feeling that this man was cold and dispassionate melted as fast as it had come. Far from being cold, he was as sincere and as moving a speaker as I had ever heard. I walked toward him so I could hear better.

"Our President, newly-elected, stood on a platform of unity."

The crowd roared, "*God bless President Lincoln!*" "*God save the union!*"

"He promised to hold together these United States of America. He swore that, if elected, he would uphold the

Constitution and keep our nation whole. This is what the majority of citizens in this land called for. But there are some among us who do not hold to these views…"

Cries of, "*Traitors! Traitors!*"

"… and whose thoughts and actions threaten all that we hold dear. We cannot allow their views to prevail. We cannot allow it!"

His voice rose to a thunderous roar which electrified the crowd. More cries of "*Union forever!*" Someone in the band yelled, "*Hurrahs boys, hurrah!*"

As the cheering died down, the captain's words rang out again, "None of us wants war! None of us sought it out! None of us wanted anything more than to live in peace with our brethren! But there are those who threaten our very way of life! Who would tear asunder all that we hold dear! They cannot prevail! They shall not prevail!" More roars and cheers from the crowd. I felt my heart pounding in my chest, and a constriction in my throat that threatened my very breathing!

"Our President has told us that 'the Union is perpetual, confirmed by the history of the Union itself. That, no state, upon its own mere motion, can lawfully get out of the Union; that resolves and ordinances to that effect are legally void, and that acts of violence, within any state or states, against the authority of the United States, are insurrectionary or revolutionary, according to circumstances.'"

"*Lawbreakers! Lawbreakers!*"

Furthermore," he raised his arm, staring round at the crowd as if he would look every one of us in the eye, "he has told us that there needs to be no bloodshed or violence. And there shall be none. There shall be NONE," the captain emphasized, "unless it be 'forced upon the national authority.'"

He surveyed the crowd once more. We seemed as one to be holding our breaths, attending to his every word.

"'Unless- it- be- forced- upon- us,' "he slowly emphasized.

He looked upon us, with a world-weariness that spoke volumes about all he had seen and heard in his short life.

"Ladies and gentlemen, I am no stranger to war. I fought for my country in the West," here he paused, seeming to gaze into some fathomless horror too terrible to contemplate. "I have seen what cannon can do to a man. I have seen wounds too terrible to remember. I have seen men tremble with fear. I have seen men suffer. I have seen them cry for their mothers, I have seen them bleed and die. ..."

Not a sound was made by the crowd. Nobody moved. Nobody coughed. It would have been sacrilegious.

"But I have also seen bravery. I have seen courage. I have seen men stand and fight together because the cause for which they stood was righteous and just. Because they were honorable men. Because they did their duty!"

The crowd was in an uproar. There was a frenzy of cheering and shouting and applauding. I was cheering and shouting along with everyone. We were screaming, *"Long Live the Union!" "Down with the rebellion!" "The Union forever!"*

"Ladies and gentlemen, we did not ask for this fight! We urged our brethren in the South again and again to come to their senses, to settle their differences with us like men. They did not! They chose the path of blood and tears! They chose to fight against the very Union that sustains us all, as good Americans!"

Cries of *"Traitors!" "Villains!" "Southern scoundrels!"* pierced the air.

"Are you with me?"

"We are!" the crowd yelled.

"Will you fight to preserve all that you hold dear?"

"Yes! Yes, we will!"

"Who will join me?" yelled the captain, his fist held high, his face red and his eyes bulging.

"I will!" "I will," cried men throughout the crowd.

"They are waiting for you!" the captain pointed in the direction of the tent behind us. "They are waiting!"

Suddenly, the crowd broke. In a mad confusion of bodies and dust and pushing and yelling, the crowd surged towards us and made for the tent. Caps flew asunder. Men fell to the ground and were climbed over. We turned and ran ahead of them, reaching the line, each of us clinging to the man ahead of us. There were now seven or eight ahead of us. I was pushed hard from behind into my brother, Nate. My mouth crushed into his back and I felt myself struggling for air.

Out of nowhere, a line of soldiers in blue appeared. They let lose a volley of gunfire that stopped the crowd in its tracks, and focused all attention on a man I now recognized as a sergeant.

"Get in line! Settle down, you fellahs! Steady there! Wait your turn! Stand aside! Over here, young man!" Within minutes, he had restored control. The crowd was split into four lines. I was gently led aside and the men were called forward, one at a time, to where four others sat at small wooden tables. The men were asked if they were over eighteen, and after saying that, yes, they were, they signed their names or made their mark, signaling them ready to enlist.

"That boy there scarce looks eighteen," I whispered to Nate.

"Reckon there's a few here who don't," he replied, indicating a blond-haired boy, whose head scarcely reached the jacket of the man in front of him.

The signing seemed to take but a minute. From there the men were directed into a double line, moving slowly towards a harassed-looking doctor, who looked back and forth from right to left, bidding them to open their mouths and to stare into his eyes.

"I understand about the eyes, but why does he look inside their mouths?" the man next to me asked.

"You need a tooth to undo your powder," I told him, making the gesture of ripping a powder bag. He stared back at me blankly.

"When you load your musket..," I tried. "You pour in the black powder?" Clearly the man had never so much as seen as musket, let alone fired one. I wondered how a man could live nowadays without knowing his way around a weapon!

"I'm from Chicago," he said in a low voice. "I want to serve my country."

I saw then that his hands were white and soft-looking, as if he had spent his life holding books.

"What is it you do?" I asked him.

"I'm a teacher," he whispered. "But I want to fight!"

"Lord, save him!" I thought to myself. "He won't last a minute in a battle!"

Just then, they called Eli forward. I watched my brother's back as he bent over the table. In an instant it was done. And Nate was right behind him.

I watched numbly as the doctor examined first Eli and then his brother. They turned and each, full of excitement and pride, gave a hearty wave before they disappeared inside the tent. I was left to stare at the line of men slowly making its way forward. More than a few of them looked old, and past any useful service to their country. Several had seen service once before and sported bits and pieces of their uniforms from the Mexican War. A grizzled veteran limping on one good leg signed up with a flourish. The doctor took one look at him and waved him on without so much as a by your leave. So this was the state of the army! The line moved forward, the men and boys chattering with excitement, their heads stuffed full of romantic notions of saving the Union. I was torn, bitterly torn, between pride and a sense of the righteousness of the fight, and a deep-seated, selfish fear, I was about to lose the only people I cared about in this world.

I was shaken from my reverie by the noisy arrival of a wagon full of ladies. They were young, pretty and giddy with excitement. They called out that they had come, "to wave at our brave volunteers!" At which news, an eruption of whooping and throwing of hats started among the men. The girls smiled and waved and made bold eyes. They called out that they would wait for any man brave enough to fight for his country! Hearing this, the men became louder and even more excited. One called boldly for a kiss, "To send me on my way!" Another cried out, "Marry me! And I'll leave a happy man!" The girls pretended to be shocked, hiding their heads and turning away from so bold a suggestion. But they peeked back at the men, giggling and blushing in a most unseemly way. I thought them silly beyond measure. I took myself over to a bench, out of the sun, and sat looking at the ground, drawing idly in the dirt with my boot.

I looked up to see Nate, decked out in a union blue shell jacket with a forage cap on his head. Behind him, Eli wore a similar uniform. They both saluted proudly. Privates Eli and Nate Reinhardt reporting for duty," they said in unison. Despite my misgivings, I laughed and my heart swelled with pride at the sight of them.

"You look…"

"Like soldiers?" Eli suggested.

"Like soldiers!" I agreed. "So what happens next?"

"We have our orders," Eli pulled a sheet of paper from his jacket and handed it to me. "We leave this afternoon, as soon as the enlistment is completed. We are marching south of here to Camp Douglas. There we will undergo training and be issued further orders. This is it, sis. We are really on our way! Oh, and we received *this*." He pulled a handful of bills from his pocket. "A thirteen dollar advance, just for signing up. Take it, sis. Put it towards the purchase of a farm."

"And take mine too," Nate said, stuffing more dollars into my hands. "We'll have the farm before you know it!"

"I'll not take every dollar you have between you," I said through tears. "Here, take a few dollars, both of you. You never know what you'll be needing."

"We'll be needing socks and underwear."

I looked at them blankly.

"The army doesn't supply them. Nor shirts neither. Good job we both came wearing ours!"

"Write to me and I'll send them," I said quietly. "Making underwear is what women are good for!"

Nate punched me good-naturedly. "Thanks, sis," he added softly. "I know this is hard for you."

I felt a tear sting my eye.

We haggled over money for a moment. Then each of them reluctantly agreed to keep three dollars for himself, but I was to keep the rest."

"It's for the farm, Becky. It's what we're fighting for," Eli said.

"You're fighting for that and for …"

"Privates! Report for duty!" a voice boomed from across the yard, cutting off my words. At once, a wailing cry went up from the women gathered all over the square. The men still in line yelled at those ahead of them to "Move faster!" Mothers held babies up to their fathers for one last kiss. Sweethearts embraced. Wives held back tears.

"I'm surprised Lena Kaltenbach wasn't here to say goodbye," I said pointedly.

Eli blushed, and thought better of denying the attachment. "I should have known better than to think it would remain a secret from you, sis."

"Why isn't she here then?" I persisted.

"We thought…I thought it might be easier if we said our goodbyes last night," he blushed violently. "It can be a little public out here, don't you think?"

Looking around us at the shocking lack of decorum, I could not help but applaud his good sense.

"Indeed it can, brother. Is there anything you wish me to tell her?" It was cruel of me to tease him so.

"No, no indeed…I believe I have said all that needed to be …"

"It's all right, Eli, I am playin' with you." I patted his arm.

"You take care of yourself now, Beck," Nate declared. I could almost feel how badly he wanted to be off.

"Wait a minute," I suddenly said, "Where are they sending you again?"

"For training!" Eli said proudly, "To a place called Camp Douglas."

"Yeah, it's in Chicago! And we're walking!" Nate was beaming ear to ear. I wished I could share his joy.

We hugged one another again, but it wasn't the same. They were soldiers now and I had been left behind.

Chapter Six

The only comfort to be had in church that Sunday was a poor one. Lena's pale, unhappy face was a mirror of my own. Indeed, it was hard to tell which of us was the sadder, her or me. On the surface, life continued much as it had the month before, only nothing was the same. Whereas I was, in general, of a sunny disposition, when I came back from Deerfield I was other than myself. Which, is as much to say, that I was sad, miserable or despondent, depending upon the time of day. This did bring about one pleasant outcome, namely that, in consequence, Otto gave up in his effort to "brighten my life," as he put it, and more or less left me alone.

"One day you'll come and seek me out," he said sadly.

"That will be a cold day in hell!" I thought, but I kept my counsel. No point in aggravating the situation.

We were now well into the summer. Warm weather and frequent rainfall had caused the corn to grow fast. It stood almost as tall as I was, and threw shadows on the ground as I walked across the field. Around the dinner table, talk was all of the war: who had enlisted, who was going to enlist, which men spoke of enlistment but were widely thought to be cowardly. Rumors spread like wildfire, fueled by anxiety, curiosity, pride and anger at the rebel states. We all fervently believed in the justness of our cause. None of us ever doubted that the rebel states were in the wrong. From the pulpits in every neighborhood, exhortations to join the righteous cause rang out across the land. Ministers and pastors loudly declared that our President's words, at his inauguration, had been truly spoken and that, "no state upon its own mere motion could lawfully get out of the Union." Much as I hated to have my brothers leave, and much as I feared for their safety and for the safety of all the Northern boys, I came to see we had no choice but to fight. Not to do so would jeopardize everything.

"Just imagine where we would be, had this country not existed," exclaimed the pastor one Sunday. "How many of you men would own your own land? Not many, I'll be bound. And rather than sitting here today, free men, able to determine your own futures by the dint of hard work and sacrifice, you would be working twice, nein, three times as hard but for the good of the landowner, not to put bread on your own tables! We owe this country everything, my friends. And now, in her hour of need, it behooves us to defend her!"

The pastor's words stirred my blood. Everywhere I went, I kept thinking how different life would have been, had my parents never left the old country. True, it was men, and not women, who held power in this new land. But, it had always been so, although I doubted it would stay that way for ever. Meanwhile, we had riches beyond our grandparents' wildest dreams. And even though that villain Kessler had taken our land from us, I knew we would win it back. One way or another, we would win it back or die trying!

The days and weeks passed slowly. There was little news out of Camp Douglas. In the absence of solid fact, rumor rank amuck. Someone heard there was illness in the camp and that all who went there perished. Another person heard the men were short of food and shoes and still another heard that the 1st Illinois had left the camp and were fighting for their very lives at Pittsburgh Landing. No one knew which batteries, if any, had been deployed. Plunged into an agony of uncertainty, I determined to find out as much as I could of the army and the battles that absorbed it.

My skill with the wagon had not gone unnoticed and several times a month, once the chores were done, I was allowed to drive into Northfield and over to the general store, where Mr. McMurphy kept a copy of *The Herald* displayed in the window. A crowd would gather every time he changed the paper. Someone in front would read the stories to the crowd behind, with everyone exclaiming and commenting on the progress of the war.

Despite their promises to write, there was still no word from my brothers. In order to stay close to them, I became obsessed with learning everything I possibly could about artillery service. I picked the brains of every man known to have served in the Mexican War, who was now too old to fight. I read and reread the pages of *The Herald*. And most helpful of all, I found a small book entitled *Artillery for the United States Land Service*, at the back of the general store. Published in 1849, it was said to be the bible of every artillery man, whether he served the cause of the North or the South. I resolved to understand it. But this was no easy task. It was a difficult book. There was page after page of miniscule print, replete with words and terms I had never before heard of. But I put my mind to the task, and by reading and reading its dull pages, I received something of an education in the military mind. Indeed, I was so often turning the pages of that obscure little book, that Mr. McMurphy suggested I take it home and pay for it later, when I was able. Which, bless the man, was many years after I started reading.

The book became my inseparable companion. I carried it in my apron everywhere I went. Any time there was a lull in the chores, I would pull it out and study a few more pages.

I learned there were two kinds of artillery, mounted and horse. Mounted meant that the officers and drivers rode and horse meant that everyone did. My brothers' unit, being light artillery, represented the mounted kind.

The smallest unit in the volunteer army was a battery and a battery fired canon. For some reason, the army called canons "guns." A battery comprised six guns, each under the command of a sergeant. Every pair of guns was commanded by a lieutenant and seven or eight men were needed to keep a single gun in the field. Since each gun required two corporals to serve it, one served as the gunner, the man who fired the piece, and the other was in charge of the caisson, a fancy name for the ammunition wagon.

I found that the army set great store by the kind of uniform worn, and the shape, color and placement of ribbons and trim worn on the jacket. Try as I might, I couldn't see the point of so many ribbons and epaulettes. But the manual devoted many pages to describing the differences between them, so it must have been important.

Cross canons were the badge of the artillery service, but the cross was nothing like the symbol of our Lord. Rather, it presented a set of dulls Vs, the top and bottom of which were wider than the other sides.

I learned that enlisted men wore a brass version of the canon on their hats, along with a number indicating their artillery regiment and a letter designating the battery. My brothers, then, would be wearing a 1 and a G.

I struggled mightily to understand how batteries became sections, sections became regiments and regiments became armies. I threw the book down more than once, frustrated with a system so cumbersome and obscure that outsiders couldn't grasp it. But I would not allow the nonsense to defeat me. One afternoon, I sat on the ground with a stick in one hand and the book in the other, and drew the formations and combinations of men until I had it clear in my mind. Then I recited it over and over until I knew it back and forth and forth and back. In time, I guess I knew as much about army matters as any civilian could possibly know.

By early September, news of the Union's disastrous showing at Second Bull Run was widely known. Union General John Pope had led our troops to near disaster and many in the North secretly felt General Lee's army undefeatable, though it were treason to say so. When Lee's army crossed the Potomac to invade Maryland, there was near pandemonium in certain quarters. Around the dinner table, the Bischoff men argued loudly over the strategies of the opposing armies. When I suggested the key would be rivers and railroad junctions there was a stunned silence. Karl laughed out loud, as if I, a mere woman, had no right to speak of such things. But when Konrad, his father challenged me, I replied that the movement of troops and supplies would win or lose the war for the South.

"How so, little girl," he said, eyes twinkling.

I stiffened at the condescension. "Because the North has more of both, and if the naval blockade continues, we will strangle the South and win the war."

"That's a great theory," Karl said, scathingly. "I suppose you haven't noticed Lee winning every fight!"

"He's good, possibly the best general in the field," I replied firmly," But even Lee can't feed his men on air. Neither can he shoot without guns or powder. If we hold the rivers and the railroads, we'll defeat him. It's just a matter of time."

"Now you're an expert on the war, just because your brothers enlisted?"

"Karl! There's no call to be rude to Miss Reinhardt!"

"It's all right, Mr. Bischoff," I told him. "I am sure Karl means well." I thought no such thing, but I had no wish to upset Annamarie. Even so, I shot a look at Karl, who had the sense to keep his mouth shut..

"You seem to be well informed," Konrad continued. "Unusual…"

"For a woman?"

"Well, yes, I suppose so."

"Why shouldn't a woman know these things?"

"Rebekkah reads a lot," Otto said proudly, "about the war."

Obviously he had been watching me.

"Why would she read about the war?" Karl demanded. "It isn't natural."

"It isn't natural to fight!" I retorted. "Or that's what the preacher says. But we do it anyway."

"Why d'you read about the army then? It's not as if you're going to enlist or anything."

"And why shouldn't I?"

There was a stunned silence.

Karl sniggered.

"Why shouldn't a woman enlist?" I glared at them. "We are as patriotic as the rest of you!"

"It's not about being patriotic, Rebekkah," said Konrad. "Women don't join armies."

"Well, why don't they?"

"Rebekkah, don't be silly," he sounded genuinely puzzled. "Why would a woman join the army?"

"Why would a man?"

"Because it's his duty."

"And why not hers?"

He shook his head.

Annamarie looked up from the hearth where she was heating up the iron.

"You really want to know, Rebekkah?"

"Yes, I really want to know. I want a good reason why women can't fight just the same as men."

"Well, for the same reason they do not draw the plough or chop down trees," she said.

"And that is?"

"God made women to have babies," she said simply," and to mind the family. He didn't mean us to go running off with guns shooting people."

"He didn't mean for men to either and they do it just the same!"

The subject was quickly and irrevocably changed. Henceforth, we were to talk about the harvest, the weather, Sunday prayers. In short, *anything* other than the war and fighting.

I sat in silence. I hadn't heard an answer to my question, and I couldn't for the life of me supply one. Why *couldn't* women fight just the same as men? The question wouldn't go away. Late into the night, I found myself wondering about it. No answer I gave myself settled the matter to my satisfaction.

Chapter Seven

Sometimes the most momentous decisions of our life are not made, they simply arise. Thus, it is with some difficulty, that I attempt to describe how I found myself one morning outside a recruiting tent in Chicago. I had left the Bischoff's farm hours earlier after borrowing one of their horses, and arranging with a stable in Chicago to house it there until it could be collected. I had left a note on my bed, thanking the family for their hospitality and apologizing for the use of their horse. I assured them, I would pay for his sojourn in the city. With any luck, they would collect him before the money for his keep ran out. I'm afraid I then told a terrible lie. I wrote that I had received word from my father and that I was to join him in California immediately and was to travel there by any means possible. I left it to them to figure out which route I could have taken, hoping that by the time they exhausted all possibilities, I would have long since disappeared.

After writing my thank yous, I then took another piece of paper, wrote the number eighteen on it and placed it underneath my foot, between myself and my sock. I had not wanted to go to hell for telling two untruths in the same morning, and being a few months shy of my eighteenth birthday, I had thought to be honest about my standing at the time. With this concession to the truth, I took a blade and by the light of a flickering candlelight, I cut my long hair as close to the skin as possible. I then collected it all, in a piece of cloth, to be disposed of along the way. Examining myself in the mirror, I saw standing before me a slender young man of average height, with close-cropped light brown hair and bright blue eyes set in pale skin. He was dressed conventionally in faded brown work pants, a red and green checked shirt and brown boots. He was clean-shaven and looked healthy, though a little tired. I watched as he pulled on an old brown beehive, checking his reflection left and right and seeing not a stray wisp of hair. Satisfied with what I saw, I picked up my leather satchel from the floor, turned from the mirror and slipped out of the room without a backwards glance. Deep inside the satchel were my mother's locket and brush, the only outward signs of the old life I was leaving, making my way to the stable, I took the oldest horse I could find. I threw an old saddle and reins onto him, before walking him quietly down the path to the north/south road, where I then threw myself into the saddle.

I had thought to arrive in the city at first light, but riding in the dark was harder than I imagined. Besides, the horse I had so thoughtfully chosen was not in the best of shape. Thus, it was approaching eight the next morning when I arrived outside the recruiting office in Chicago. I had not troubled to enlist at the recruiting office closest to the stables, just in case my story about pa and California struck the Bischoffs as false. Instead, I walked past two other offices and headed for one further away, figuring no one would be looking for me so far south.

As soon as I arrived, I thought I would be undone. No one was on line inside and the corporal in charge looked up expectantly when I opened the door, ready to give me his full attention. But I was mistaken. Happy to direct "yet another one" to the enlistment line, he bade me leave the storefront and turn at once to my right, where I would find "plenty waiting" before me.

To my immense relief, as soon as I turned the corner, I came upon a throng of men who were pushing and jostling one another in their haste to enlist. No one paid me the slightest mind. When I pulled my hat down further over my face, I happily blended in among them, grateful for the shoving and shouting and general air of confusion.

"Where you from then, young 'un?" I turned to find a man, in his mid to late thirties, with a grizzled face and a gap-toothed grin staring at me in a not unfriendly manner. I had given my story a lot of thought and I hoped it would serve me well.

"I'm from south of here," I told him, "south of the city."

"Farm boy are ye?"

"That's right, sir. I was raised on a farm."

"I thank ye kindly, but there's no need to be calling me sir," the man laughed, revealing a mouthful of discolored teeth. He reached in his pocket, stuffed a wad of tobacco into his mouth and started chewing. "Want some?" He shoved the wad in my direction.

"Very neighborly of ye, but I think I'll pass," I said, giving what I hoped to be a diffident shrug. The man only laughed.

"You're too young to have gained any bad habits then, are ye? I'll warrant you'll be taking up the weed sooner than not, once they start shooting at ye!" He seemed to find this most amusing. He was soon laughing and coughing in equal measure, drawing a great deal of attention down upon the two of us. Luckily, most people were laughing at him and few seemed to mind me, standing beside him. He glared at them, spat a wad of yellow-looking phlegm at the feet of the nearest man and wiped his hand on his pants before offering it to me. I swallowed my dismay and stuck out mine in return.

"Fritz Vogel," he said pleasantly.

"Josef Schmidt," I replied. "Pleased to meet you!"

"Pleased to me you too, son," he said. "Why you joining?"

"For my country," I said quickly.

Fritz threw back his head and laughed.

"For the money, son," he spat again. "I want to buy me a piece of land and raise hogs."

"You don't own land now?"

"'Fraid not, son. Had me a bit of bad luck…" he mimicked an arm going up and down and made a slurping sound…," if you get my meaning. I've been dry these many years, but I ain't never gotten my land back. Lost my family too. Work where I can." Brightening, he added, "But this fight's gonna put me back where I wanna be."

"Raising hogs?"

"Like my granddaddy before me and his father before that! In the old country!"

"That's good, Fritz! That's good. I'm sure you'll make it!"

While we were talking, the line was moving and suddenly Fritz was pushing me forward.

"Your turn, Josef!"

"Great! Great!"

My heart was pounding as I stepped up to the desk, certain that every eye was upon me. But the sergeant sitting at the small table didn't even raise his head. I pulled the satchel close against my side. It was all I had left of home.

"You over eighteen and in good health?"

Gratefully, I thought of the letter laying snug under my sock.

"Yes, sir!" I answered truthfully.

"You know this is an artillery unit?"

I looked up at the banner over his head. "2nd ILLINOIS LIGHT ARTILLERY CAPT. JIM MAGGIORE'S BATTERY C ATTACHED TO COL. STEVEN CURTIS' 3rd REGIMENT." I would have been sarcastic, but I didn't want the attention. "Yes, sir!" I said simply.

"I'm a sergeant, son. You don't address me as sir."

"Okay…"

"Sergeant." He had an amused look on his face, as if my discomfort was the highlight of his day. My temper was rising, and I fought to hold my tongue.

"…sergeant."

"You know how to use a gun?"

"Yes, sergeant."

"You any good?" he smirked.

"I get by."

"We'll see. Sign here." He pointed at the last line on the page. The page was filled with scrawled signatures and a few marks, where men hadn't known their letters. I signed "Josef Schmidt," with a flourish.

"Next!" He nodded behind him by way of dismissing me. I moved on to the medical exam. I could hardly believe I had gotten this far.

My brothers' exams had gone quickly. I was hoping for the same. But to my dismay, I saw that several lines of recruits were being channeled into one long line for the medical examiner, who seemed to be taking his time examining recruits. Behind me, I heard raised voices. I looked back to see Fritz and the sergeant staring at one another with tense expressions on their faces. Fritz said something about being a young know it all. At which the sergeant sprang to his feet and Fritz adopted a pose like a cockerel in a henhouse. Then both men leaned forward until they were practically nose to nose. A captain rushed over to see what all the fuss was about, followed closely by two privates.

"What's going on?" the captain demanded, sounding out of breath.

"Your sergeant here is an arrogant ass!" Fritz replied.

"And this man's not fit for duty!"

"Says who, ye young…!"

"Now, now," said the captain smoothly. "I am sure this good man…what's your name, sir? Fritz, you say? I am sure Fritz here misunderstood what you were meaning, sergeant. After all," he gave the sergeant a knowing look, "this army needs all the good men it can get."

The sergeant spluttered, but didn't dare say anything. I was hard put not to laugh. The two men looked ridiculous by now. They were posturing in the sunlight while a crowd of people were waiting to move forward. But neither man would budge. There they stood, nose to nose, mouthing insults at one another. The captain wasted no more time. He pulled the sergeant off the line and replaced him with another. Apologizing to Fritz for his trouble, he made some conciliatory remarks and encouraged the signing of the document. As Fritz walked forward, the captain's expression hardened. The displaced sergeant stood to one side, licking his wounds. His expression was vicious. I wondered what punishment would be exacted on Fritz should their paths cross again. As the line moved forward, my immediate concern turned to my own fate. I was less than six men away from the front of the line. The doctor seemed to be taking his time examining every enlistee. To my dismay, several of the men were asked to remove their shirts, at which point he examined their chests. If that happened to me, there would be no escape. With a sinking heart, I realized I was done for. I might as well leave the line. There was no way I could remove my shirt and escape detection. While I was wondering how I should explain my change of heart to the Bischoffs, the line shuffled forward and it was too late to back out. Suddenly the doctor stood before me. A pleasant man in his fifties, he asked me to open my mouth, where upon he examined my teeth. Next, he placed his fingers on my face and peered first into the left, then into the right eye. His hands felt exceeding cool for a man and smooth too. I was used to the roughened hands of a field worker. These were the hands of a pampered girl!

Hmm?" He looked at me expectantly. With a start, I realized he had asked me a question.

"Would you mind repeating…" I began.

"Don't be nervous, son," he laughed. "I'll not hurt ye."

"Dr. McGreggor? You're wanted over here!" someone yelled. With a sigh, he patted me on the back. "You're fit enough, lad. May God bless ye." And with that, he was gone! I was through!

"Go on, will yer" the man behind me, said. "You're holding up the line!"

I glared at him. "It's hard to be examined when the doctor's over there!"

The man shrugged. "Move forward, that's all!"

I shook my head and walked forward. Next stop was the uniform tent.

I had never been under canvas before. Though the tent was large and high, inside it was very hot and musty and carried a distinct odor. A series of wooden rails had been suspended from the ceiling on which were hung dozens of jackets and pants and long blue coats. Around the walls of the tent, several rows of shelving had been constructed, upon which were stacked all manner of boots and belts and buckles. In one corner, there was a half curtain that acted as changing room. Above it, I could clearly see a bare-chested man pulling on a pair of pants. I had no sooner taken this in, than I was called to a long table at which sat two privates. One was very large, the other was a very slender man. They were such an odd looking pair, that I laughed out loud at the sight of them.

"You have a problem?" the large man asked.

"He seems to have a problem," the thin one echoed.

"You have a problem?" the large man repeated.

"He seems to have a problem," the thinner man echoed again.

I was so astonished that I think my mouth dropped open.

"He seems to have a problem," the thin one said again.

"I…I don't have a problem," I managed to say.

"He doesn't have a problem," the thin one said. I starred at him for any sign he was joking with me, but his expression betrayed not the slightest hint of a sense of humor.

"Um….I came for a uniform," I began.

"He came for a uniform," the thin one echoed.

I was all ready for the larger man to repeat this information, when he surprised me by pointing to the rail on his left.

"You'll take a jacket from that rack and a pair of pants," he pointed to his left, "from that rack there. A belt you'll find over here…"pointing, "and a hat there."

"Do you want to measure me?" I asked.

"He wants to know if we want to measure him," the thin one echoed.

They both started laughing.

"You're in the army son," said the fatter one." This ain't no fashion show!"

"But…"

"Over there!"

One glance at his expression and I knew further dialogue would get me nowhere but into a fight. I had no wish to draw attention to myself. So without further ado, I collected the items he suggested and was pointed to the curtain at the back of the tent. I pulled the flap aside, and found myself in a small space where three other men were in various states of undress. They paid me no mind at all, which was just as well, for I found myself flushing at the sight of three half naked strangers. In front of me was a small bench upon which I set my knapsack and my uniform.

I already knew that the army issued no shirts, socks or underwear and I had come prepared. When I took off my jacket and civilian pants, my brother's knee-length drawers and shirt covered me sufficiently. Even so, I turned my back to the room before I pulled on my new woolen pants. This did not escape notice by the others in the room, all three of whom had a good laugh at my expense.

"Ah, you're modest now, but wait 'til you get in the field, lad!" the fastest of the three laughed. "There's many a man starts out modest and ends up with his pants down in front of everyone just the same!"

Try as I might, I could say nothing to that. I hoped my flaming face would not betray me when I turned around. As quickly as I could, I pulled up the army pants. I had never been so exposed to a man before. And here I was, half undressed, within several feet of three of them! With trembling fingers I fastened the three top buttons. The pants fit perfectly! Even the legs were not too long. I fastened the belt around my waist, pulled on the shell jacket- another near perfect fit- and exchanged my work cap for an army kepi. Picking up my knapsack and my civilian clothes, I stepped into the main tent again and examined myself in the mirror. I gasped at the transformation. Standing before me was Private Josef Schmidt!

"Over here, lad! Where shall we send your clothing?" the large man asked.

"You…you may as well keep it, thank you kindly. My folks are deceased."

He nodded, as if this were a frequent occurrence. "Over here!" he said. He had already moved on to the next person.

"That way," the thin one said, nodding at the exit. Amazing. I got out of bed that morning a woman. I left the house a man. I stepped out of the tent a union soldier. And, it was not yet noon.

Chapter Eight

To reach Camp Douglas, my brothers had marched some twenty miles. We, being already in southernmost Chicago, were to march a mere two. There looked to be seventy men, commanded by a captain and three lieutenants. Behind them were half a dozen sergeants and a group of corporals. I didn't recognize any of them from that morning.

They directed us to line up two abreast. I fell into line with the man immediately to my right. He was only an inch taller than me, although considerably wider. He acknowledged me with a nod of his head.

"Gottfried Lange," he said.

"Josef Schmidt."

"Where you from?"

"Upstate. Near Wisconsin. You?"

"South of here."

A lieutenant stepped forward. Despite his proud manner, I sensed at once he didn't know what he was doing. The others sensed it too. There was an imperceptible shift in the crowd.

"I am Lieutenant Yanke," he announced, with an air of self-importance. His voice was high-pitched for a man, which didn't help him much in his bid to control the unruly crowd.

"We're headed for Camp Douglas!"

Judging by the muttering and exchanged shrugs, it seemed few of the men had heard of it. He didn't enlighten us, he just kept barking orders. "Now get into line!" We looked at one another.

"We're already in line, lieutenant!" someone yelled from behind me.

"Let's get out of line and back again!" someone else suggested.

There was wide- scale laughter. A line of red moved swiftly across the lieutenant's face, down to his collar. His nostrils flared and he shouted even louder, "Stop laughing! Stop laughing, I said! Stand up straight! Stand up straight!"

Behind him, even the sergeants were laughing. None of them made any move to aid the man, who stood there ridiculed by one and all. When the line was finally quiet, he slapped his arm against his leg and screamed a few obscenities in our direction.

"Pay attention, you men!" he yelled, looking to the sergeants for assistance. A large man finally stepped forward. One look at him and everyone was quiet and stood to attention.

"Take over, sergeant!"

"Yes, sir!" barked the man, saluting.

"My name is Billings," barked the sergeant, looking us over slowly. He seemed to be an officious little man, although he clearly knew what he was doing, I took an immediate dislike to him. His manner was imperious and "fussy", as if he cared way too much about unimportant matters. His tongue moved slowly around his mouth as if he were considering what to say next. No one moved a muscle. All was silence.

"When I say 'Halt', plant your left foot firmly on the ground like so and bring your right foot next to it!" he barked. I noticed his beady little eyes were darting to and fro along the line, like a startled rabbit. I suppressed a giggle.

"Stand to attention, back straight, eyes forward and await further instructions. When I say 'March', lead with your left foot. Keep in step with the man directly in front of you. Eyes front. Is that clear?"

"Yes, sergeant," we all yelled.

"Yes, Sergeant Billings!"

"Yes, Sergeant Billings!" we repeated. Clearly, this was a man used to being obeyed.

Billings gave the order to start marching. Although Yankowitz marched at the head of the line, it was clear to all of us the sergeant was in charge. I wondered who Yankowitz was and how he got appointed. It couldn't have been on merit.

We set off around noon, the lieutenant in front, followed by the sergeants and the corporals, who flanked our line to both left and right. The sun was overhead, and, despite the short distance between us and the camp, after about ten minutes, I found myself breaking a sweat. Pretty soon, my face, arms and legs were damp. I felt water trickling between my breasts, underneath the cotton work shirt. I tried my best not to wipe myself, but once or twice I wriggled my shoulders to try and ease the discomfort. My companion laughed and told me to go ahead and scratch. Which I did.

I was not used to the feel of wool next to my skin. The heat from the sun bore into me and puddles of sweat were forming now on my back, arms and legs. I wondered how long I could bear it. But to my amazement, after a while it began to feel less, not more intense. It began to feel almost bearable. In fact, the more I sweated, the better I felt. We were fairly spread out along the road and the nearest corporal was several men away.

"How d'you find the wool, Josef?" Gottfried whispered.

"I'm getting used to it."

He grinned.

Minutes later we arrived at the camp, marching in formation through the wide wooden gates. We found ourselves in a large square dominated by the Union flag and filled with soldiers, wagons and horses. It was wildly chaotic but Billings directed us quickly through the maze of people and equipment. We burst through the crowd and found ourselves on a make-shift shift dirt road leading between two rows of wooden huts. He stopped before the third one.

"Take care of your men, corporal!"

A trim-looking man with sandy hair stepped forward. "Yes, Sergeant Billings."

"Okay, men. I'm Corporal McWherter and *this* (indicating with a sweep of his arm) will be your quarters from now until you muster out. Find a bed. Take a rest. We drill at three."

"But we missed lunch, corporal," yelled the man who had interrupted earlier.

"You could probably do with missing a meal, Hager!" he retorted to widespread laughter.

"Oh.....but the army cooks so good!"

I looked over at the private. He seemed the jovial type, a big man, with a large belly and bushy red hair.

"Then you'll be all the more ready for your tea, won't you!" the corporal finished. The two men seemed to share a mutual respect born, I found out, of long term acquaintance. This was more than could be said for sergeant, who seemed almost universally despised.

Without further ado, we were summarily dismissed into the hut, which they called a barracks and which looked to be a place designed for thirty men. By my reckoning, there were a hundred of us. Inside, four rows of cots were arranged in double tiers, four single beds on their own at the front of the room. These, I surmised, were for the sergeants. In the center there was a chimney that doubled as a stove. On top of it stood a griddle stacked high with pots and kettles, some of which were steaming. It was August and the temperature in the room was somewhere north of unbearable. Many of the beds were occupied by men in various stages of undress, on account of the heat. The stench of sweat and unwashed bodies knocked me sideways the moment I entered.

"Toughen up, lad, you'll get used to it," someone told me, not unkindly. "Find yourself an empty bed and take a load off."

I found a spot, on the top of a bed near the back of the room. I was furthest away from the door and any hint of fresh air. I threw my satchel up first and used my arms to haul my body up. Then I pealed off my jacket and my boots and rubbed my feet.

"Take your shirt off, lad, you'll regret it if you don't," the man in the next bed advised. He was lying not a foot away, looking straight at me and lying buck naked like the day he was born.

I flushed bright red at that and looked away, but not before he caught a glimpse of my flaming face and roared at the sight of me. "Lord what have we here! Virgin eyes, lads!"

The men in the surrounding beds had a good laugh at my expense and I was mortified by the unexpected and unwelcome attention. The last thing I wanted was to be singled out from the others. I was feeling panic, but the man next to me laughed and said, "Relax, kid, you'll get used to it."

I lay back on my bunk, hot and miserable. Sweat was pouring off me, and my freshly-washed shirt was a soaking ball of sweaty cotton. The heat and smells in the room were nauseating. Men were smoking, yelling and using language better suited to a hog farm. I was not accustomed to hearing men talking in this way. It was uncomfortable and embarrassing. Before I knew it, I had swung my legs over the side of the bed, jumped down and was headed for the door.

"Where you off to, Virgin Eyes?" someone yelled.

"To find something better looking than you," I yelled back, pitching my voice as low as I could.

The men's easy laughter told me this was a good response.

Outside the air was fresher, if no less hot. I breathed in deeply, trying to shake off the smell of dankness and sweat. I walked away from the barracks, pushing through the streams of men in uniform, while heading back towards the main square. It was no less crowded than before, with men in uniform coming and going at a frenzied pace. Horse-drawn wagons were driving in and out of the gates, loaded down with supplies. Officers were barking orders. Men were shouting greetings, and not a few curses, from one side of the square to the other. There was a general air of chaos and disorder.

I was shaken from my reveries by an urgent screaming and whooping. Pushing myself back against the safety of a brick building just behind me, I watched in amazement as a horde of drunken-seeming men, with sabers drawn, whooped through gates shouting and brandishing their swords. Unimpressed by the attempts of two sentries to halt their progress, they proceeded to challenge any soldier or officer who dared stand in their way. Screaming and shouting abuse, they galloped noisily out of sight, disappearing down a dirt track to the left. The sounds of whooping and cheering could be heard above the noise, along with some scattered gunshots. I was pretty shaken up by the whole thing.

"Who *were* they?" I asked no one in particular.

"That would be Colonel Ritchie's men," a soldier replied. They're back from a two day furlough and I daresay they spent most of it in a bar down the street."

"They're allowed to drink in uniform?" I asked, amazed.

"Drinking, shooting, fighting duels...It's stopping them that's the issue, not giving them permission."

"But they're in uniform!" I repeated.

"You must be new, lad," the man chuckled. "You've got a lot to learn!" Shaking his head and laughing he wandered off into the crowd. I continued my inspection of the camp, wondering what kind of army I had signed on for.

"Hold it there, private!"

With a start, I realized the barked order was directed at me. I turned and found myself starring at a well-dressed, angry-looking captain of artillery, his light blue eyes full of fury and his mouth set in a hard line.

"Well, private, what have you to say for yourself?" he demanded.

"I... I'm sorry, sir. I don't understand the question."

"Don't understand the question? Well, young man, the question, as you put it, is this. Since when does a private walk past an officer without saluting? That, son, is the question!"

His action and his manner of forming words was strange to me. I didn't know what to say.

"I..I'm sorry sir, I'm afraid I didn't see you."

"Didn't see me!" he blustered. "Aren't I big enough for you?"

"Yes, sir. I mean. No sir."

"Well, which is it, yes or no?"

"I don't know, sir. I'm afraid I wasn't paying attention," I said, feeling stupid. "I just didn't see you."

"Remind me to keep well away from you on the battle field."

"Yes, sir," I relied. Not one day in the army and already I was failing miserably.

He turned on his heel then turned back. "And if you had seen me, what would you have done?" he barked.

"I …would have said good afternoon, sir."

"Good afternoon!" he blustered, turning so red, I thought he should have burst all the buttons off his jacket.

"What should I have said then, sir?"

"You shouldn't have *said* anything, young man. You *should* have saluted. This is the army, young man, not some goddamned social club! You pass an officer, you salute him, god damn it! Don't they teach you people anything! How the hell are we going to win a war with idiots like you for an army? Which unit are with anyway? When did you join up?"

I felt my temper rising at the absurdity of the thing. "I'm with the 2nd Illinois Light Artillery. Captain Jim Maggiore's Battery C. And I joined this morning… SIR," I said indignantly. "I'm sorry I didn't see you. And I didn't know I was meant to salute. Everything's kinda new right now. I was just curious about the camp, that's all! And then those men started shooting..." For a moment, we stared one another down. It occurred to me, that this was not a good idea. Then all at once his expression changed. To my amazement, he threw back his head and roared with laughter.

"Are you always this spunky, boy?"

"Reckon I am, sir."

"Hmm." He stared at me a while. "We'll make a soldier of you yet, boy. The enemy's in trouble surely, if you attack them with this intensity!"

I bit my lip.

"What's your name?"

"Josef Schmidt, sir."

"Where'd you hail from, son?"

"Upstate, sir."

"Hmm."

He turned on his heel and again thought better of it.

"And by the way...?"

"Sir?"

"Next time you see, me, salute, would you?"

I saluted smartly. "Yes, sir! Indeed sir!"

The captain turned and walked briskly away.

"Wow! You got balls, kid. Either that, or you're missing a few brain cells."

I looked round into the face of a boy about my age, with red hair and a very freckled nose.

"Virgil. Virgil Jones."

He stuck out his hand.

"Josef, Josef Schmidt," I said.

"So I heard. Any idea who you was talking to?"

"Captain someone or other."

He snorted. "Captain someone! That was Captain Mallory. One of the toughest guys around here. Very ambitious for higher office. You sure made an impression on *him*!"

"I didn't mean to. I was just minding my own business. Why does he speak like that?"

"He's from England. They all talk that way."

"Oh."

"Anyway, the new rule is you salute every officer, every time!"

"I didn't know the old rule. What was that? Salute every other officer, every other time?"

"You sure are strange! You're gonna get yourself in a heap of trouble with an attitude like that!"

"I don't know what you mean," I said. "Alls I'm doing is trying to figure this place out."

"You'll find out soon enough! For instance, every afternoon…"

He was interrupted by the sound of a bugle. All eyes were directed to the middle of the square, where a bugler and half a dozen drummers were marching and playing a loud, military-sounding tune.

"Like I was saying, every afternoon we have drill. Four straight hours."

"Four hours!"

"At least, yeah. Better get back to your unit." He set off at a trot.

"Wait!" I called after him. "What's your unit?"

"Same as yours!" he flashed me a grin.

I trotted after him.

"Great!" I said.

I caught up with him. "So, you seem to know what's going on. What are we drilling so much for?"

"It's how they teach us to be soldiers."

"Don't we have to study battle plans and things?"

"Heck, no!" He seemed to find this very amusing. "That's not for the likes of us! Why should *we* know what we're doing! Alls we need to know is how to follow orders. That means marching and stopping, marching and stopping."

"But what about shooting?"

He stopped in his tracks, and shot me a look that was part surprise and part scorn. "That's pretty simple. Shoot them aforen they shoot you!"

"Wait a minute, I have to write that down!"

"You what...?"

"It's a joke, Virgil!"

I trotted on.

"Wait a minute!" he shouted after me. "You can write?"

"Ha, ha!" I yelled.

Something caused me to stop and look back at him.

"You mean you can't?"

"Not hardly," he said. "Maybe you could learn me?"

"Sure," I said. "Of course I can!"

His face brightened then. We trotted side by side, back to the front of the barracks, where the battery was assembling hastily.

Men of every shape and condition were struggling into wet shirts and damp wool jackets. I ran inside, grabbed my jacket and had it buttoned up by the time I got back outside. Four lines of men were forming under the shouted direction of the sergeants. I took my place at the end of a line, behind a wiry man with a gray moustache and a thick head of curly gray/brown hair.

In no time at all we were marching down the dirt track and round the square. Left leg, right leg, halt. When we got to the end of the square, the corporals had the line tack left, directing the men at the front of the line to march in baby steps, while the men behind them swung the line around them. When we banked right, he had the men at the rear swing the opposite way. Despite the heat and the dust thrown up by the marching of so many feet, I enjoyed the drill. It was exhilarating to be part of a unit. I had never been with so many others before, performing a common task. It was a new experience and it was totally absorbing. Four hours passed in no time and despite the grumbling and complaining of those around me, I enjoyed myself a great deal.

"Stupid, ain't it?" a man grumbled as he shuffled past. "My feet is killing me! My boots are too small and my socks got holes in them."

"Least you got socks. What are you complaining about, you old goat!"

"Ah, mind your manners, will ye. Alls I'm saying is we didn't ought to be marching around all afternoon. Never caught no enemy by marching."

"Officers got nothing better to do than make us march all afternoon. Reckon they wanna keep us busy."

"Don't make no sense to me!"

"Wanna play a hand of cards?"

"You bet. But you cheat me this time, and I'll have ye."

"I beat you fair and square."

"The heck you did!"

As they moved past me, I was startled by a familiar voice.

"So young man, what did you think of your first drill?"

I turned to find myself staring into the face of Captain Mallory. I stopped dead in my tracks and saluted briskly. "I enjoyed it, sir."

"And why was that, private?"

"It had a sort of … majesty to it." I blushed awkwardly.

He stared at me and I feared I had made an ass of myself again.

"That is …" I began.

"I know what you mean, son. There's nothing like the feel of a hundred men marching in unison."

I nodded vigorously.

"It's even better when you get a thousand marching as one."

"I should like to see that, sir."

"So you shall, private. So you shall."

He walked on past the line of stragglers making their way to the tent. Sergeant Billings came over and snarled at me. "Sucking up to the captain, are you! Don't think it'll win you points with me!"

"But I wasn't, sergeant!"

"Why would the captain speak to the likes of you!"

"I'm sure I don't know, sergeant."

"Pretty pleased with yourself for a private, aren't you!"

"But, I was only…"

"You was only…" he bellowed. "You can clean the officers' boots!"

I opened my mouth, but thought better of it.

"You were saying?"

"I was saying, at once, sergeant!.."

" Hrump! The boots are in my quarters….That way, before you ask."

"Yes, sergeant."

I made my way wearily to the barracks behind ours, where at least a dozen pair of boots lay scattered on the floor. The corporal followed me into the building, pointed to a pile of rags and a bucket of waxy looking substance.

"Make sure you do a good job!" he smirked. "Since you like army life so much, I'll be sure to give you lots of extra jobs to keep you happy!"

"Thank you…sergeant," I said cheerfully, setting about my task.

I stuck my tongue out and muttered "you hateful man!" under my breath the moment his back was turned.

"I guess I'm in the army now!" I grimaced as I set to work.

Sergeant Billings had clearly taken a real dislike to me, prompted no doubt by my over-zealous drilling and by Captain Mallory's attention. Whatever the case, he had me clean the same pair of boots no fewer than four times, and I could see no good reason for it. Nevertheless, I accepted my fate with a cheerful demeanor. I was encouraged, no doubt, by the fact that the more cheerful I became, the angrier HE became, his face turning beet red as he stomped his foot with temper.

"I don't know why he cares so much for riding boots," I muttered to myself after he left for the fourth time. "He's an artillery officer. He doesn't go anywhere."

"Don't let him bug ye, Virgin Eyes," the man in the bunk next to me muttered, sleepily, as I pulled off my boots. "He'll get shot in the back soon enough."

He rolled over and started snoring. I wondered if he meant it- the part about shooting the sergeant in the back.

"Thanks for the food...er ...?"

I thought he was asleep when he turned towards me and muttered loudly,

"Kessler," he said abruptly.

"You don't have a first name?"

"Just Kessler"

"Oh."

"Sleep tight, Virgin Eyes!"

Chapter Nine

Reveille came early the next morning. I groaned and fought my way into consciousness. All around me men were grumbling, thrusting legs into woolen pants and tired feet into boots. I forced myself upright, willing my eyes to focus and my feet to touch the floor. All the while, I was thinking how splendid it would be just to have another hour, no, maybe just another ten minutes of sleep. My feet, that had so recently left my brother's hand-me-down boots, would not return to their customary place. With difficulty, I pushed them back in, as blistered and sore as they were. I winced a little as blister rubbed against leather, wishing for some of ma's poultice that was so soothing on a body's tired and aching feet.

Once outside, I breathed deeply of the morning air and joined my brother soldiers while slapping my face to get the circulation moving.

"Tired are you, Schmidt?" Billings sneered from somewhere behind me.

"Bright as a button, thank you sergeant!" came my deliberately cheerful reply. I would be damned if he would smirk at *my* expense!

"Let me look at that shirt!" he said. Suddenly he was right in my face. His breath smelt stale as he pushed his face into mine and my whole body stiffened as he pushed himself into me. I must have grimaced because his face contorted and a flash of hatred flew across his features and was quickly covered with a sneer.

"Something botherin' you boy?" he spat. I sensed him baiting me at that point. I wanted so badly to put my fist right through his face, but I knew it would be the end of me to strike a superior.

"Well?" he said.

I shook my head and said cheerfully, "I was hoping we would be marching all day, sergeant. Looks like it might be another hot one!"

"Damn you little pip squeak!" he snarled through clenched teeth. "Don't think I won't break you down, because I will!"

He turned on his heel and marched off. I stood rigid, mouthing some obscenities and giving him a rude gesture to boot. All around me the men were laughing.

"Goddamn it, Virgin Eyes, you sure have gotten onto the wrong side of him!"

"What d'you do, turn him down?" a man asked.

I laughed, unsure of their meaning.

"He don't know, does 'e?" someone said.

"Don't know what?" I asked.

"Everyone knows, lad, that man's as crooked as a stile. You know…" his hand flapped up and down. "He likes boys. He lies with every piece of pretty young meat that comes through the camp and you're as fresh-faced as a young girl!"

"And he wants you!"

I felt my eyes widen in disbelief.

"And you're ignoring him, the poor thing!" someone said. "Couldn't you do it this once, just to be nice!"

There were roars of laughter. I knew I looked horrified. I think my mouth even dropped open and I felt my eyes widen in my face. Men were pointing and laughing at my distress. I couldn't imagine a worse thing to have happened, even if they had they stripped me naked in the middle of the square.

"Just look at his face!" pointing at me. "I don't think he likes the idea!"

"Course, if you *were* a girl, you'd be safe from him. Too bad for you, son!" And he slapped me so hard on the back, I about choked. Just as well, because the ensuing laughter and confusion covered my embarrassment. My body had become an object and they didn't even know who I really was! This was so awful. I wasn't sure how to talk my way out of it. And the men had hold of it like a wild dog with a piece of meat.

"That's why he's always on you, boy!" someone quipped. "It's because he wants to be on you boy! And he laughed real loud at his own joke. Great! As if I didn't have enough to deal with, now I had to protect my female bones from a soldier whose taste ran to young men. I would have laughed if I hadn't felt sick to my stomach.

Just then, thank God, a group of sergeants came running to see what all the yelling was about. Everyone stopped laughing and shuffled themselves into line. The command was given to start marching. Slowly, I felt my heart rate drop and the flush in my face pass away. I was sobered by the thought of Billings lusting after what he thought was my male physique. Urgh! And he was such an unattractive man to start with! The thought of lying with a man like that was enough to send me screaming out of the camp. I knew had to get away from him if I was ever going to survive the army and find my brothers.

"Sorry, lad," Kessler whispered kindly. "Sometimes you run across men whose thinking ain't quite proper."

"Why?" I whispered back. I was totally bewildered.

"Where else are they gonna find lots and lots of nice young men missing their mamas and looking for a bit of affection?"

"Ohhhh!!!" I said, understanding at last.

Gradually the sounds around me overtook my mind. "STEP, step, STEP, step" went our boots as we marched along. The sound calmed me. I forced my mind off of Billings and focused on the blue wool in front of me. We fell into an easy rhythm: LEFT, right. LEFT, right. Once again, I found myself soothed by the act of marching in tandem with my fellow soldiers, and the exhilaration of moving amidst a hundred bodies as if we were one. I liked the discipline of army life. For an hour or two we marched in unison, up and down the main square, banking right and left on command. Our first attempts at banking were none too good, of course, but we soon fell into the habit of watching the men on our flank. When we banked left, the left flank stayed in place, marching in two-step, while the right flank stepped wider until it had wheeled around the left. When we banked right, the right flank stayed put, while the left flank swung around. In no time at all, we were marching like veterans! Even Billings seemed pleased.

I glanced to my right as we did a last turn around the square. A group of senior officers was standing outside headquarters, perusing the square. Standing tall among them, I recognized a pair of bright blue eyes and a trim moustache. I smiled despite myself when I caught his eye. To my surprise, he nodded. As my eyes returned to the back of the man in front of me, I was dismayed to see Billings glowering at me again. He seemed to take the captain's approval of me as a personal affront to him. No! What if...I couldn't think such thoughts. But, darn it!

Over the next few days, we fell into a pattern. The day started early with drill. After morning drill came breakfast, then daily chores. After chores came afternoon drill. We ate in the early evening. There were few complaints on that score. Many of the men were grateful to be fed on a regular basis. Most were equally pleased to be freed for a while from the rigors of life on the farm, with its attendant uncertainties.

In addition to our regular chores, such as sweeping out the barracks, maintaining our uniforms and the like, we rotated through kitchen duty, taking it in turn to make the meals and clean the huge pots. Of all the chores, I hated kitchen rotation the most. It was replete with tedium. We typically peeled several hundred potatoes or shucked a mountain of corn. Cutting and frying the pork was tolerable, as was dicing the mangy birds that passed for chicken at the time. Being mostly farm-raised, we were more than used to hard work and tedium, but my calloused hands took poorly to the amount of peeling and chopping required for the feeding of this many men. I volunteered, when I could, to clean the pots and chop the firewood needed to keep the cauldrons well stoked and the water bubbling.

Five days after we arrived in camp, there was near pandemonium prompted by the delivery of several weapons. A large crowd of men was running towards the back of the camp grounds and I fell in alongside the others, asking anyone who would listen what the hubbub was about. No one seemed to know for sure, but when I turned the corner, I found out. At the back of the camp, on the edge of a clearing, were several twelve- pound howitzers left over from the Mexican-American War. Despite their age, they were in surprisingly good condition, having been lovingly preserved by men who knew better than to let them go to ruin. You could feel the excitement in the air and cries of, "Look at them guns! Look at them guns!" echoed up and down the line. There was a palpable shiver when the officers arrived and ordered us to line up at the edge of a field so we could start drilling. Lieutenant Yankowitz was flanked by several sergeants, including Billings, who wore his usual sour expression. The other three were introduced as Lessing, McWherter and Smith.

Yankowitz divided us smartly into groups of eight, each assigned a number and directed towards a different gun. There seemed to be no rhyme or reason to the groupings, each formed by the accident of standing next to a particular person. Had any of us known how much our very lives would depend upon the seven others in our group, we might have taken more care about whom we stood beside that warm morning. But as it turned out, few of us could have chosen any better than chance did that day.

In my group there were: me, of course; Virgil, who was stand-ing next to me; Kurt Kessler, my gravel-voiced bunk neighbor, who had followed us out of the barracks; Ernst Weinlaeder, a sickly-looking man in his fifties who coughed a lot; Gustaf Oluffson, a tall, taciturn Swede with sandy- blond hair who kept pretty much to himself; Corporal Thomas Peterson, a jovial Englishman from a city called Bristol, who had light brown hair, ruddy red cheeks and bright blue eyes; Ryan Hager, the huge, fun- loving Irishman with the red hair, booming voice and an endless supply of stories (most of them filthy and having to do with women and farm animals); and our Corporal, Johannes Fried, a trim, proper, school teacher by profession, who had a stiff manner and a habit of addressing us all as if we were errant school children and he our master. I didn't care for him at all. All told, we were four Germans, two English, an Irish and a Swede.

"If we was on the other side of the water, I'd be kicking your arse," Ryan said to Tom and Virgil with no particular rancor.

"If we were on the other side, we wouldn't even know you!" Tom replied cheerfully.

"If we weren't in the army, I'd probably shoot you!" replied Ryan.

"We ARE in the army and I'll probably shoot the bunch of yers anyway!" Ryan cut in.

"Something to look forward to," I said dryly, ending the matter.

As luck would have it, our group was number four and we were assigned to McWherter, who, it turned out, had a sense of humor.

"Okay, men, we will start drilling on the gun right away," McWherter shouted. "Take your positions!"

None of us moved. Behind me, I heard someone whispering.

"What are you waiting for?" McWherter barked.

When no one else answered, I volunteered that we were awaiting his instructions.

"What do you mean, private?" he bore down on me.

"I mean, we don't know what to do, sergeant," I said, more forcefully than I felt. "You..er…haven't told us."

"Haven't told you? Waiting for me to show you?" he repeated slowly.

Cursing my foolish honesty, I waited for the ax to fall. The next stop was surely the stockade and twenty lashes applied to my sure- to- be naked back. But an instant later, McWherter laughed.

"Quite right, son," he said good-naturedly. "How come the rest of you didn't say that?" Beaming broadly, he nodded us in the direction of the gun. You could have knocked me down with a feather, I was that surprised at his change in tone. I looked at him sheepishly.

"Relax, son, it was a joke," he said matter-of-factly, as if he made a habit of such things. "Of course you don't know what to do." As for myself, I didn't think it that funny. Neither did my pounding heart, when I realized how close I'd just come to being discovered. Damn me and my big mouth. No one else seemed to notice my discomfort.

"All right men, gather round!" McWherter yelled decisively. "You're about to receive your first lesson in artillery."

The eight of us crushed forward, each man wanting to be the first to touch the strange-looking object. I found myself at the end, pushed nearly into the barrel, which was black and evil-smelling, despite the coldness of the metal underneath my hand.

"I'm going to assign positions," McWherter continued. You'll be one, two…," he turned to me, "three, four…."

I wondered why he had broken the order to make me number three.

"Okay men, you have your eight positions. You are now in a gun crew. The numbers I gave out represent positions on the gun. When I yell your number, you complete the task assigned you for that number. Every man on every crew will learn every position. At a moment's notice, you may be called upon to fill any position. The life of every man among you will depend upon your knowing your job, and every other job, back to front and inside out. Therefore, we will drill all day, every day, until you know these positions better than you know your own mothers."

Several of the men groaned. One cried out, "But I don't like my mother!"

"Goddamn it, man, I don't like mine either!" McWherter snapped, "but I'm damn well stuck with her and you're damn well stuck with the drill!"

After that he explained in general terms what each man did and walked us through the basics involved in loading a gun. Then he told us all to post. We stood to attention, alongside the silent metal witness to so much suffering and so much glory, those many years before. Since I had been assigned position number three, my job was to prick and prime the powder bag so it was ready to fire when the lanyard was pulled. Kessler and Ryan stood at the front of the gun, holding upright the long, sponge rammer. Gustaf and I were ready to prime and fire the piece. Virgil was playing "monkey" and running powder. Thomas and Ernst were responsible for the ammunition box. We already knew Johannes Fried had been promoted to corporal and assigned to another gun. I was pleased to see him go, of course, but I knew the promotion would only make him harder to take than ever. I made a face.

My reverie was interrupted when we were given the order to "Load!" My heart lurched. I was nervous, excited and proud in a heady combination.

Straightaway Kessler stepped in front of the gun, shoving the sponge end of a long pole into the water bucket. Then, thrusting it vigorously into the muzzle of the gun, he rammed it up and down with energy and vigor.

"Um Gottes Willen!" Fried yelled. He hadn't quite made it over to the other gun. McWherter gave him a friendly push in the right direction. "Good job, Private Kessler," he said, walking over. "Only one problem. Anyone guess?"

He looked around. No one said anything.

"Well?" his tone demanded a response. Four pair of eyes bore into mine.

"His back was to the enemy," I said quietly.

"And what else?"

"He rammed the sponge too hard?" I suggested.

"Exactly! Not only did you get yourself shot while you were standing there, Kessler, but you blew up the rest of your crew when you rammed the sponge into a smoldering ember and ignited some spilled powder! *This* is how you sponge, men." He demonstrated a leftwards thrust into the gun barrel, moving the sponge gently up and down the length of the muzzle, never entirely exposing his back to the enemy, who were presumably aiming right at us.

Kessler caught my eye and shrugged. I shrugged back apologetically. Watching McWherter, it was clear that the man loved guns and enjoyed teaching us.

"Continue!" he yelled. He was walking towards the caisson when he turned abruptly and came back towards us.

"Course, all this goes away in the heat of battle, men," he said softly. "In a choice between a clean, safe gun and a bullet through your head, it's okay to cut corners!" He grinned at Kessler.

Peterson yelled for a twelve pound shell at two hundred yards. Ernst opened the box and pulled one out. Virgil ran back to the limber, his leather satchel swinging by his side. Fried yelled an obscenity from his position on the adjacent gun.

"For the love of God, number five, walk when you're near ammunition!"

Virgil looked miserable. McWherter put an arm on his shoulder and walked over to Fried, bending to say something in the man's ear. No one could hear *what* was said, but when McWherter stood up again, Fried's face was beet red. After that, there were no more comments.

Virgil was smiling when he handed the round to Kessler. As number two, Kessler's job was to place the round in the muzzle and step aside so number one could ram it into position. Meanwhile, I had my thumb firmly over the vent hole, to prevent any escaping air from sparking a premature explosion. Number three's job was fairly straightforward. As soon as the round was seated, I withdrew a metal pick from the leather pouch around my neck and pushed it carefully into the vent on the top of the gun. I was warned repeatedly not to position my fingers over the vent, in case of explosions or escaping flames, which would remove my hand or badly burn it. I came to see the immediate concern was not for the welfare of the man concerned, but only for his function on the team.

As I plunged the pick down through the vent hole, I felt the give in the muslin bag. The purpose of my pricking was to pierce the cloth containing the gun powder and ready the powder for firing. As soon as I was done, I was to look at number four, who would then insert the firing pin into the vent, pulling clear the attached string or lanyard. With my left hand, I held the lanyard steady while Gustaf stepped back into firing position. Then he nodded me out, checked that we were all clear of the gun's deadly wheels, and awaited the corporal's command to fire.

We were warned to cover our ears.

When the gun fired, it took me very much by surprise. The noise was deafening. My ears were ringing and for a moment I thought I had lost all capacity to hear. But worse than the danger from the boom of the gunpowder was the danger from the gun's massive wheels, for the moment the canon fired, the gun leapt backwards headed right for me and threatened to knock me down. I leaped aside by the grace of God. Everyone thought my desperate yelp and subsequent leap most amusing. Kessler threatened to change my name from Virgin Eyes to Leaping Lad.

"Ha, ha, ha!" I spat.

"Oh, the lad has a temper!" he countered.

"Damn right, I do!" I replied, my eyes flashing. Then and there, I was ready to take on the lot of them.

Sensing how angry I was, he backed down.

"Calm yourself, I was only teasing!" Kessler said. "Couda happened to any of us."

The others murmured in agreement.

"Then you're all damn fools!" Billings spat, walking up behind me. "Might have guessed it was you, Schmidt! Don't know everything yet, I see!"

I didn't bother to answer him.

"Keep your goddamn feet clear of the wheels, people! You're no good to me with crushed feet!"

His concern was touching.

"Take a break men!" McWherter offered. I could tell there was no love lost between him and Sergeant Billings.

We fell out and threw ourselves to the ground. Some reached for their canteens, some lay back on the ground, caps over their eyes to shield them from the sun. I propped myself on one elbow and squinted over at the other gun crews.

"You did fine," Virgil muttered, walking past me. He appeared to be sulking. Like me, he claimed to be eighteen, but, unlike me, he was small, not quite five feet tall. To my eye he looked to be no more than fourteen. Number five had a dangerous job, not for the faint of heart. The Powder Monkey ran the powder from relative safety at the rear up to the front of the gun. Unlike everyone else, he was to show his back to the enemy's guns using his body as a shield to protect the round from enemy fire. Small and swift of foot, Virgil was ideally suited to the task, unperturbed by the imminent danger to his person. I thought him very brave and resolved to tell him so at the nearest opportunity.

The days passed quickly, but my joy and excitement at the live firing was short lived. As they told all of us, several times, there was no ammunition to be spared for training the likes of us. It was all needed in the field. After the first loud boom, we had to content ourselves with Kessler's loud "Boom!" And it just wasn't the same. No matter that he shouted at the top of his lungs and Virgil took to running in front of the gun and falling down "dead" every few minutes, it never was as exciting as the real thing.

I came to know Kessler, Ryan, Gustaf and the others better than I ever dreamed possible in so short a time. Every night, after supper, a group of us sat around the camp fire, sputtering out smoke and fighting over whose turn it was to fetch more wood or empty the slop pail. And one by one we would wander over in the direction of the gun. Pretty soon the whole group would be there and someone would say, "We might as well drill, seeing as how we are here," and so we would drill. Other groups would stop by and laugh at us, but we didn't care. It got so that me and the others were so comfortable loading and reloading those imaginary rounds, that we could do it blindfold or in the dark. Certainly, we could do it without speaking or exchanging so much as a glance. We would just kinda sense when someone needed a pick, or a glove, or a round, or any other thing. Sometimes I would look up and find Sergeant Billings looking over at us, and once I found him staring right at me. And I couldn't help myself. Before I even knew what I was doing, I found myself waving hello. As soon as I raised my hand, I cursed myself for being a foolish woman. No young man would wave at a fellow the way I had, especially at one who was known to like young boys! I flushed then and busied myself with the task at hand, all the while waiting his angry denouncement. But it never came. When I dared look up again, there was no trace of him. Whatever he thought of my foolishness, it was never mentioned. And I resolved to keep my womanly impulses in check, lest they betray me.

The drilling continued unabated. We drilled misfires and smoke in the barrel and the enemy charging and three men down, then four, then five. We changed positions over and over until every last one of us knew every position better than he knew his own name. I reckon we were firing, or pretending to fire, three rounds a minute when we hit our stride-and we often hit our stride-and then some. And as dear to me as were my own brothers, these men came to feel like family to me also. Unlike the rest of us, Ryan was pretty large but he moved with the grace of a man half his size. Gustaf, on the other hand, was as tall and thin and wiry as a man could be without snapping in half. And although I had seen him tuck away enough bread and meat to stuff a man three times his size, he never seemed to fatten up. Instead, he looked perpetually hungry. Gustaf was pretty quiet, and difficult to draw out. Quite often, Fried would come over and, for some reason, would insinuate himself into the group. No one ever spoke to him, but he never seemed to take the hint. He just sat there, silent. From time to time, he would make rude or sarcastic remarks. Then he would retreat back into himself. The others ignored him, but I chaffed under his spitefulness and lack of good humor.

As for me, I had many a reason to stay quietly in the background, but I have never been one to keep my opinions to myself. In any group conversation, I usually speak up forcefully and, even though I was supposed to be hiding in plain sight, somehow, I could never force myself to keep quiet.

Sergeant McWherter worked us hard, far harder than the other teams had to work. We drilled seven straight days, even on the Sabbath. Although Yankie gave us leave to go to church on "God's Holy Day," McWherter had us meet on the field in the afternoon. For, as he explained it, "You will be doing God's work keeping the union together." Thus it was we found ourselves up earlier and to bed later than any of the other crews. Yankie, of course, approved heartily. He declared that we would be better prepared than the others when the time came that our skills were needed. Time was to prove him right. But we didn't know that then. All we knew was we that were tired and hungry all day long and even I was sick of drilling by dark on the fifth day. Little did I know how soon all this was to change.

On the sixth day, we were woken early by a steady drum beat sounding outside the barracks. In the darkness of a muggy July morning, we lined up outside and were given the orders to "ship out to Corinth." None of us had any idea who it was that gave the order, and where it was we were going. Behind me, someone whispered that Corinth was a railway junction somewhere in the South. I had no other sense of where the place was, or of the horrors that would await me when we arrived. All I knew was that we were finished with drilling and onto the fighting. The sooner the better, as far as I was concerned. The longer I stayed in, the more I got paid. And the more I got paid, the more I saved and the closer I got to reuniting with my brothers and buying back our farm. But there was one small issue.

Every day when I did my business, I was careful to do it when no other man was around. Being slender and small breasted, I could pass for a man in certain respects. But there was no mistaking what was below the waist and no way could I imitate the men, passing water the way they did, firing at targets and squirting one another when the spirit moved them. I already had a reputation as being squeamish when it came to certain things and that worked in my favor. In general, the men respected me, so they allowed me discretion in daily "personal" matters. But I lived in dread of my monthly flow, the more so since it was irregular and came with nary a warning.

The night before we shipped out, it came to me in a sudden rush of warmth between my legs. Excusing myself discretely, I worked my way to a quiet corner of camp. No one was around at the present. I quickly removed my sole shirt and tore it into long strips as best I could. Three of these I tied together to form a belt, which I secured low around my waist; another two I stretched between my legs, securing the ends to the belt to form a makeshift band. Then I pulled up my woolen pants, re-buttoned them and stuffed the remaining rags into my pockets for when we would need them. I hoped no one would notice the small bulge and ask to share whatever food I must have squirreled away against a rainy day. As a final precaution, I re-buttoned my jacket, the wool distressing my now naked skin. But the situation had been dire and my options minimal. Much as I had needed my one cotton shirt, I had nothing else with which to bind myself. I knew not how to explain its disappearance, nor how to make one shirt do the job of several cloths over the next few days. But as luck would have it, the flow was short and inconsequential. And since he was lucky enough to have a spare, Virgil gave me a replacement shirt when he saw mine had been "lost." Better still, he asked no questions.

Chapter Ten

I was so happy to be finally moving out, that I scarcely slept for excitement. But my dreams of a triumphant march out of camp were immediately squashed when I awoke next morning to the sounds of rain beating on the roof of the barracks. It was hard to hear reveille above the sergeants' urgent screams for us to assemble outside, but their stern voices were at odds with their bedraggled appearance. Indeed, they seemed more like hens and goats left out in the rain than non-commissioned officers worthy of respect. A muddy, forlorn and ill-tempered group of men presented themselves before us. There was so sign of McWherter. As we pulled on our jackets and rushed into formation outside, we soon acquired the same bedraggled look as them and altogether we formed a sorry picture of a company readying for war.

"Guess what, Virgin Eyes?" Kessler whispered.

"What is it?" I hissed, my eyes facing front

"They changed Billings' assignment!"

"Oh no," I said, "to what?" Now he had my attention.

"Field artillery. He's coming with us. And McWherter too! But he's been reassigned."

"No! Why?" My mouth dropped open. Kessler laughed but I groaned at the thought of Billings dogging my trail forever. I vowed not to talk to him again. That lasted for at least a mile. After that we were friends again. I could never be mad at anyone for long.

And so we left the camp, me marching alongside Virgil. We were growing into close friends, drawn together, no doubt, by our closeness in age. He reminded me a little of my brother Nate, with the same lean build and mischievous smile, though none of his trademark good looks. We started out cheerfully enough, but by the time we reached the gates of the camp, I had decided I did not care for the smell of wet wool. In the space of only a short march, the legs of my pants were thoroughly sodden and a combination of heavy, wet wool and mud clung to my legs, impeding my stride. I prayed the sodden wad of fabric between my legs would stay put long enough until I could adjust it. As we passed under the gates of the camp, we were directed by the sergeants to look right and I turned my head to see a row of officers saluting the flag as we filed past. Captain Mallory caught my eye at once, standing tall beside an older gentleman I took to be the colonel. I thought he would have minded the soldiers marching off to war before him, but he was attentive to the conversation of a young woman standing beside him, her face concealed by a parasol shielding her against the rain.

"Reckon that's the colonel's daughter, Miss Rainier," Virgil whispered, following my glance, "Rumor has it, they are soon to be engaged. It wouldn't hurt his chances for promotion none if he were connected to the colonel, would it now?"

"I suppose not," I replied stiffly, "I really wouldn't know."

Just then a stiff gust of wind pulled at the parasol, revealing a dark-haired woman with a horsy face and a mouth too wide to be attractive.

"What a plain-looking woman!" I said ungraciously.

"They say she is kind and very well- schooled."

"I dare say she is!" I retorted, resolving to think no more of Captain Mallory and his military ambitions.

Ahead of us, a great tumult broke out as we cleared the camp gates.

"Hey up, fellahs, we're out of camp!" Ryan yelled. "Let's go shoot us some Rebs!"

Cheers of "Hurrah for the Union! God bless Lincoln! Hurrah, Hurrah! Hurrah!" went up and down the line. Suddenly, as if at God's behest, the sun broke from behind a cloud and a rainbow spread its vibrant colors clear across the sky. It nearly took my breath away and I wasn't alone in feeling a quickening of my heart and a glistening in my eyes. At that moment, there wasn't a man (or a woman) among us who wasn't ready to give his all for the cause.

Several miles later, our enthusiasm somewhat dimmed by the mud and the rain, we struggled into the Central Chicago train station. I felt my mouth drop open in wonder at the size of it. The ceiling was higher than anything I had ever seen until this point. And the noise! The noise was almost incomprehensible. When we arrived, the place was a swirling hubbub of humanity. There were more people, in that cavernous space, than I had ever seen in my life. Most of them were dressed in the uniform of Northern soldiers and there seemed to be scant order to their coming and going across the wide expanse. Our battery was to join up with two others: Captain John Long's Battery A and Captain Adolph Wirt's Battery G. Altogether we would be about four hundred and fifty men. That is, if we could find one another amidst this confusion of humanity! I began to feel oppressed by the sheer number of people pressing against me. Despite my relative height, I could not see, due to the sheer size of some in the crowd.

Behind us, someone called Captain Maggiore's Battery C into formation. It was an order difficult to obey under the circumstances. The officers could scarce make themselves heard above the noise. Abandoning the call to formation, and with some difficulty, they herded us across the vestibule and in the direction of a platform where I beheld a train for the first time in my young life! I was struck dumb by the magnificence of the thing. With no warning, it spurted steam and snorted and snarled as it awaited its consignment. And with very little ceremony, we were directed to get ourselves on board. I was one of the lucky ones who found a seat and, jammed between a large, foul-smelling man from Niles and a thin, bony man from Wheeling. I took a deep breath and steeled myself for the first ride of my life. As the train lurched out of the station, gathering speed at a dizzying pace, I reflected that I had never imagined myself hurtling across the landscape at such a speed. I wondered what mother would have made of any of this, had she been alive to see it. And not for the first time, I was struck by the number of changes that had turned my small life upside down. Had it not been for an accident of fate, neither my brothers nor I would have ever have enlisted in a war about which we had no particular feelings, but which was now beginning to make a strange kind of sense. My fellow soldiers had imbued in me a sense of duty to the land and to the cause of freedom for which we fought. At this point,

I could no more have pictured myself sitting the war out on the sidelines, than I could imagine waiting back home for my brothers to return.

I must have dozed off at that point, for when I awoke, I was propped up against the thin man to my right, our two heads gently banging with the rhythm of the train. I sat up and looked around me. The larger, unpleasant gentleman was nowhere to be seen. In his stead, there sat a plain-looking man from "downstate" with a firm handshake and a friendly demeanor.

It looked to be around noon and the landscape outside was as flat and dull as any I have ever seen. My new neighbor offered me a slice of ham and a chunk of hard bread. I gladly took them as there was no telling when my stomach would next see food. I was grateful for any I could get. Outside, there was nothing to admire but mile after mile of cornfields with an occasional farmhouse off in the distance. The contrast to the teeming city we had just left could not have been starker. As I slowly chewed on the hard crust, I became aware of the bareness of the land I was raised on. I thought it strange that I had never noticed such a thing before.

The journey went on. It seemed we would never get there. I was feeling cramped in my seat and I longed to be able to rise and stretch my legs when the train began to slow down, and word was passed along that we were there.

"We're there?" I asked. Outside the window, everything looked pretty much as it had for the last several hours. The fields were still flat and the corn spread out for miles, as far as the eye could see. The fields met the horizon and the blue sky stretched up towards eternity. In short, there was nothing to indicate in any way shape or form that we were "there."

"Where exactly, is *there*?" I asked no one in particular.

We were all on our feet by now, noses pressed to the glass.

"I can't see much of nuthin'," said the man to my left.

"Don't look like anything other than a field." said another.

As the train slowed to a crawl, the tracks took a gentle turn to the right and we moved in view of a water tower and a clearing in the fields. There were several wooden huts and something that looked to be wood pilings stacked on the side of the tracks. There was a much larger building rising at least two stories high beyond the water tower, it had a balcony stretching round it on two sides and a sign across the front. I could only read .....Y INN.

A corporal yelled us all to, "Grab yer stuff and git off the train."

We all grabbed our rolls. I moved in pigeon steps towards the door, caught in the crush of men as eager as I was to get off the train and on to wherever it was we were going.

"Can't wait to fight me some Rebs!" someone cried.

"You'll be fightin' them soon enough!" another replied.

"Long live the union!" a third exclaimed.

It was pretty exciting to be in a new place. We were traveling into unfamiliar territory with fighting and rebels and so much unknown in front of us. Some of the men covered their nervousness with a continuous stream of banter; others kept pretty much to themselves. I found myself staring around me, wide eyed as I climbed off into the swirling throng of blue. We were standing on a dirt clearing in front of a gray water tower that looked to be some eighty feet high. The building I had seen from the train window had a sign across the front that read, COZY INN. To my way of thinking, a cozy inn would be a welcoming place with window boxes and flowers, and some homely touches like ma used to add to the kitchen to make it friendly and welcoming. This Cozy Inn was anything but. Its white paint was peeling and had turned a nasty shade of gray. Instead of window boxes and flowers, the front porch boasted a couple of worn steps and an old rocking chair that had seen better days. And the whole place screamed, "Keep away!", rather than "Welcome traveler!" I made a face. We seemed to have arrived at a deserted corner of God's universe. There was nothing here but a collection of rail lines ending at a run down hotel.

"Are we getting on another train?" I asked one of the corporals.

"Beats the heck outta me, son." He spat onto the ground. "They don't tell me nothin'."

"And nothin's all you need to know, corporal," came the unmistakable voice of Sergeant Billings. "Just do as you're told and follow orders."

"Yes, sergeant. Right, sergeant," the man saluted. As soon as Billings passed by, I heard him mutter, "There's some people as won't last too long when the shooting starts. Mark my words!"

Much as I disliked Billings, I wasn't sure I wanted to see him shot deliberately. I shook my head. This was all very different than I thought it would be.

The order came to assemble on a flat field off to the right. I reckon we were four to five hundred strong, counting everyone in the three batteries. We were introduced to our commander, Captain Maggiore. He was one of three captains flanking a stern-looking man in fancy civilian clothing, who announced himself as Lieutenant Governor M... He seemed very pleased with himself. Maggiore was a tall, robust man with a graying beard and a full handsome face. His strong voice made him a mesmerizing speaker.

"Good afternoon, men," he began. The assembled troops were so quiet that you could hear the wind blowing across the fields behind us.

"You are about to embark on a great adventure," he continued. "The Southern states have seceded from the union, threatening to tear our mighty nation asunder. They have declared war on us and we have no choice but to answer the call and go to war against them.

"You brave men have volunteered to serve your country, putting your lives on the line to make sure this great nation never splits in two and that our way of life is preserved from this day forth and forever more!

Cheers and cries of God bless the Union.

"I know you go forth to face great peril. But your officers are here to see that you receive all the training you need to defeat the enemy!

Hurrah!

"Do not be afraid…and I know you are not. The enemy is bold, but he is no better trained than you! The enemy is brave, but he is no braver than you! What the enemy lacks is justice. The rebels do not have Right on their side. *YOU* have right on your side! We will fight this war, men, and we will *win* it! Long live the Union!!

Hurrah! Hurrah! Long live the Union!!!

"Sergeants! Assemble your men!"

We fell into rank behind the sergeants, every one of us filled with euphoria after the captain's rousing speech. All around me, I could hear men's excited chatter:

"That man sure can speak!"

"We're gonna beat them Rebs right back to Charleston!"

"They don't know who they's fightin with!"

"Let's get on with it and get this war over with!"

Despite our great number, we were well-disciplined and every man seemed to know his duty. In short order, the officers broke us into companies, and from there into lines and finally into gun crews. Ours was a fine looking gun with a large black barrel and a proud shine to her. We were glad to see one another, all the way down here in southern Illinois. None of us had been so far from home before and the familiar faces standing round the gun reassured us that everything was all right. Yankowitz was as dull and officious as ever as he turned the gun over to Billings. Inwardly I groaned.

"I miss McWherter already!" I hissed.

"You're not kidding!" Kessler retorted. "Oh great!"

I looked up in time to see Johannes Fried approaching.

"Sergeant Billings, take command of the gun!"

"Yes, sir Lieutenant!"

"Good luck, men!" Yankowitz barked. It was the closest he had come to anything personal since we'd met him

"Ain't that touching?" Kessler said dryly.

"Makes you wanna weep," echoed Ryan.

"Now men! Settle down!" Billings shouted, seeing we were not all focused on him. "You all know Corporal Fried. He will be replacing Corporal Peterson."

If Billings had been expecting cheers of delight, he would have been disappointed. No one said a word. He cleared his throat.

"Corporal, let's see how much of the drill the men know. Don't forget they were trained by someone other than me."

"For which we are eternally thankful," Ryan muttered behind me.

Er, Sergeant?" Kessler wondered aloud. "Is the man on the right number one or number two? Only I was thinking, since I'm right handed, that would make my right hand number one and my left hand number two."

"Ah, but it all depends if you're looking at the gun or at the field," Ryan put in. "After all, if you're facing right, then your right hand would be number one, but if you're facing the other way, then…"

"Shut up! Shut up you men!" Billings face was turning a strange shade of purple. Kessler and Ryan looked at him as if butter wouldn't melt in their mouths.

"It's a genuine question, sarg." Kessler continued, only…"

Billings raised his hand as if to strike Kessler, but thought better of it. He grit his teeth and shook his head violently from side to side.

"It's Ser*geant*," he spat. "Now, git into position and start the drill! One more word from *either* of you and I'll bring you up on charges!"

Kessler turned his back on the sergeant, walking towards the gun. "It was an innocent question," he shrugged.

It was as much as I could do to keep a straight face. "Shut up, Kessler," I whispered. "He's about to blow!"

"Stupid arse," Kessler muttered. Even Gustaf cracked a smile.

We drilled into the late afternoon. We were so used to working together by now, that no one missed a beat as we moved the dummy ammo back and forth from the caisson, to the gun and pretended to fire.

"No live rounds, men," Billings had explained. "We have to save powder for the real thing."

That made sense to all of us.

Billings walked over to another gun and fell into conversation with the sergeant. We pretended to misfire and took a break.

"You know any of the guys over there on the caisson?" I asked.

"I seen the fellah with the beard before. Don't know the others, though," Ryan said.

"I know the tall one. He's a landsman from my town," Ernst said.

"He okay?"

Johannes made a face. "Too much German. Not enough American." He shrugged as if we all knew what that meant. Behind his back, Kessler motioned to let it pass. We did.

As we rested, we fell into casual conversation. Ryan told us about his farm on the Wisconsin border. Gustaf told us about his wife and twin daughters, Elsa and Ilsa. Even Fried said he was married, but didn't say to whom.

"How about you, Virgin Eyes?" Kessler asked, "where'd you come from?"

"Everywhere and nowhere" I said softly. "Don't like to talk about it."

He nodded. No one pushed and I said nothing more.

"My father was a farmer. I got five brothers and no sisters," Kessler boasted.

"What about yer ma?" Ryan wondered.

"She's a token man." Kessler volunteered. "Big and round and can arm wrestle anyone. She can plough and swing an ax and down a beer faster 'n anyone."

"Sounds like a man to me!"

"Got that right!"

"No wonder you turned out the way you did!" Ryan observed.

"Shame what happened to you, though," Kessler replied.

They carried on like this all afternoon.

It was dusk when the sergeants finally relented. We broke ranks and were directed back to a side of the clearing where we were told to bunk down for the night. The tents and most of the other gear followed on a separate train. We were told to use our blankets and be grateful it wasn't raining. Several fires were already lit and supper looked to be a fine stew, with some kind of meat smelling awfully good to my hungry belly. After a steaming plateful of beef and a hunk of bread and cheese washed down with a cup of bitter coffee, the thought of a good night's sleep was awfully appealing. Even though there were no tents and no covering of any kind, the ground was fairly even and still retained some warmth from the summer sun. They promised us tents the following day and bacon for breakfast. I had the smell of it in my nostrils long before my head touched the ground.

It was near dawn when I was dragged out of a deep sleep by the screaming of horses and shouting and general confusion.

There was a mist coming across the fields and sporadic gunfire off in the distance beyond the tree line, and then a blood-curdling yelping that sounded like all the hounds of hell were suddenly unleashed upon us.

"The Rebs are here! The Rebs are here!" someone yelled and suddenly men were rising and pulling on their clothes and boots in a frantic race against death. I was up and pulling on my boots, hopping on one leg and cursing the thing for not sliding on right. My hands were all thumbs and my heart was pounding so hard in my mouth, I thought I would choke on it. My mind was telling me the Rebs would cut me down where I stood, before I even got my boots on, and my terror made me clumsy and inefficient. One man fell to the ground next to me with a gaping hole through his forehead, and I stared stupidly at the trickle of blood as it dripped across his cheek onto the edge of my blanket. Then I was into my boots and running like the devil towards the gun, though it felt as if I was moving under water and as slowly as I have ever moved.

All around me men were panting and snorting as they ran, jackets flapping or shirt-sleeve bare. One man ran in his undergarments, barefoot and disheveled. No one paid him any mind.

I reached the gun right behind Kessler, with Ryan and Gustaf flanking me. It was aimed down field, right to where a line of Rebs were rushing upon us with muskets firing, and that terrible cry coming from one side of the line to another. Kessler was screaming for ammunition and Virgil came out of nowhere, thrusting the ball into his hands before anyone was aware of him. Then we were loading and firing, our rhythm lost, everyone fumbling at first, so keen to get that gun firing that we forgot all our drilling and started shouting at one another. Suddenly McWherter was there.

"I believe in you, Josef" he said calmly. "You can do it!"

To this day, I can't say for sure whether he really *was* there, or whether I imagined it. But suddenly, I got into it. My movements became less jerky and my heartbeat slowed. Around me, the other men seemed to catch their rhythm too. Suddenly we were loading and firing, loading and firing, just as we had practiced. Time stood still. In the distance, I could hear the screams and explosions of guns to right and left of me. I saw through the smoke, pictures of rebels in grey and brown, roaring at us and past us, like in a dream. I lost my fear. All I knew was the gun and the men around me. Prick and prime, prick and prime. My life narrowed down to just that spot right there before me. All I knew was the vent in the gun, the feel of the steel prick in my hand, the smell of the gunpowder. Men were screaming and dying all around me. I heard it, I saw it, yet it didn't touch me. I existed only for the crew and for my job. Prick and prime, prick and prime. From the front of the gun, Kessler turned and stared at me, his hand raised as if in supplication.

I swear I saw him mouth, "So long, Virgin Eyes." Then blood cascaded up from somewhere deep inside him, and his eyes lost their sheen, and he crumpled right down where he stood. And then he was gone.

I stared at the empty spot where seconds before he had been standing. He wasn't there. The field was full of rushing, snarling men charging right at us. I nodded at Ernst, and he pulled the lanyard and fired. Gustaf rushed to the front of the gun, grabbed the ball from Virgil and rammed it into the barrel. We kept firing. They told us later the fight lasted less than an hour. It seemed like years.

Over in the distance, I could see Billings running hither and thither and flapping his arms in the air. I felt nothing but contempt for him. The shooting went on and on. Plumes of black smoke hung in the air, clouding my vision and adding a ghostly, dreamlike quality to the whole thing. One time, through the haze, I saw a man shot through the head. Half his face flew off and he stood there, transfixed for a second or two, until his legs collapsed under him as he fell to the ground. Another time, I saw Yankowitz in the middle of the storm, his sword raised, exhorting the men forward. It should have been heroic. But the men ignored him. He just ran back and forth in the midst of them all, shouting and turning red in the face, the way he always did. It was strange to watch him.

Young men dressed in grey raced past me, screaming and whooping. They looked scared and determined and seemed in an awful hurry to get across the field.

Behind Virgil, a Reb raised his sword and looked to run him straight through. McWherter came out of nowhere, pulled out his pistol and shot the man clean through the head without even blinking. He just pulled out his weapon and shot the man dead. Virgil's eyes widened as he turned and realized what the sergeant had done. McWherter stepped into his former role, exhorting us to load and stay calm and focused on the field ahead. I loved him right then and there for his calm and his direction and his cool under fire. I watched and I learned. I was determined to be just like him, if I survived.

"Oh, Lord, oh Lord, let me live through this day," I whispered. "Please, please let me live through this day!"

By and by, the shooting died down. Gradually I became aware of the sights and sounds around me. Guns were firing here and there in the distance. A musket fired close by, its singular "pop" a strange sound after the barrage of gunfire. The acrid smell of powder blew in my face and my nose. The unmistakable smells of death and fear rose from the ground as the morning sun climbed in the sky.

Those of us left by the gun grew still and stared at one another in wonder.

"Kessler's gone," Virgil said dully. We nodded, as if this were new information. Virgil looked down at his arm, his sleeve was torn and the arm was bleeding hard.

"Better see to that arm, lad," said McWherter kindly. "There's some sheets and water over by the tents- leastways, they was there when we started all this."

Virgil tottered as if to find his balance. Ernst took his arm and they set off slowly in the direction of the tents. I looked toward the front of the gun where Kessler was lying. I couldn't bring myself to go over there. Instead, I turned and set out after Virgil, seeing if I could help him out. Behind me, the men were silent. Seems none of us could stomach seeing Kessler that way. No one said much of anything. McWherter was over with the other sergeants, surveying the field and watching the tree line in case the Rebs came back.

"What happened to Billings?" Ryan asked. "Ain't he 'sposed to stay with the gun?"

I shrugged. "He ran off somewhere and McWherter stepped in."

"Where did the Rebs go?"

Reckon they're lickin' theys wounds," Ryan spat on the ground. "Can't fight fer nothin'."

"Fight good enough to take out Kessler," Gustaf said morosely. It was the most emotional speech we had ever heard him make.

A bugle sounded. We looked over to where Lieutenant Yankowitz was struggling to make himself heard above the crowds of dazed and confused soldiers:

"Great job, men! The rebels have retreated. But they'll be back! Get in formation. Over here, men, but watch your guns. Hurry! Stay wary."

We greeted the news with stunned dismay. The field all around was littered with the dead and dying, both ours and theirs. Groans and sobbing pierced the air. The air reeked with the smell of feces and blood and fear. At the edges of the field, I could hear the cries of horses whinnying in terror and pain. I stepped among the dead and dying, wanting to help, under orders to pull back and reassemble so we could take stock. Someone said to watch the guns. Someone said we should move the guns. Someone said we should leave the guns be. Rumors ran wild. The captains were dead. The captains were alive. The captains were hostage. The rebel captains were hostage. No one knew what was true and what was not.

Some of our fears were put to rest when we stood to attention, and Captain Maggiore, flanked by Captains Long and Wirt, stood before us.

Standing tall in his dress blues, his black beard flecked with grey and his steel blue eyes flashing in the sun, Maggiore's loud voice bellowed over our heads:

"You made us proud today, men!" he began. "I am proud of you and the Union is proud of you! Those cowardly heels couldn't wait to attack you when you had your boots on!"

"*Too right!*"

"They had to hit you when you were asleep. They were scared they'd lose if you were awake when they started!"

Laughter and applause.

"They'll be back, lads!"

"*We'll be ready!*"

"You'll be ready for them!"

"*Yeah, too right! Damn cowards!*"

"*Push them back to Georgia!*"

"*Rebs go home!*"

"*And Carolina!*"

"*Go pick your own cotton!*"

"And Alabama!"

"*Try working in your own fields, you slave mongers!*"

"You'll beat them back! Now go rest, get yourselves some food!"

"*Yeah, if they left us any!*"

"We will find supplies. You'll eat! You'll rest! And you'll be ready for them next time they come!!!"

Damn right we will!

"Lieutenant Yankowitz?"

Yankowitz stepped forward.

"Take over, Lieutenant!"

Yankowitz puffed out his chest. "Right men, fall back to the guns!"

General groaning. What about breakfast! Yeah, we gotta eat!"

"While you are cleaning and repairing the guns…"

Groans

"…we will make sure that food is read for you!"

Hurrah for Lieutenant Yankowitz! Good old Yankie! Let's hear it for Yankie! One, two, three!

To our enormous surprise, we all let a mighty cheer for the man most of us found foolish and wanting in every way. Truth was, he hadn't been bad in the battle. He had shown considerable courage and, speaking for myself, the fact I lived through the fighting made me feel warm and friendly towards every living creature who wasn't about to kill me, Yankie included.

"What about the fallen, lieutenant? What's gonna happen to them?" The quiet voice came from the back of the line. Chastened, we all looked over at Yankowitz. There was silence for a moment.

"First, see to the guns," he said after a moment. "Then we'll eat." After that, the corporals will assign you into details and we'll take care of our dead. Hospital detail will see to the wounded."

"Ours or theirs, lieutenant?"

"Ours, stupid! We don't want them gittin' better and shooting at us agin, now do we?"

Wearily, we fell out and cleaned the guns while the cooks among us, that is, the men who burned the food the least, set to and made us some food. It was small consolation for the groaning and dying souls on the field, lying unattended in the smoldering sun, waiting their turn for water, aid and some modicum of relief from their agonies. No one talked about the burial detail and no one was about to volunteer. The more time past, the less and less I wanted to see Kessler lying there on the field looking into my "virgin eyes" for the last time. I shook my head. Uh, uh. The less I thought about that body, the less chance there was he was really and truly dead.

Chapter Eleven

We waited all day for the next rebel attack. It never came. Not that day. Not that night. Not the following day. I took my turn standing watch. I drilled on the gun. I ate, and I stared into space. What I didn't do is sleep. When night came, I forced myself to stay awake, no matter no badly my eyes wanted to close. I didn't want to fall asleep. More than anything, I didn't want to dream. Sleep came to me at last, when I was too exhausted to fight it any more. I drifted off where I sat, bowl on my lap half- heatedly spooning my dinner into my mouth. Someone must have taken pity on me and set the bowl down after finishing off my meal. That was okay; I wasn't hungry any way. I wasn't tired either. Leastways, I didn't think I was. But I fell into an exhausted sleep anyway, and I didn't dream, until I was near done with it. Rising back into consciousness, surfacing after hours of peaceful, dreamless slumber, I was suddenly aware of Kessler, staring across at me, grinning that big grin despite half his face being blown away.

"How's things goin', Virgin Eyes?" he laughed. "Still enjoying life?"

"How can you laugh like that when you're dead?" I asked. My sleep-locked self demanded, "What's it like being dead anyway?"

"Oh it ain't so bad, Virgin Eyes," Kessler laughed again, "you meet some pretty nice people this side of the great divide!"

"How can you be so cheerful? What is there to laugh about? You're dead!"

"Ah, come on, Virgin Eyes! You get to do some neat tricks when you're dead!" he exclaimed. And right then and there, he started pulling at his face until the skin peeled right off and worms came pouring through the gaping hole. I started screaming and screaming until strong arms shook me roughly by the shoulders.

"Wake up! Wake up, Josef! It's all right! It's all right!"

"God, stop it! Stop it! Stop it! Stop it Kessler!" I yelled at the top of my lungs, flailing away at the vice-like grip upon me. Then he was gone, and I was staring up into Ryan's large face bent over me.

I sat up abruptly.

"You had a bad dream, that's all. It's okay."

I shuddered and looked around me. A dozen faces quickly looked away.

"Great!" I thought to myself. "Now they think I'm soft."

I felt hot tears stinging at my eyes. That was all I needed! If I cried now, I was finished. Angrily, I stood up and strode towards the woods.

"Let him go," I heard Ryan say. "He's just a lad."

I was pushing through the woods at quite a clip when I became aware of sounds behind me. I looked over my shoulder and saw Virgil running through the undergrowth.

"Wait up, Josef," he called out. "You're goin' too fast!"

"Never asked you to follow me," I said unkindly, turning and walking on. Suddenly I was in a clearing. It was stunning. The land fell away right in front of me and the woods wandered on alongside a small river. A deer looked up from her grazing, startled by the sudden noise. Seeing I meant her no harm, she went back to eating. Virgil crashed through the woods beside me and landed breathless at my side. The deer took off, running.

"You could a waited for me," Virgil gasped.

"Didn't ask you to come," I said, punching his arm. "Thanks."

We sat down side by side in the grass, looking over the idyllic scene. Neither of us spoke for a long while.

"Lost my pa two years ago," Virgil said. "Ma's new husband doesn't take to me too well."

"Lost ma this year," I said. "Me and my brothers are all we got."

"How many brothers?"

"I got two."

"Older or younger?"

"Older."

"They join up?"

I was about to answer honestly, but thought better of it.

"Don't know for sure. I joined up soon as I could. Maybe they joined up too."

"What d'you join up fer then?"

"Wanted to see what it was like," I said dishonestly.

"I wanted the money," Virgil said. "Buy me a farm someday."

"That, too," I nodded. "Me and my brothers can live on it together."

"You wanna live with your brothers?"

"Somethin' wrong with that?"

He looked puzzled. "Most fellahs wanna live with a woman."

I realized my mistake. "Yeah, well, that'll be part of it too, I guess."

"You guess? You don't seem too sure!"

"Well sure I am. I don't have a woman yet, that's all."

"Neither do I, but it don't stop me looking!"

"You're too young to be looking!"

"The hell I am!" Virgil started, "I …."

At that moment in the clearing down below us, a line of rebels came through the trees, muskets drawn. They were moving swiftly and silently along the edge of the river. I threw myself onto Virgil, clamping my hand tight over his mouth. His eyes widened in astonishment beneath my hand, and as he started to struggle, I bent and whispered, "Rebels! Rebels!" He nodded and quietened at once. I removed my hand. We turned quietly onto our stomachs and wriggled forward so we could watch them undetected.

"How many do you reckon?" Virgil whispered.

"No more than twenty."

"They're scouting," he said. They want to see if we've moved our guns."

"The main force must be right behind them."

"We've got to warn the others."

"I'll go back," I said. "You stay here, see how many are behind them."

"You got it," Virgil whispered, grabbing my arm. "Be careful running back there, hear!"

"Sure," I said.

"I ain't never had a brother," he said. "Just sisters."

"Sisters are great," I replied, with feeling.

"Well it ain't the same."

I shrugged. Then I was wiggling backwards, keeping my body low to the ground so as not to call attention to myself up on the rise. When I felt it was safe to do so, I stood up and ran as fast as I could back in the direction of the camp. Wherever the rebels' main force was, it was within minutes of hitting our camp. This time, we were going to be ready for them!

Suddenly a shout rang out and a bullet whizzed past me, embedding itself in the tree right in front of me.

"They've seen you, Josef! Run! Run!" Virgil screamed. I had no time to think of him and his fate. I had to warn the others. Branches and leaves struck my face as I raced through the woods. Bullets were flying around me. I was sure I would be struck down any minute. I kept running. At one point, I tripped over a tree limb hidden in the undergrowth and fell, but I was up in a heartbeat. I was up and running on, heart pounding with the fear of what was behind me!

I burst through the tree line onto the open ground, running at full tilt, waving my arms and shouting at the top of my lungs.

"Rebels! Rebels right behind me! Man the guns! Man the guns!"

Across the field, the officers stood together, laughing and smoking. You could tell the last thing on their minds was another rebel attack. They looked up as I came crashing through the trees. Yankowitz stared at me, frozen for a moment, his cigar butt halfway to his mouth. But, McWherter and Lessing sprang into action and ran for the guns. McWherter and I reached ours at the same time. Swiftly, McWherter and I lifted the heavy arm of the Howitzer and swung it around like it was nothing, pointing the muzzle straight at the tree line. "Take number four!" he yelled. I grabbed the lanyard. He took three. Ryan and Gustaf were there in seconds. Ernst ran up with ammunition. Ryan loaded while he ran back for more. The Rebs burst through the trees and I pulled the lanyard. Smoke exploded out the front of the gun. Five men at the front of the rebel line fell down.

We reloaded, fired again. Beyond us, other guns fired. The noise and smoke were indescribable. Wave after wave of rebel troops came pouring through the trees a hundred yards from where we stood, muskets pointed straight at us. I expected to die at any second, cut down by rebel bullets. There was no time for fear. We loaded and fired loaded and fired. Something stung my arm. A red blotch spread down my sleeve and onto my wrist. I kept firing. Rebels ran past us. McWherter pulled out a knife and began slashing and cutting at men as they ran. Several fell. We were become beasts, stabbing and snarling at everything in our path.

With Ernst running powder, I knew Virgil hadn't made it. He had been behind me when we first spotted the scouts. They must've heard him warning me. No way he could have escaped. Cut down before he had a woman, or even a brother to call his own!

I fired madly, hating the rebels, hating every one of their cowardly hearts! I hoped they all died! I hoped they all died and went to hell!

Then it was over. The field grew eerily quiet. No more rebels came bursting through the trees, yelling their blood-curdling cries and pointing their guns straight at our hearts.

The air grew still. Smoke curled in wisps up into the sky. All around me men were coughing, and I could hear groaning now. A shot rang out here and there as angry soldiers shot at the thing that had hurt them.

McWherter looked over and acknowledged me. Across from us, Sergeant Lessing smiled, inclining his head to the back of the gun where Virgil stood grinning. I shuddered with pleasure. My friend had made it! Virgil had made it, albeit on the wrong gun!

The field around us was strewn with bodies of dead and dying men. This time, no horses' screams pierced the air. The horses had been too far behind us to have been in any immediate danger. This time, the men had taken the brunt of it, fighting, and dying, and praying to the Lord for victory.

"I wonder if the rebels pray to God for victory also." I thought suddenly.

"You saved us all!" McWherter said, coming over and extending his hand. "You're going to go far in the army, son. I'm recommending you for promotion."

"It wasn't just me," I said quickly. "If it hadn't been for Virgil…"

"He'll get there too, I'm sure," McWherter laughed. "Right now, you're getting a field promotion if I have anything to say about it!"

After that, things happened rather quickly. While a bunch of men were detailed to collect weapons and ammunition from the fallen, others walked the field attending to our wounded. Once again, the Rebs were left to suffer where they lay. Their pitiful cries shook me to the core. I found I could no longer hold my peace.

"Aren't we going to help them, Sergeant McWherter?" I asked.

"You feel sorry for them then?" he asked.

"I've no time for Rebs!" I replied hotly. "In battle, lord knows, I'd shoot 'em down. But they're no threat to anyone now. They're still God's creatures, after all."

He stopped walking and turned towards me, seeming to reflect on my words. "If it wasn't for their stubborn rebellious hearts and the greed and selfishness of the slave owners, we wouldn't be here fighting this war. And dying…They'll get comfort when we're good and ready. And that will be when we've seen to our own."

"But sergeant, they're dying! If we don't help them…"

"Don't you worry about that, son," he patted my shoulder. "A few more dead on the field today is a few less shooting our boys tomorrow. Come along with me. There are people waiting to meet you!"

And he strode off towards the officers' tent. With a heavy heart, I followed him. The logic of his words was irrefutable, but the sin of it lay heavy on my heart. The nagging feeling stayed with me as I followed McWherter across the field. Men stood and formed a line and cheered as I walked by. I flushed and wished myself invisible.

"I didn't do anything," I tried to tell them. But they kept cheering. Then we were at the tent. McWherter pulled aside the flap and motioned me inside.

"So this is the young man who saved the day!" a voice rang out. With a start I saw Captain Mallory standing where

Maggiore should have been. I couldn't help it. I felt a rush of pleasure when I saw him.

"I might have guessed you'd be the one to do something special!" he grinned. "And in case you're wondering why I'm here and not Captain Maggiore, the army reassigned me. From now on, you're in Captain Mallory's Battery C! Now, tell us in your own words how you came to raise the alarm."

"It was nothing," I started to say and then felt myself swaying.

"Whoa, there, young lad," Mallory said, stepping forward smartly and throwing out a hand. I found myself in the disquieting position of lying near prostate, propped up in the captain's arms. I flushed as red as I have ever flushed in my life and struggled to sit up.

"Not so fast, young fellah," Mallory said solicitously, feeling my arms and legs for wounds. "Well lookeee here. The young man has been shot."

Deftly he swung me out of my jacket and tore the sleeve of my shirt to reveal an ugly hole where a bullet had pierced the skin.

"Looks like it passed right through yer, son. You were lucky," he said grimly. "McWherter, you better get this seen to."

His face was so close to mine as I lay there that I could see the pencil thin hairs of a moustache growing on his upper lip. I felt awkward and embarrassed, but he was oblivious to my discomfort. It occurred to me that what I wanted from Mallory was his good opinion, not his affection. He was the first powerful man to recognize my talent. What a shame it had happened when he believed me to be a fellow male.

"Yes, sir, Captain Mallory. Come on lad!" And McWherter pulled me unceremoniously out from the captain's grip. "Begging your pardon, sir," to Captain Mallory, "but what the lad did was far from 'nothing'," McWherter insisted. "If it hadn't been for this young man's quick thinking, our whole line would have been cut down before we manned a single gun! Not only was he scouting rebel positions in the woods…"

"I wasn't…"

McWherter shot me a warning look "…but he ran back to raise the alarm, then rushed onto the field, trained the gun on the enemy and killed their first line of offense!"

"Well, done Josef!" Mallory beamed.

Seeing him smile at me, all thoughts of his fiancée slipped from my mind. I basked in the joy of his attention. For a moment we were frozen in position, smiling at one another. Then the captain took a step backwards, accepted two stripes from the adjutant and pinned them on my jacket.

"We've decided such valor deserves a reward. Congratulations, Corporal Schmidt!" he beamed. "Well done! Now go and get that arm seen to."

The assembled officers clapped and cheered. I felt foolish and proud all at the same time.

"Thank God I am keeping a low profile," I said to myself as McWherter thrust his arm underneath mine and half supported me towards the door of the tent. "No one is ever going to notice *me!*"

Chapter Twelve

Only after we left the officers' tent did I become aware of the parching thirst that was gripping me. McWherter was ahead, and walking over towards the hospital tent, when I stumbled a little and felt a rush of nausea come over me. I must have made some noise, because he turned and grabbed me and immediately pulled out his canteen.

"Drink up, lad. You need water."

Sure enough, as soon as the cool liquid hit my throat, I became aware of a desperate need for it. After a few quick gulps, I pushed the canteen back into his hands, so he could drink and continued drinking from my own. For a few minutes, all I could hear were the sounds of our gulping.

"You have to watch that, lad," McWherter advised. "Nothing weakens a soldier more than lack of water. It's even worse than lack of food. You need to drink two or three of these a day. Remember that."

The hospital tent was pitched at the rear of the camp. It was well known, among the men, as the last place on earth you ever wanted to go. No one in his right mind, and body, ever went near it. As we approached, I could hear the groans and screams of men in various degrees of agony. I grabbed McWherter's arm.

"Look, I know the Captain said to get myself seen to, but he didn't say anything specific about the hospital tent." I gave McWherter a pleading look. "I don't want to go there. You know as well as I do what goes on. They'll as soon cut off my arm as see to it. And this is a flesh wound. I've lost some blood, but the bullet passed straight through me and the only danger is from the wound festering. I've seen mama treat wounds down on the farm. She heats up a knife real hot and then she sticks it on the wound and it burns the poison right out of it. Heals up real well after that."

McWherter turned towards the tent.

"Sergeant, for pity's sake, don't make me go in there!" I wailed.

There was a long pause while I stared at his back and prayed with all my strength. With obvious reluctance, he turned to me.

"You say your mama's cure works real well?"

"Real well!" I asserted. "Real, real well!"

"Okay," he said slowly. "Okay."

We walked back towards the men. I hardly knew whether to laugh or cry. I had escaped the dreaded hospital tent…but the thought of burning my arm with a scalding knife wasn't pleasing either.

We reached the camp fire. Everyone was glad to see us, and Ryan gave me a good- natured ribbing about my being a corporal. Then he noticed my arm.

"What d'you do there, corporal?"

"I shot myself through the arm so I could get some sympathy."

"Stupid thing to do," he retorted. "No one here gives a damn!"

"Oh ha!" I said, all the while looking at McWherter, who was bending down by the fire, sticking his knife in the flame. I saw that his hands were dirty.

"You might want to hold the corporal down," McWherter said tersely. Gustaf and Johannes each grabbed an arm. Ryan thrust his arms around my waist.

"Yer sure are a skinny fella," he jibbed.

"Yeah, well, I don't care that much for…" I didn't have time to finish for McWherter came at me suddenly with the knife and thrust it onto my arm. There was a sizzle, like when bacon fat hits the flame. The pain was so extreme that I must have lost consciousness for a moment. The next thing I remember was looking up at Johannes with the smell of burning flesh in my nostrils.

"God, I smell better than most of the stuff you cook!" I gasped.

"Maybe we should have let them cut your arm off," McWherter said. He was standing there with an exhausted look on his face.

"Thanks, Sergeant. I appreciate what you did for me."

"Yeah and don't bother doing it for the rest of us," Ryan said. They all looked subdued.

"Why'd you do that anyway?" Ryan asked McWherter. If he noticed the informality, McWherter let it go.

"Schmidt here thought it was a good idea."

"Leastways, my ma did," I said. "Listen, it could have been worse, one of *you* coulda been shot in the arm."

"What happens now?" McWherter asked, staring at the burn mark on my arm.

"I keep my sleeve rolled up and wait for a crust to grow," I said.

"This was your ma's practice?" Johannes asked. "And it worked?"

"Oh every time!" I boasted, not telling him the only time ma used this technique it was on a wounded sow, and it hadn't turned out so well…but it was worth the risk. And the pain. I wasn't going to lose my arm inside that hospital tent, not for anyone.

Pretty soon the guys had thrown some sort of stew together, and we took turns fixing ourselves a bowl. My left arm hurt like the dickens. Good job I'm right handed. We sat together on the ground, eating the stew and trying to get our thoughts back together. The evidence of heavy fighting was all around us, from the dead and dying lying on the ground, to the dazed and exhausted faces of the living. Not too far from where we sat, several men lay with their bellies split open, their eyes wearing the vacant stares of the dead. One man lay prostrate, weeping and beating the ground with his fist. I wanted to go over and help him, but the others told me to leave him be.

"There's others that will see to him," Tom advised. "We have to get our strength back, case they attack again."

I stared over at the man. He lay still for a moment, then started up again. "Help me! Help me! Oh for pity's sake, can you spare me some water?"

I looked over at the water jug. Ryan followed my look and raised his eyebrows.

"One less Reb," he said simply.

"He can't hurt us now," someone said in a quiet voice.

"That's as may be," Ryan said, "but you give him water, he'll git better. He gits better, he's gonna fight us again…" He spat on the ground. "Besides," he added, "we shoot collaborators."

We all sat there, silently. After a while, the rebel's voice grew softer. Then he stopped calling out altogether. None of us spoke. My heart was deeply troubled. The strength of Ryan's argument was undeniable. The man had been our enemy, plain and simple. But the suffering of the poor soul, just feet away from us, was also undeniable. My heart fought with my head 'til I was plain exhausted.

After a while, I threw the contents of my bowl onto the fire, wiped my bowl and spoon, and put them back in my roll. Then I went for walk. I could see Virgil over by the edge of the clearing and I walked over to join him. He looked up when he heard me approaching, but quickly looked away again.

"What gives, brother?" I shouted. Despite his apparent aloofness, I was happy to see him.

"Virgil?" I asked, "Is something the matter?"

"Congratulations, corporal," he said softly. I could tell he wasn't pleased with the change though.

"What's the matter?"

"Nuthin'," he said, too quickly.

"No, really, what is it? Do you think this was unfair?" I grabbed his shoulder, trying to make him look at me. "I agree with you! I tried to tell them it was both of us and…"

"It's not that," he said quickly, pulling away from me.

"Sure it is," I said. "And you're right to feel cheated."

"I don't feel cheated," Virgil said hotly. "You did more than me. And you'll make a good corporal. Better than I would."

"What is it then?" I asked.

"It changes everything, that's all."

"What does it change?"

"Everything."

"Like what?"

"Us. You know."

"What do you mean, it changes us?"

"There's a difference between corporals and regulars. You know it."

I was puzzled.

"We can't be friends no more," he continued.

"Why not?"

"Cause corporals and regulars can't be friends."

"Sure they can!"

"No they can't!"

"Says who?"

"Says the rules."

"Where does it say that? I read the rules. There's nothin' says corporals can't be friends with regulars," I laughed.

"Not them rules."

"What rules, then? What rules are you talking about?"

"They ain't written down, Josef. It's just the way things are."

"Then we'll change the way things are!" I said hotly.

"You can't change the way things are."

"Why ever not?"

"Because you can't, that's all!"

"That's not a reason!"

"It's how it is," he said quietly, kicking at the ground with his foot. "We was friends and now we ain't."

"That's ridiculous! I'm still your friend!"

"No, Josef, you ain't. You're a corporal and I'm a regular."

I watched him walk away, head down, kicking at the ground. For the second time in only a few minutes, someone had lectured me about the way things were and the way they had to be. For the second time in as many minutes, I felt they were all crazy for not trying to change what wasn't right.

Later that morning, McWherter assembled us for drill.

"Sergeant Billings has been reassigned to gun five…" he explained.

"Oh, what a shame…" Ryan said dryly, "Just when we were beginning to bond with the man!"

"I heard that Hager!" McWherter snapped. "You will refer to your superiors with respect."

"Yes, Sergeant, McWherter!" Ryan replied. There was a pause. "Thank bloody God!"

Even McWherter laughed at that one.

"Okay, men. And you all know that Schmidt here," indicating me, "has been promoted to corporal!"

"Great job!" "Knew this was comin'." "Well deserved."

I grinned happily.

"From now on," McWherter continued, "Corporal Schmidt will share a tent with the Corporal of the Caisson."

"Nice for you, lad," Ryan winked, while I tried desperately to recall the name of the man in charge back there. I couldn't remember him at all.

After drill, I moved my pack into the wedge tent the corporals shared next to the sergeant's larger one. Inside, I found an older man of perhaps five and forty years lying on his side on a blanket, reading from a well-thumbed bible. He sat upright when I entered and extended a thin, effeminate hand.

"Whiley," he said pleasantly. "Corporal of the Caisson. You must be the new Corporal of the Piece. "

"That's right," I replied, taking the proffered hand and shaking it vigorously, "Josef Schmidt."

"I trust we are going to be good friends."

"I am sure we will," I said.

"Well, that depends, young man," he said, pointedly looking down at the open bible and then looking back at me. "Do you believe?" he asked.

There was a pregnant pause. I suppressed an urgent impulse to laugh.

"Well, um, yes, sure I do!"

"Good. That is good, young man," he returned brightly. "Then we can pray together."

"Well...I...um..."

His eyes narrowed.

"Are you wavering in your faith, Corporal Schmidt?"

"No, no of course not! It's just that I was raised to pray silently to the Lord. I speak to him privately. When I am alone." I struggled to explain myself. Whiley sat bolt upright on the blanket across from me.

"I see," he said, clearing his throat "It says in scripture that the Lord blesses those who come together, as one in a congregation of the blessed."

"It does?" I said. "I mean, yes, it does, of course." Privately I wondered what I was in for, having to share a space with this man. I pulled my blanket roll off my pack and lay it on the ground. After dropping the rest of my pack at the end of my improvised bed, I threw myself onto the blanket and promptly fell asleep. I slept clear through until supper.

We fought the rebels two more times in the same number of days. Each time, we repelled them with casualties about equal on both sides. I took to being in charge like a duck to water. Being the only girl in a family of brothers, I was used to holding my own with a bunch of boys. Nor did I have to raise my voice. The men knew their jobs as well as I did, and there was no need for me to mix in and tell them different. For their part, they took to me running the gun as well as I took to running it. My only problem was back in the tent with Whiley, and his ever-lasting praying. If he wasn't on his knees, he expected me to be on mine. Finally, I told him I was becoming a heathen just to shut him up. From that time on, he took to scowling at me or praying for me but not, thank God, to talking to me. We maintained a strict silence whenever we were together in the tent, which I made sure was as seldom as possible. On the third day, our scouts told us the rebel forces were pulling back. Orders came to break camp and follow them.

It was a long but orderly line of soldiers that marched out of camp that spring morning. It was still dark when we awake. But, as we were knocking down the breakfast fire and untethering the horses, the sun rose.

This time I walked alongside the men, instead of among them like last time. Captain Mallory rode at the head of the line, the sun glinting off his saber. In front of me marched the sergeants and behind me the corporals of the line. The men were orderly and quiet. We made ten miles before breaking for lunch and another ten before dusk. The scouts rode back and reported the rebels were some ten miles ahead of us, still unaware of our movements. We broke rank and slipped into the woods for the night. No one lit fires and no one complained.

"Rather an empty belly than a belly full of lead," as the saying goes. With the danger that rebel scouts might see our fires and catch us unawares as we slept, the men settled for hard tack soaked in canteen water and forgot their coffee.

"They're a good group," McWherter said.

I nodded my agreement.

I was in a deep, dreamless sleep, when an unfamiliar sound woke me around three a.m.. Raising myself up on my elbow, I looked around me. The men were sleeping soundly, spread out among the trees, no point in pitching tents, we might have to abandon, in the event of an attack. I couldn't determine the source of the noise and, wondering if I had imagined it, I was about to lie down again when I heard it again: a moaning, so quiet, you could barely hear it. Grabbing my hunting knife, I slipped out of the tent heading in the direction where I had last heard the noise.

The trees were close together in this part of the woods. But the full moon shone through the tree tops, guiding my way through the gloom. It grew darker as I moved away from the road, and the sound was barely discernible. Then I heard it, the groan of an animal in pain. I crept forward some more, only to stumble as I hit against a mound of something large and soft. With my knife ready to strike, I reached forward with my left hand and felt what seemed to be the body of a man. It was cool and still. A man scarcely alive.

Suddenly a hand shot out and grabbed my wrist. I pulled back sharply

"Help me," a voice croaked. "Help me, please!"

My heart pounded. I thought it was the ghost of the man we let die, coming back to haunt me. I near fainted with fright. Then the moon moved from behind a cloud and revealed the coat of a rebel artillery officer, a captain.

"My god, you're a rebel!" I whispered.

"Aye, to you I may be," croaked the man. "But to my kin, I'm a patriot, same as you. So. you gonna help me or shoot me?"

"I reached forward and felt the man's head. It was cold and clammy to the touch. Whoever he was, the man had but hours of life left, unless he got help very quickly.

I pulled out my flask, holding it to his lips and forcing the cool water gently into his mouth. He drank eagerly, and then choked it all back.

"Shh! Someone will hear you!" I whispered between clenched teeth, then we're both done for! Now, try again, but slowly this time!"

I held the man's head steady with my left hand, and guided the flask to his lips with my right. The strain on my bad arm made it difficult, but the man was in too much pain himself to notice. He seemed young, maybe my older brother's age. I couldn't see much in the darkness: only the growth of several days' beard, a head of curly black hair and a faint masculine smell.

"What's your name?" I asked suddenly.

"Eli," he gasped. My name's Eli."

"Same as my brother," I replied.

"Then you was sent to save me," he said weakly, seeming to smile. "It can't be coincidence."

I pondered that.

Voices behind me alerted me to the danger this man was in.

"Quiet! Quiet!" I hissed. If they find you, they'll kill you."

I heard him swallow back his pain. I wondered how bad his wounds were, and if he could be saved.

Behind us, two people came crashing through the trees then stopped about fifty yards away. There was a rustle and then I heard the sound of water hitting undergrowth.

"Yer never could piss fer shit!" came one voice.

"Good job yer proud of yer pissing then, 'cos yer wieners no good fer nuthin else!"

"Says who?"

"Says yer wife!"

More good natured banter of this type, more rustling of clothes and the two men made their clumsy way back towards their sleeping companions. The forest grew still once more. I turned back to the fallen man.

"Where are you wounded?" I whispered.

"Hurts all over," he said.

"No, specifically, *where* are you hurt?"

"In the chest and upper thigh."

"Okay. Okay, that's good."

"Good?" he gasped. "There's nothing good about it!"

His breathing was labored, as if the exertion of talking was sapping what was left of his strength.

"It's good because I have a reason to cut your clothes off of you."

"Oh yes, I see," he said.

Slipping my knife out of my pocket, I began cutting away his jacket and pants, taking care not to cut him or hurt him any more than he was hurt already. The fabric resisted in places, soaked though with damp or dried blood. As I cut, I saw him bite his lip, struggling not to cry out against the pain. It was difficult cutting through so much fabric, with a man lying on top of everything I was trying to pull away. At times I had to roll him gently this way and that to get the fabric away from him. Each time I moved him, he moaned. His face felt damp and clammy against my hand. I knew this was not a good sign. In due course, I had the remains of his jacket and pants in my hand. I quickly rose, and took them a ways away and buried them underneath a thick clump of bushes about two hundred yards from where he lay. Then I hurried back to his side.

"Thought you left me," he said, bravely. "Glad you came back."

Above us, the sun was trying to rise. For the first time, the light through the trees allowed me a good look at the man I was trying to save. I was taken aback when I could see him properly. It was a very handsome face that stared up at me from the forest floor. I was hard pressed not to smile.

"Hey, I don't look that bad, do I," he wondered. "Only, you're staring kinda hard at me."

"Um, sorry," I said. "It's just that I haven't seen the enemy this close before."

"That makes two of us," he winced.

"Listen," I said. "I have to go and get help. But I can't tell them you're…"

"The enemy?" he suggested.

"Yeah," I said. "Just follow my lead when I get here, okay?"

"Okay," he managed. But son, before you go?"

"Yes? "

"What's *your* name?"

"Schmidt," I said. "Corporal Josef Schmidt."

"Clydemore," he replied. "Captain Elijah Robert Clydemore the Fourth of the Third Alabama Light Artillery."

"That's quite a mouthful!"

"No kidding," he gasped. "If you met my parents you'd understand."

Not knowing what to reply, I was silent.

"My friends call me, Eli," he said after a moment. "Not that we're friends!" He gave a rueful grin.

I couldn't help laughing. "Not hardly!"

"Are you going to shoot me?"

I stared at him with something like horror on my face.

"Goodness, no!"

"I think you should!"

"Really?"

"Yep," he winced. "Except I'm an officer. We're worth more alive."

"Oh?"

"Uh, huh. As bargaining chips."

It was obvious he was in a lot of pain.

"I'll be back."

"You will?" he winced again.

"Yep."

"I'll be here!" He smiled wanly.

"Make sure you are," I said.

I turned and ran back the way I came, realizing with a start, that I was becoming used to running through the woods of late and always with some urgent purpose in mind.

This time a man's life was at stake, and maybe more than one life, if they found I was offering succor to the enemy.

There was no time to think through what I doing. Looking back on my actions that night, I think perhaps I was trying to atone, with that one life, for the many lives I had taken or had failed to save during and after battle. Whatever the case, I was driven by a sense of urgency, of decency perhaps, and by the immediacy of the man's plight.

When I got back to the area where most of our men were lying, I saw that Captain Mallory, his lieutenants and staff were gathered in a tight knot deep in conversation. Screwing up my courage, I broke through the woods and hurried over to them.

"Sorry to disturb you, Captain Mallory," I began.

"Why, Corporal Schmidt," he said with a start, "what urgent business leads you to interrupt a meeting of the senior staff at this ungodly hour of the day?"

"I…yes, I'm sorry, sir," I began, searching desperately for an entrée. "It's just that I was in the woods…because…because…"

"Yes."

"And I came across a wounded officer. He's hurt pretty bad."

"We need to get him to the first aid tent at once," Mallory said. "Lieutenant?"

"Yes, sir!" Yankowitz sprang to Mallory's side.

"Organize a detail to get this man attended to!"

"Yes, sir! Right away, sir!"

Within minutes, Yankowitz had stretcher crew behind me and we were all running back into the woods in the direction of the fallen officer.

"Amazing," I reflected, "I never had to lie about the man's affiliation because Mallory never asked. He just assumed the man was one of ours."

I reached Captain Clydemore's side moments before the others. I bent down anxiously, sure he had passed on and that we were too late.

"You came back!" he whispered.

"Sssh," I said, "Don't say a word!"

"You men, he's alive!" I called to the men behind me. "But he's lost a lot of blood and he can't talk"

"Where's he from?"

"Don't know," I said. "He was out of it before I could ask him."

"How d'you know he's an officer then?" the larger of the two men asked. "Looks to me like he's lost his uniform."

"Can't explain *that* one," I said, hoping I sounded perplexed, "but he said he was a captain before he passed out. I didn't catch his unit."

"Shame," they said. "He got any identification on 'im?"

"None," I said, with conviction.

I followed them back to the wagons, where the wounded lay in varying degrees of pain and distress. Being an officer, Clydemore was accorded far better treatment than were the ordinary soldiers. Within seconds of our arrival, the doctor was all over him, examining his wounds and calling for assistance. Before I left, I squeezed the captain's hand and mouthed "Good Luck!" The captain looked up at me, his forehead wrinkled in pain, his clear blue eyes smiling their thanks.

As I walked back to my tent, I reflected that amidst all the hell and insanity of war, I had finally done something good.

Chapter Thirteen

We broke camp before the sun cleared the top of the trees. As usual, I woke up tired. It seems I was always tired these days. There was never time to rest during the day and at night, I fell into an exhausted and dreamless sleep which the bugle or the drum always dragged me from too soon.

As soon as I opened my eyes, I could feel the tension in the air. We knew from our scouts the rebels were still unaware we were trailing them. We kept about ten miles between us and them and maintained a steady stream of intelligence as to their movements and disposition. We aimed to attack them as soon as the terrain gave us the advantage. About thirty miles ahead, the road became a narrow pass squeezed between the mountains. With their backs pressed to the river and their flanks pinned in by the mountains, we would have the better of them. Until that time we kept our distance, moving at a steady pace behind our prey, ever attentive less they sensed the danger behind them.

It would have struck everyone as strange if I had gone to visit the injured captain before we moved out, but I found myself wondering if he had made it through the night. I turned once or twice to see if I could make out the hospital wagon following behind. I couldn't help but remember his deep blue eyes and how his mouth crinkled as he said his name was Elijah Robert Clydemore the Fourth. How the heck did a man get so many names anyway? I laughed out loud.

"What you laughing at, corp?" one of the men asked me.

"I was thinking about the Rebs' faces when they see we're right behind them," I answered.

There was loud approval at that one.

We marched all morning and late into the afternoon. It was hot. The men were tired and the lack of rainfall this time of the year made the road dusty and unpleasant. A fine film got into our clothes and mouths making it hard to keep going. It was almost dusk when the thunder of hoofs told us horses were approaching. We looked up as Captain Mallory and two of his adjutants sped past headed for the front of the line. Mallory made a fine impression, riding tall, his sword flashing in the afternoon sun.

"What a fine figure of a man!" someone sneered. "He rose to greatness fast."

"He did it the old way," another volunteered.

"Yeah. 'E engaged himself to money!"

"Stop it!" I ordered, unnerved by the bitter tone and by the sneers of the men around us.

"Corp, don't you go defendin' 'im now," one of them men advised. "Men like 'im aren't worth the time of day!"

My eyes widened in my head, and I raised my hand to give the man a good cuff about the ears.

"You shut up, now you hear, fellah! One more word along those lines and there'll be a beatin' in it for you!"

"No need for that, corporal," the man sniffed. "We was just havin' a bit o fun! We didn't mean no disrespect. Leastways, none against yerself."

"I'm not sure that's of any comfort, private…?"

"Jennings."

"…Private Jennings. Captain Mallory's a superior officer. You will refer to him accordingly!"

"Yes sir, corporal," the man said.

As I turned on my heel, I heard him mutter in a low voice, "Captain or no, the man's a lowlife anyhow, rising on the hem of a petticoat!"

I let it go this time. It had to be the men's jealousy. After all, not everyone rose to the rank of captain in so short a time. And he was rich! And good-looking! It would make any man green.

"It is how far we are marching today, corporal?" a thin young private next to me wondered. He didn't look much older than I was, but where I was muscular and out-going, he was thin and seemed unsure of himself. I almost felt sorry for him, knowing how the men would seize on that weakness right away. Sure enough, someone jumped all over him.

"Corporal, you gotta teach Fritz 'ere to speak proper English! It's marching, mate, not are marching," a rough-looking man offered.

"What's your name?" I snapped.

"Ernie," the man replied cheerfully. "Ernie Painter from London."

"Is right what I ask," the young man insisted, "how far we are marching today?"

"Dumb German!"

"What? What are you saying this for?" the man flushed.

"Stop it, now!" I snapped. "There's room for all of us in this army and plenty of us need to learn to talk properly!" I glared at the first man.

"Wha'd I do, corp?" he asked, all wide- eyed and innocent-looking.

"You know darn well what!" I bent close to his face. "Now cut it out, Ernie! The man's unsure of himself to start with!"

"You got no sense of humor, corp!"

"Goes with your lack of h's then, doesn't it!"

"Oh, good one, corp!" Ernie's wide mouthed grin revealed a mouth missing several teeth. "I'll try and be nice to Fritz 'ere."

"Stop calling him Fritz!" I hissed.

"Why's that, corp? Fritz is 'is name! Ain't it Fritz?" Ernie slapped him on the back.

"Ain't your name Fritz?"

The man stumbled but saved himself. "Fritz, ja, Fritz is my name!"

"Oh very funny!" I snapped at Ernie.

"Please, why is this funny? Fritz is what I am called," the young man said sincerely.

"That's fine…er Fritz!" I said. Behind his back, Ernie and his friends were laughing. I gave them a withering look.

At that very moment, Captain Mallory and his entourage came galloping back down the line. When he saw me, he drew his horse up sharply and sat beaming down at me. I saluted.

For a moment, being the object of his obvious and exclusive attention felt distinctly uncomfortable.

"Good morning, Corporal Schmidt."

"Morning to yer, Captain Mallory, sir!" Ernie yelled.

A look of irritation swept across the captain's face as he turned towards Ernie. "Good morning, private! Corporal!" Inclining his head briefly in my direction, he reined his horse abruptly, spurred its side and galloped off down the line as his entourage followed. I watched as his form grew smaller. Little did I know this was one of the last times I would see the good captain. He disappeared during the battle of C…and no one was able to say with certainty whether he had fallen in battle or been captured by the enemy. But none of this was known to me that fine morning as I watched him ride off with his fellow officers.

I spun to look at Ernie.

"Whad I say?" Ernie gave an innocent shrug. "I was just wishing the captain a fine mornin'!"

"Yeah, right!"

"And a fine mornin' to you too, corporal!" the man next to Ernie added in a fine Irish brogue. "I'm James, Ernie's friend."

"Yeah, Mick 'ere, is my Irish friend," Ernie said, pushing him. Despite the slur, I could sense a real affection in his voice.

"You're not totally prejudiced then?" I raised my eyebrows.

"Me, prejudiced? Whatcher talkin' about, corp? I love Mick 'ere like he was me own brother!"

"Yes and he near killed his own brother for stealin' 'is girl."

"Now Mick, that were somethin' else." Ernie's voice had an edge to it but he quickly covered it. "Besides, he deserved it!"

"She was a beauty and make no mistake," Michael flashed back. "I could tell you stories…"

"But you won't, will yer!" Ernie snapped.

Maybe it was just as well the order came to halt. The rebels' pace had slowed and we had to fall back accordingly. We were within a few miles of the valley now. The men knew a fight was coming and they were ready.

"Are we gonna finish them off this time, corp?" a large man, known as Jake, asked me.

"I think so, Jake, I think this is it!"

We fell out by the side of the road, with our gear handy, in case the order came to press forward. Small groups formed, but where there would have been campfires and a hot meal or coffee, there was hard tack and water. Again, we were too close to the rebel army to risk them seeing our smoke. Someone took out a mouth organ and softly played a tune. A few of the men got a game of dice going. Still others took out paper and pencil and wrote letters home. I excused myself and made my way back through the tangles of men towards the rear of the camp. It took me a while to find the right tent. There were several tents filled with groaning men and a wagon where the most severely wounded lay. I found Captain Clydemore near the back of the tent reserved for officers. It was clean and served by two women wearing blue dresses, one a good deal older than the other. They looked to be mother and daughter. Their hair was tied back under white kerchiefs, with union flags pinned to their bosoms. There were blood stains all over their aprons and their faces wore the harried looks of those who have seen too much. I asked the younger woman where I could find the injured officer. She asked his name.

"I don't know his name. I know he is a captain." I looked at her hopefully. "Um, he can't speak," I added.

"Oh, him," she said haltingly. My heart gave a lurch, as if something terrible was about to happen. But she turned and pointed to a cot in the corner.

"He's over there." Her face was pale and drawn. She looked exhausted. "He still hasn't said anything."

"Thank you!" I strode towards the cot. As I squeezed between the rows and rows of injured men, I smelled the blood and fear of battle. Faces turned towards me pleading for recognition. Voices cried out for water, for comfort, for their mothers. One man grabbed my arm, but I pulled away, knowing there was nothing I could do that the nurses weren't already doing. And then I saw him, on a cot in the corner.

"So you remembered me," he said, wincing.

"Lie still," I said, bending low over the cot. "They mustn't see us talking. How are you feeling?"

"Better for seeing a friendly face," he smiled. "How goes the war?"

I shrugged.

"There's talk of attacking the rebels sometime soon."

"You know I can't speak to that."

"It is true then." He stared at me wistfully. "Where I come from, you all would be the enemy, you know."

"I know. Are you in pain?"

"Not that you want to change the subject!" A shiver passed across his face. "Okay then, yes, I'm in pain."

"Are they taking care of you?"

"They do their best."

"I'm glad to hear it."

"They wouldn't be so helpful if they heard my accent."

"Make sure they don't then!"

There was a comfortable silence.

"You hear anything from home?"

"There's no one left. My brothers and I are all in the war."

"No parents then?"

"They passed away." It was easier than explaining all about pa. He was dead to me anyway.

"But you have your brothers?"

"Two of them, Nate and Eli." As soon as I said it, I wished I hadn't.

"What units are they with?"

"I don't rightly know."

"You mean you won't tell a Southerner?"

"I mean I don't rightly know. They ran off and joined the army afore I had the chance to stop them."

"You the oldest then?"

"The youngest. Do you have siblings?"

"One younger sister."

"And where is she?"

"Back home with our folks. She's only twelve."

"A lot younger then."

"A lot. Did you grow up on a farm?"

"Sure did. How about you?"

"I guess you could call it a farm of sorts. We call them plantations."

I felt my eyes grow rounder. "Are you telling me you keep slaves?"

"Well…yes."

"I don't believe it! How many of them?"

"I'm not saying."

"Two? Three?"

He said nothing.

"More than ten?"

"Maybe…eighty."

"Eighty!"

He shrugged apologetically. "Give or take. Are you going to turn me in now?"

"I ought to!"

"It's how we live down there."

"But you're keeping *people*! As property!"

"That's not how we see things."

"Then how *do* you see things?"

"We treat our people well, treat them like family."

"Do they live in your house?"

"Certainly not!"

"Then they aren't like family!"

"It's a matter of degree."

"So you tell yourself."

"What about you?"

"I don't keep slaves."

"Not you personally. People in the North. Factory owners."

"What about them?"

"They hire and fire people like so much chattel. Throw them out when they don't need them. Hire them back just when they want them. And pay them whatever they feel like paying! And then lecture the South for keeping slaves! At least we care for our people."

"Northerners are free. Free to leave and get better jobs."

"If there are jobs to be had."

"If there are jobs to be had."

"And if not? People starve. By us, no one starves."

"It isn't freedom."

"But it's not starvation."

We thought about it for a while.

"It isn't right!" I said firmly.

"Neither is starvation!"

We thought about it some more.

"You have a girl?" he asked suddenly.

"Of course not!" I said, taken aback.

"Why, of course not!"

"Not just one," I answered, thinking quickly.

"Oh!" he laughed. Me neither. Nothing serious. Much to my family's distress."

"Why distress?"

"Clydemores marry young," he said ruefully. "Carry on the family line."

"And you haven't? Why not then?"

He leaned forward conspiratorially, " Between us men…"

I could feel his breath on my face. "Yes?" I whispered.

"They bore me stupid."

"Who do?"

"Women," he said simply.

"Women?"

"Women! Leastways, Southern women."

"Why do they bore you?"

"Well let's see," he looked up at the roof of the tent. "Their idea of conversation is to talk about hats or fashion. Our country's at war and their biggest fear is that their magazines and Parisian fabrics may be delayed. Their idea of news is the latest gossip about who's courting whom. Shall I go on?"

"Oh my!" I said.

"Oh good one! You sound like a girl!"

I grinned. "Exactly! Look, not all women are that narrow or that dull!"

"Find me one who isn't!"

I laughed. "One may be closer than you know!"

"I'd like to think so!"

"Oh, I'm sure of it!"

"Seriously now. You really think there are women out there with brains and a little spunk?"

"I really think so! Maybe you should try looking North!"

"Maybe one day I will! When this darn war ends."

"Amen to that!" I laughed.

"You never did tell me your name."

"I didn't? I thought I did?"

"Perhaps I forgot. I…I'm sorry. You've done so much for me."

"S'okay!" I laughed. "In your shoes, I might have forgotten also. It's Josef."

"I will call you Jo!"

"And I will call you Elijah Robert!"

"You will call me no such thing," he laughed, sucking in his breath against the sharp jab of pain. "My friends call me Eli."

"Nice knowing you, Eli."

"Be careful out there, Jo," he said.

"You're s'posed to *hate* us."

"I know."

Chapter Fourteen

They sent men to wake us just before dawn. Rough hands shook me from a deep sleep when word came we would attack within the hour. The rebels were sleeping not two miles from where we lay, and the air was tense with the sound of a thousand men trying to move quietly. A rush of bile filled my mouth and I swallowed it back. My stomach ached from want of solid food. I remembered countless mornings back on the farm, returning from the barn with frozen fingers, to find mama bent over the fire with a plate full of steaming eggs or sausage to greet us after our chores. With a start I pictured Eli and Nate, gulping down their food and ragging good-naturedly on one another or me. I hadn't thought of my brothers these several days, and I wondered how the thought of their dear faces had slipped away. It was as if the very reason for my being here hadn't been to find them in the first place.

All around me, men were tensing for battle. I could feel mama's locket pressed against my skin. I patted my jacket and said a prayer for mama, for myself, my brothers and my men. We moved forward slowly, dragging the guns behind us. We couldn't risk having horses pull them, for fear their neighing would give us away. So we dragged them ourselves over two miles of uneven land, sweating and grunting in the pre dawn air. Alongside our fears, there was a feeling of excitement, and my breath quickened despite the bile in my throat. Suddenly, I was back home. It was fall and farmers from all over the area had gathered for a hunt. Women and children wore bright colored clothing and carried baskets filled with fruit and beer. There was bread and cheese, and they got together and made a huge fire in the middle of the green, so they could cook the meat brought back by the men. I was as a good a shot as any of them, and I was wearing breeches and a jacket, same as my brothers. Martha Tildiger laughed at me, and said I would never get a man parading around like that in men's clothing. And I told her she would never get herself a brain, seeing as she was so narrow- minded and there wasn't room.

We set off for the hunt pretty eager. Some of the men had dogs and some rode horses. Most of us were on foot and we trekked into the forest after the dogs. It was warm day, late in August, and the colors were already turning. I marveled at the beauty of God's creation, and took pleasure in the warmth of the sun as it touched me through the trees.

Up ahead, I heard a terrible commotion, squealing and shouting and the baying of dogs. Men came crashing through the trees towards me, shouting and waving their hands. A deer, maybe two years old, was running straight at me. Its nostrils were flaring and its eyes were wide with terror. A shot rang out, just before it reached me. It froze in motion. I saw its eyes widen in fear and it crashed to the ground before me. A dog leapt instantly onto its back, followed by another. I looked right into its eyes as the slaughter started. It seemed to plead with me for its life. I stood frozen as the life drained out of it, its eyes dulling and the drool from its mouth changing to a bloody red. The dogs were merciless, ripping and tearing at the flesh while the creature screamed. It was a sight terrible to behold. Mercifully, someone shot it and took away its pain. But mine stayed with me. The thought of that poor creature, and its agony, spoilt the day for me and several after that. The crowd seemed pleased with its bounty, carrying the huge carcass back to the green in joyful celebration. But while others whooped and cheered and tucked into their fleshy feast, I wandered alone in the forest, wondering how we could bear to inflict such agony on another of God's creatures.

Now here I was, a corporal in the Northern army, stalking my Southern prey, knowing they were trapped and helpless in the valley up ahead. All around me the men sensed victory. They longed to avenge themselves for fallen comrades, and for their own feelings of terror and helplessness days before. Now it was their turn to terrorize, their turn to rain horror from black steel mouths.

"You okay, corp?" Ryan's voice snapped me from my reverie. "Only you look a bit green."

"Stomach's sour," I offered by way of explanation.

"Gottcher on that one. Lack of food ain't helping. After this is over, I'm gonna cook us up a plate of steaming bacon. Maybe a sausage or two."

"Maybe you can bake us a pie!" someone offered.

"Hey, git off, yer bleeders," Ryan said. "If I wanted yer darn opinions, I'd a asked for them."

"Too dumb to know you need 'em."

"I was talking to the corporal! Not to the likes of you!"

"Okay, enough of this!" I managed, forcing myself to focus on the task at hand. Slowly we rumbled towards the enemy. At last the guns were in place, the men in position. Somewhere in the half light, men lay sleeping, dreaming of loved ones and of days back home. For now, I stood with the men, waiting the order to fire. There was an eerie silence in the forest. No birds sang to greet the morning. No creature stirred in the undergrowth. Those of us born and raised on the land knew this meant danger. The forest is never silent, unless something terrible is about to happen. But the men sleeping not five hundred yards from us knew nothing of this. And while they slept, we stood, poised and ready. Suddenly, the order came. I dropped my arm and the gun spat out angry fire. To my left and right, eleven others did the same. We struck with no warning. Gunpowder rose in the air, mingling with the morning air and forming pretty patterns above the trees. Time slowed and every wisp of smoke and every patch of light danced in my memory.

In the rebel camp, men came running from every tent before us. Like ants disturbed by a stick in an ant hill, they swarmed hither and thither trying to escape. Men rose from the ground where they had been sleeping, and were cut down, without mercy, before they could grab their boots and run for the safety of the trees. We fired, we reloaded, we fired again. The first of our foot soldiers reached the camp, firing at almost point blank range. Men fell then, and pools of blood spread out on the ground where they lay in death or in agony. Meanwhile, some of the lucky ones reached the trees and the foothills of the valley, and started manning their guns. From every corner of the battleground, guns started firing back at us. Some of our ground troops fell, their blood mixing with the rebels' blood, staining the soil where they lay. Then a big gun started firing on our right flank. The men firing it were good, mowing down our front assault line and building a steady pile of corpses that blocked the way for the men behind, making it easier to kill them in turn. Rebel sharp shooters took aim then at the trapped and panicked soldiers. Chaos ensued and our men ran back and forth between the piles of corpses, struggling to get out of the trap they had entered, while a steady rain of bullets cut them down without mercy. It all happened in an instant. One minute, our men were rushing victorious through the camp. The next, they were being slaughtered where they stood.

I yelled at the men to turn the gun and aim it straight up the slope towards the twelve pounder. I had to silence that gun! My eye focused on the man in charge, a short fellow whose experience on the battlefield was obvious and deadly. I gave the command to fire. The first shot hit their numbers three and four. They fell and were still. But the corporal stepped into place and the gun kept firing. And we fired back. Shot after shot. Some missed, some hit their target. Ernst, Ryan Gustaf and I worked like one man; one brain, one heart between us. Again and again we fired: three; four; five; six times. At last the gun fell silent and we looked around us. Everywhere we turned, there were bodies, hundreds of them. There was only sporadic firing now. Small pockets of resistance continued and were quickly silenced. Our men had broken through the barrier of corpses and continued on through the rebel camp, until there was no one left on the other side to fire at. All was silence and death.

I stepped backwards, running my fingers through my short cropped hair. Ernst and Ryan were smiling. They were proud of us; proud of the victory and glad to be alive. Gustaf said nothing. He leaned back against the gun, took a wad of something out of his pocket, and stuffed it into his mouth. Then he stood and chewed morosely, staring out over the battlefield in quiet contemplation. I knew we had to clean the gun and keep it battle ready. So I gave the order.

"Come on, corp! There's no one left to shoot at!"

"Ryan, until this darn war ends, there will *always* be someone left to shoot at. Now clean the damn gun! That's an order!"

Reluctantly and obviously exhausted, the men set about their task, pulling out the water bucket and swabbing out the soot-filled barrel.

I wanted the men to rest after so much exertion, but I couldn't risk it. There was no way of knowing if and when another rebel force might appear. For the first time, I wondered if I might have what it took to be in charge. It was a depressing and chilling idea. As soon as the gun was set, I told the men to stand down. Word had gone out that the camp fires were starting and there would be hot food and coffee as soon as the pots could be warmed. This brightened our mood considerably.

Behind us, tents were being pitched and I could make out three or four camp fires already. I followed Ryan and the others back towards them. I felt sick to my stomach. This was no victory, this was a slaughter. It had been an unfair fight. All around me men were cheering. "We won! We won!" Men slapped me on the back. Men shook my hand vigorously, grinning from ear to ear. Even Ernst was grinning.

"Is a great victory, ja?" he grinned.

I looked at him in horror. I felt we were all covered in blood. We were sinners, sinners on a vast and cosmic scale. I didn't know what to say or do. I turned to walk away. I was the spoiler in the party. I was…

"Hey, there, Corporal!"

Captain Mallory was striding towards me, his uniform pressed and his sword gleaming. Beside him were two other captains, and a man I didn't recognize, a tall man dressed in civilian clothes and wearing an impressive hat.

"Gentlemen, I am honored to present to you Corporal Schmidt!" Mallory beamed. "Corporal, this is the Speaker of the House."

The tall, thin gentleman extended his hand. I took it and we shook hands vigorously. His hand felt cold and clammy. His eyes were gray and watery He smiled with his mouth, not his eyes.

"Good job today, corporal," he said. "I saw you working that gun! You were extraordinary! Extraordinary!"

"Killed the whole lot! Good job, lad! Your future is set with work like this!" one of the captains beamed. "Your quick thinking saved a lot of men. Well done, lad!"

"We're recommending a promotion to sergeant," said the other.

Mallory grinned broadly and beamed down at me as if I were his special project. Despite myself, I felt a glow of pride.

"Are you blushing lad?" the other captain said, clearly astonished. "Why look at that! He's blushing like a girl!"

"Sorry, sir," I said in as low a voice as I could manage.

"He's embarrassed," Mallory beamed. "Lad's as modest as he is brave!"

The civilian and the captains strode on past me, Mallory's hand resting on my shoulder as he passed. "I'm proud of you!" he said, and he squeezed my shoulder.

I stood for a moment, wallowing in the special feeling that being near him always brought. And then the feelings of shame and consternation took over. I didn't know what to think. Why was a superior officer paying me attention? Was I a good soldier or not? I felt like an impostor. Besides, to him I was a man, so his attentions meant nothing. And had he known I was a woman, he was engaged to another, so what difference would it have made anyway-except that it would have led to my expulsion and disgrace!

I was so confused. And my bowels felt loose. I excused myself. I made it a habit to relieve myself within the deepest confines of the forest, for fear of detection. But since I had left the crowds behind me, I let my guard down and simply went. I was fixing my shirt back into my pants when a cough behind me alerted me to another presence. I was discovered!

"How're *you* holding up?" a deep voice.

I glanced behind me. The voice seemed to be coming from behind a tree.

"All right…I guess. You?"

"As well as can be expected."

Silence filled the space between us.

"You ever done this before?"

"What? Fighting?"

"Yeah."

"No. You?"

"No. My old man fought in the Mexican American War."

"How was that?"

"He never talked about it."

"I didn't think it would be this…"

"Brutal?"

"Yes."

"Today was pretty bad," he offered.

"It was awful."

"They never had a chance."

"If they had, we might not be standing here."

"I know."

More silence.

"I didn't join up for this," he offered after a while. "I thought we was fighting for our freedom. Not slaughtering people like hogs."

"They would have done the same to us," I said, reflexively.

"So why do I feel this bad about it?"

"We both do."

"Funny that."

"Yeah."

After a while, I heard him get up and walk slowly back towards camp. Some time later, I did the same. I was never sure whether he had discovered my secret or not. Either way, I guess, he didn't tell anyone. I never did find out who he was.

Chapter Fifteen

"They're promoting you again!" Clydemore whispered. We were huddled together in a corner of the hospital tent, him lying on a cot and me bending over, so the nurses could not see us talking. Clydemore was clearly struggling not to laugh. "Ouch! You're not here trying to kill more enemy soldiers, are you? Because when I laugh, it hurts! I feel I'm in danger!"

"Oh very funny!"

He slapped his hand playfully over his mouth. Above his fingers, I could see his blue eyes twinkle.

"Don't laugh! This is terrible!"

"What's so terrible, Joseph? You're smart. Anyone can see that. You keep your cool under pressure. The men respect you."

"How would you know? You're in here!"

"I know men," he answered. "And I know battle. If they didn't respect you, they'd have sabotaged you, or worse. The fact they listen, and obey you, tells me all. You'll be a sergeant, yes, and a captain too, I'd wager. Maybe even higher."

"This is crazy!" I said, more to myself than to him. "I joined up to find my brothers. Not to be a leader!"

"But a leader is what you've become, yes and a hero too, I'll be bound. Those …Southerners…" he said the word carefully, "were decimating your men. You took action that stopped them in their tracks. And for that…"

"Stopped them in their tracks! I killed them! I killed them all, Eli, as surely as if I'd hacked them to pieces with my sword!" I turned away, fearful I might cry and give myself away.

"Don't hide your emotions, lad. This isn't a fist fight on the village green. This is war. And men get killed."

"It was *your* kind I killed!" I looked at him again.

He grimaced. "I know. Had you been born in the South, you'd have been killing Northerners!"

"I believe in the Northern cause!" I said fiercely, thinking on my brothers and on our heated debates concerning the roots of the war.

"Of course you do, Joseph," he said sadly. "You were born to it. But just imagine for a moment, what if you'd been born in the South, on a plantation, like me? Would you have supported the North then?"

"Of course!" I said without thinking. Then, "I hope so! Ours is the righteous cause!"

"Sure it is!"

I glared at him. "Are you suggesting you would have supported the North if you had perchance been born there?"

"I'm saying I might well have done. The North would have been all I knew. I wouldn't have *seen* a plantation or *dreamt* of keeping slaves. It would all have been alien to me."

"So none of us have principles? It's all an accident of birth?"

"I don't know, Joseph. It was just a suggestion." He sounded weary.

I looked around, anxious lest the sound of our voices may have carried further than we intended. But the faces around us were wracked with their own private pain. No one had cause to, or interest in, attending to us.

"Shh. No one must hear you," I whispered.

"And still you defend me," he smiled. "This Southern slave owner!"

"Are you really a slave owner? Please tell me you're not!"

"Not yet, I suppose. Not strictly speaking. I'm the heir apparent. My father is the owner. I'll take over. Unless we lose the war."

"You will!" I said simply. "Of course you will!"

We stared at one another glumly.

"How come," I said after a moment, "when I'm out *there* it all seems straightforward and when I'm in *here*," I gestured round the tent, " I get all muddled up?"

"It isn't *here*," he said emphatically, "it's *us*. You and me. We're no longer strangers. And you can't kill a friend now, can you?"

"People do it all the time! Cain killed his brother!"

"Yes, but God called it murder! He didn't call it justice!"

"How come you're always right?"

"I'm not, but I've got nothing else to do these days save think. And the more I think, the less and less I know why the two of us are fighting."

"You and I?"

"North and South. It's all one country."

"Not according to Jefferson Davies."

"Oh yeah, him."

Like every conversation with my new Southern friend, this one left me energized and confused. I had entered the tent feeling unworthy of promotion; I left feeling confused about the whole war.

"Maybe I'm just a confused person," I suddenly thought. "After all, I'm not even the man they think I am, let alone a man fit to be a corporal in the Northern army! Why should a little thing like the causes of the war disturb me?"

"Corporal?"

"Oh!" I hadn't heard the young nurse calling me, and when she grabbed my arm to get my attention, I started violently.

"I didn't mean to startle yer."

"It's fine, nurse. What can I do for you?"

"It's just that I can't help noticing you spend a lot of time with the Captain over there." She indicated Clydemore.

"Um, yes. I suppose so," I answered, wondering where this was going.

"Only, you seem to be talking to him a great deal- considering his problem."

"His problem?"

"Yes. The fact he can't talk."

"Oh, oh, *that* problem."

She looked confused.

"What of it, then?"

"It's just that I think it's awful nice of you to sit with him like that, catching him up on the war and all that!" she suddenly blushed violently.

She was a very young girl. With a shock of recognition, I realized she must like me, thinking herself talking to a young man and all. Oh dear. This was very awkward.

"Well…I…"

"I didn't mean to embarrass yer." She became very busy with whatever she was carrying at the time. "It's just that I think it's very nice of yer. I gotta be going now. There are a lot of patients to see to and all. Good day to you, corporal."

"Goodbye…?"

"Maggie," she called out. "My name's Maggie. Short for Margaret."

"Goodbye, Maggie."

I wasn't going to tell her my name. This was already strange enough. Here I was a girl, pretending to be a boy, being hailed as a hero for doing something I had grave misgivings about, in the middle of a war against people like the Southern captain, whose life I had just saved and who I was now passing off as a Northern captain. Then I was praised again by a young nurse who clearly liked me, believing me to be the male I claimed to be! It was all too much for one day. I decided I needed some sleep.

The next day was uneventful. So was the one after it. And the five that followed. Our unit continued marching south. We encountered a few Southern stragglers and engaged in some minor skirmishing, but none of it amounted to much. One of theirs shot one of ours in the foot. One of ours shot one of theirs in the leg. I saw a group of his friends carry him off into the woods, like he was a leg of beef or something. None of us were of a mind to follow them.

"Leave 'em be!" someone suggested. "It's more trouble than it's worth fighting every soldier wearing the gray."

I could not have agreed more. There would be fighting enough for everyone before too long.

My nights were spent on the ground, under the stars. I grew tired of my tent mate's biblical exhortations, preferring the hum of the crickets and the morning song of birds. He could spend all his time on his knees if he chose to. I just wouldn't be there to listen.

And then it happened. We were sitting round the campfire. A bunch of the guys were telling stories about women they knew, about the war, about their farms and their plans- when my world turned upside down twice in one day.

"I stopped by a farm not a mile from here," Peterson said suddenly. "It was filled with injured Northern soldiers. I asked if they had any food to spare. A boy called Nate Reinhardt called out. Said he was looking to catch up with his brother, Eli. They were in the fifty-first. Nate took a bullet in the leg and got left behind when his unit moved on. He was from north of Chicago. That's where you're from, ain't it Josef?"

My heart was in my mouth. I felt my face grow hot and I could scarcely speak for the pounding in my chest. As calmly as I could I said, "Nearer the Wisconsin border. I don't think I know this fellah, Nate. What's he look like?"

Tom sniffed and wiped his nose with the back of his sleeve. "Mid twenties, or thereabouts. Dark hair, tanned face. Thin fellah."

"Thin!" I thought with a start. Nate had always been on the chunky side. Army life had not favored him.

"I don't think I know him," I lied. "Was the fellah badly hurt?" My world turned on the answer.

"Looks to have been shot up pretty bad. Walks with a cane. But says he's going back into the fight. Wants to stay with his brother, I guess."

"His brother?"

"Yeah. Said something about a promise to his sister. Won't go home until the both of them can."

"Sounds like a nice young man," I said carefully, "sticking with family and all."

"They'll be lucky if both of them make it through alive," Tom said glumly. "Way we're going, none of us will make it."

"The only thing'll kill us is another year of your cooking!" Ryan growled in an obvious attempt to lighten up the mood.

Someone groaned. We all knew Tom was sensitive about his cooking.

"Well, if that's how ye feel, you can cooks the stuff yourself!" Tom threw down his cooking spoon.

"Oh come on, Tom, you know he was only joshing!"

"He's just pulling your leg!"

"You know we love your cookin'!"

"Come on, Karl, tell 'im ye was only joshin!"

Grateful for the distraction, I stared into the fire. Nate! Nate was here! Injured! And I couldn't go to him! Myriad thoughts raced through my mind: I could slip out of camp and…and do what? I couldn't walk that distance and back before we broke camp, and in view of my new rank, there was no way I could disappear without immediate detection. I couldn't tell the truth either. They shot women dressing as men, calling them treacherous whores and worse. Even if I stayed as Josef but claimed Nate as my brother, as soon as he saw me, Nate would surely give the game away. I wanted to scream and curse my fate. Instead, I sat there, discarding every thought, until the only sensible conclusion occurred to me. I must do nothing, nothing save praise the Lord for keeping my brothers alive. Despite being injured, Nate was well enough to be rejoining his unit. That was to be my comfort, my one and only comfort, this long, bleak evening.

The meal was over, conversation was waning, and men were settling down to whittle or play cards or write home to their loved ones. I excused myself and withdrew to the quiet of the woods. Walking slowly at first and then with purpose, I became aware I was walking towards the back of the camp. Suddenly, the hospital tent was exactly where I wanted to be. I increased my pace until I was practically running up to the door, bursting through into the startled presence of the young nurse who blushed with pleasure when she saw me.

"Oh, Maggie, how are you?" I asked, scarce stopping for her reply.

"Corporal! Corporal Schmidt!" she called out. I had no patience for her.

"I have to go. It's urgent that I…" I stopped in my tracks. Where I should have seen the young captain, there was an empty pallet, devoid of sheets. For the second time in less than an hour, my heart seemed to leap into my throat of its own accord. Dimly I was aware of Maggie rushing up behind me.

"That's what I'm trying to tell, ye, corporal. You're too late!"

"Too late!" I gasped.

"No, bless you, no, not that way! You're too late to see him before he's discharged. The doctor said your friend was free to go. He left here this morning He's walking back to his unit.."

"His unit?" I said, stupidly.

"Yes, the fifty first. Or was it the fifty third? I don't remember. But when we asked him where he was going, and someone mentioned the fifty something. He nodded and off he went. I am sorry you didn't get to say goodbye."

I swallowed. "Um, um yes, thank you." I turned away then, as full of emotion as at any time since mama died and I had sudden word that Nate, my brother Nate, was alive and possibly close by.

"Wait…corporal!" she said kindly, pulling at my arm. "He left something for ye."

"He did?" I said numbly. "How…"

"He gave it to me. And when I asked him if he meant me to give it to ye, he nodded and smiled," she explained. She paused then and went into a curtained place to the side of the tent where she and the other nurse no doubt had a cot of their own. She returned moments later, holding a small brown book. I took it carefully and walked out of the tent, never pausing to look down at my hand until I was well away from prying eyes. And then I looked. It was a leather bound copy of *Uncle Tom's Cabin*, the famous anti-slavery tome written just before the war. My eyes opened wide in disbelief. Inside the dust cover were the simple words, "To my dear friend." I had no way of knowing whether these were his words to me, or the words of some dear friend to himself. In any case, he had carried the book with him into war and now he had given it to me. I clutched the book to my breast and gave way to the overwhelming feelings welling up inside me. It was some long time before I left the woods that night.

Chapter Sixteen

Things got very bad, very quickly after that. The cold weather started in and with the cold came the driving winds and the snow. Like most of the men, I had long since thrown my woolen great coat to one side, figuring it too cumbersome to lug around in the heat; like most of the men, I quickly came to regret that decision. My fingers were red and blistered after days of numbing cold. My feet were scarcely better. I envied the men who received care packets from a loving mother or sister, who made them underwear and sets of woolly socks. I was wet and cold and wondering when the heck we were going to eat something more substantial than soup for dinner.

"Town's up ahead of us, we'll be eating beef for dinner!" was a frequent refrain among the officers. The reality was, after a year of fighting and of troops marching back and forth through towns and villages on the eastern seaboard, there was little enough food for the townsfolk themselves, let alone for Northern soldiers. Despite threats of fines and worse, most of the people claimed empty larders and empty purses, and there was little our officers and supply troops could do about it.

Mind you, some of the men were plenty resourceful. They took to "finding" chickens and apples and even a spare pie or two "left at the side of the road." There was many a farmer's wife who left food cooking on the hearth, only to return and find that the pot, the spoon and the dinner had disappeared on her. No wonder the locals were increasing hostile towards us. Troops came through their towns and villages on a regular basis, both the Southern boys and us Northerners. Every last man was hungry. Every last man was growing callous, hardened by the sounds and sights of battle, and by the depravity and carnage all around. Men became accustomed to taking what they saw because they wanted it. Not because they were entitled or because they ought to, but because they were hungry, tired, and angry. Men were turning into beasts. So what the locals wouldn't sell them, they helped themselves to anyway. Even when the officers tried to stop them, the men helped themselves. And since we couldn't afford to shoot every man who broke the rules, we looked the other way. This emboldened the men still further.

"Don't fret none, corporal," the men would say to me when I tried to dissuade them. "If their troops ever come North into our towns, they'll be stealing more than pies and chickens!"

"Yeah, look out for your women!" someone sneered. "Those Southern boys 'll take anything they've a mind to!" This from a man tearing into a chicken he hadn't bought and a loaf of bread he hadn't baked. Still, I was as hungry as the rest of them, and denying myself the food laid before me wasn't going to make the situation any better, it would just leave me hungrier.

The army's plan now was to march us south to the river _____ and join forces with General B's fourth army. There we would hope to engage the rebel forces in one last, fierce encounter before the winter snows made further skirmishes impossible. We had less than twenty hours to join forces with the general. And the terrain, over which we had to drag fifty cannon and several thousand men and horses along with equipment, was hilly and tree covered. Most of us had only home-made woolen gloves to cover red and blistered hands. The icy winds made the ropes sleek and slippery. It was too hard dragging the guns over just the first hill. By the time I asked them to drag it over a third and then a fourth hill, they were sullen and near exhaustion. My job became less that of a task master, and more that of a yard hen, pecking and pushing at her chicks to get them in line and over to the hen house: "Move that branch!" "Pull on that rope!" "Hold her steady now!" "Come on men, just ten yards more!" "We're cresting the hill!" "Put your backs into it!" There were two or three other corporals within shouting distance, and we were all struggling up the side of yet another hill when I had an idea. In a loud voice, so that all around could hear me, I yelled over to Corporals Lang and Heigeland that their men were a sorry sight compared to my fine crew, and that we could whip their tails any day of the week!

Lang was not the smartest of the men and he looked over with a blank expression. But Heigeland was a different sort. He and his men were a few yards ahead of Lang's on the slope of the hill and as he looked back at me, we made eye contact and the trace of a smile creased his upper lip.

"We're ahead of you now and we'll be ahead when we get to the top of the hill!" he yelled back.

"You're ahead because you had fewer trees over there. We're almost beating yer and we had to avoid three trees!"

"If your piss was as yellah as your talk, you'd be pissing real colorful!" Heigeland added.

By now we had the men's attention. They had stopped pulling and were straining to hold the guns in place, fixated on what was shaping up to be a good fight between corporals.

"You can compare piss at the top of the hill," Lang shouted up ahead. "My men are ahead of both of yers."

At this, there was a flurry of movement among the men. And what had seemed hopeless just minutes before, now seemed possible. All around us men were energized and alert. Ropes were grabbed with renewed vigor, and upwards of fifty men were now racing to see which crew was the fastest. We reached the top of the hill, and the men scarcely stopped to rest before they were maneuvering down. Zig- zagging across the tree laden hillside, finding the best places to support the heavy guns, they fought gravity and raced one another to see which crew was indeed the best. Nor did they rest at the bottom of that hill, nor at the top of the next. For several hours, aided by a steady stream of insults back and forth between myself and Corporals Heigeland and Lang, who had finally caught on to the game, they heaved and pulled the heavy weapons through the snow until I thought they should all drop from exhaustion.

"God willing, those Southern boys aren't laying in wait for us now," I muttered, looking around me. Spread out as we were across several hills, our men were vulnerable to anyone who cared to attack us. Indeed, it would have been easy to pick us off, spread across the hillside, holding onto heavy guns. Luckily, we had the snowy scene all to ourselves.

We had three days and two nights of travel over rough terrain. At night, after supper, the bitter cold forced me back into the tent with Corporal Whiley. I found him more ornery and peculiar than ever. He had taken to wearing a wooden cross under his jacket: a large, ostentatious thing, rough-hewn from pieces of tree bark. At night, he would open his jacket and shirt, whether to display his exceptional piety, or to allow the air to sooth the angry welts the cross had made across his chest, I don't know. I told him he ought to get them seen to, for the cuts were inflamed and bleeding, but he hunched up on his bed, knees drawn up to chest and scowled at me from under bushy eyebrows.

"You and your kind will go to hell, mark my words," he hissed in a low voice. I would have laughed at the man if he hadn't seemed so twisted and peculiar. I found his manner of praying strange and unforgiving, and his apparent devotion full of contradiction. Our mother had been a kind-hearted, Christian woman: a loving soul, with a generous word for everyone. She had been open to all types. I recalled a time when a peddler had called at the farm house, a dark-skinned man with a kerchief on his head and foreign-looking features. He said he came from far away in Europe. My mother invited him to pray with us before supper, but he smiled and wished us Godspeed. Mother gave him some bread and cheese and he went off on his way. Their manner of interaction was vastly different from that of myself and Corporal Whiley. I couldn't settle with his talk of hell and damnation, and he couldn't settle with my praying to my God on my own terms. To avoid the subject, I passed the time lying on my blanket, reading one of the books the Ladies of Mercy had brought to the camp for our edification. Like most of the books they supplied, this one featured stories of shy young women, with impeccable manners and good church-going habits, marrying poor farm boys with strong backs and good morals. It was the kind of thing I might have read uncritically just a few months earlier, when life was simpler and right and wrong seemed self evident. Now I lived in a murky world of lies and half truths, and I said and did things I would never have dreamed of doing in that other life. As Josef, I found the characters sickly-sweet and the stories numbingly predictable. But I read on until I was tired enough to sleep, then I turned on my side and prayed the man to my right was too God-fearing and too patriotic to kill a fellow soldier over theological differences. It was a disquieting thought. As it was, I awoke each morning to his mutterings, wondering if he had slept, wondering if this was the day he would do something peculiar. As long as I made it out of the tent alive, sharing a space with him was still slightly better than the alternative. But the gap was narrowing, and the jury was still out on the wisdom of my choice. We finally reached the last of the hills, and rejoined the road, as it weaved its way between the mountains and down into a valley. We were a battle-hardened group, toughened now by months of marching and fighting. Even so, the rugged terrain had been a challenge, and hauling the guns up and down steep hillsides had taxed the men's skills and tempers. It became second nature to curse and swear our way through the day. My hands and nails were habitually bloody and dirt stained. When they weren't blue from the cold, they were bleeding where the stem of a broken branch had snared them.

Our unit reached General B---'s encampment a few hours ahead of schedule, late in the afternoon on the fourth day. Even at that hour, the camp was a hive of activity. Some people had already settled in and some, like us, were just arriving. Scouts were riding hither and thither among the officers, bringing the latest intelligence on the movements of the Southern armies, and news from Washington and from towns and hamlets in the immediate area. I looked around and saw guns being dragged into place across the snowy field, and aligned and realigned in accordance with this captain's wishes and that sergeant's interpretation of his orders. Up here on the incline, there were trees to hide under. Behind us was a clearing where several different groups had set up camp fires and were trying to establish some sort of mess tent for the provision of meals. I had noticed that, in some camps, cooking was a communal affair with everyone pitching in as much food and as many supplies as they had on hand. Three or four men were designated as cooks for the whole group. Then in other camps, small groups of four to eight men would light their own fires, and more or less cook their own dinners. Our unit fell somewhere in between, with groups of eight to sixteen people sharing food, and one person designated as cook for the rest of us.

General B---'s camp seemed highly organized with its division of labor and land. There were even men designated to dig out "communal sanitation areas." I made a mental note to "take a lot of walks" in the forest, since communal sanitation was obviously not in my best interest, if I wished to avoid detection.

I was assigned to camp set up duty, along with two other corporals. One was a jolly fellow from Scotland, and the third an unpleasant fellow with an accent I couldn't place. We set up camp in an area to the right of the camp fires, arranging our tents in two straight lines. All around us were the usual sounds and smells of camp life: the banging in of tent pegs, the rumble of wagon wheels, the smell of wood fires, the sounds of an accordion, the shouting of officers and the grunting of men moving guns and equipment. Wafting above it all were the smells of burnt coffee and frying bacon. I realized I was hungry. When dinner came, it was most welcome.

After supper, Sergeant Howard called four of us into his tent and spread out a map. Whiley, Heigeland, Lang and I formed a line behind him and peered over his shoulder.

"The rebels will be here in two, maybe three, more days," he said. "The plan is for General G----- and a company of men to draw their army out from here," he stabbed a town, "onto the main road here. We'll draw them down towards us, using these hills here and here, to prevent their flanking the general before the terrain opens up onto this flat plain here, which is where we'll be waiting."

"What if the snow comes in before they reach us?" I asked him.

He nodded. "That's the risk we take. "Weather's come in early this year. We have to hope it holds long enough so we can cut them down before the winter snow. They can't train through the winter, so when the spring comes, we could be in better shape and hit them hard, before they can reform and regroup. It's a good plan," he added, "but it rests on the weather."

"What are our exact orders, sergeant?" Heigeland asked. He was a young man, two maybe three years older than me with an earnest expression and intelligent eyes.

"Very well," Howard said, pulling over a sheet of paper and sketching out a rough drawing. "The field of engagement extends here," he said. "General G's men will draw them in down this road, and will deploy across the field here and here. The rebel army will be drawn in down this way, and when they reach the open land, we will hit them from the right and left flank with our main forces deployed to the north here. Corporals Schmidt and Heigeland will set your guns in the woods over here, on the right flank. Corporals Lang and Whiley will stage your guns a hundred yards to the east of them. On the far side of the field, there will be more guns hidden in the tree line. When the time comes, General B will start a flanking movement around the enemy's right and left flanks, moving behind you through the trees and coming back at the enemy from the south. When you get the order, you will pull the guns forward beyond the tree line, and commence firing to support that attack."

"Doesn't that trap us between the rebels and our men?" Heigeland asked, echoing my concerns.

"Hopefully not," Howard answered crisply. "If all goes well, our troops will have passed behind you and will be engaging the enemy from the south, before the rebels even know they're there."

"But if the timings off, we will be shot at from in front and from behind."

"It could happen, I suppose," Howard said. "Let's hope it doesn't. Any more questions?"

Having none, the four of us filed out of the tent. Whiley sniffed, "God's will be done." I tried to find comfort in the thought.

Chapter Seventeen

My feelings in the hours before battle were a mixture of dread, excitement and contemplation. One minute I was in fear of my life, the next, I wondered if I would distinguish myself for bravery. Then I wondered again if the general's plan didn't condemn us to be trapped in a fiery blaze between enemy and friend.

I was standing with my men, in the pre- dawn chill under snow- laden trees, stamping my feet against the cold and thinking of winters back on the farm. With a pang of loss, I touched my hand to my neck where ma's locket sat nestled against my skin. I was too afraid the haversack would get lost in the skirmishing, and I would lose this connection to ma forever. I smiled, thinking of the stew she used to make when it got especially cold, a wondrous mixture of beef with potatoes and carrots and gravy thick enough to stand a spoon up in. I asked her once the secret of that gravy, and she said she would share the recipe on my wedding day. That day never came. Death took her away before I got around to courting. Now here I was, standing in men's clothing, before a battle where I looked to be killed.

The men around me were silent, each of them lost in thought. Some would be praying and some, like me, thinking of home. Still others, like the new boy, James, would be thinking of a girl or a wife back home. With another pang of loss, I reached for my throat, feeling the outline of mama's locket on the pad of my hand.

You can hear an approaching army long before you can see one, although on this day, the sounds were muffled on account of the snow. It had been storming pretty much all night. My mind registered a general rumbling and trembling of the ground, long before I realized I could hear it. But suddenly, the men were abuzz with the news that the rebels were coming! Our scouts arrived back in a hurry, reporting that the rebel force was rushing up behind them. We had no more got into position than they were upon us, driving forward in hopes of a quick victory. You could almost see their panic and confusion when they realized they had been drawn into a trap. Then the horses were screaming, and the men were yelling and the big guns were firing. I was aware of an intense rush of feeling through my body, a combination of fear and bile in the mouth as we stood awaiting the order to fire. There were lots of men who lost the contents of their stomachs before the corporals restored order and the training took over. It seemed like hours that the two armies engaged, before we were called into action. Alls we could do was to stand and watch from under the tree line, while the enemy poured onto the field and our men fought them from the north and the west.

"Seems to me they have many more men than we do," Heigeland observed and I couldn't help but think he was right. The plan had called for an army of several thousand men on their side, to face an army of several thousand men on ours. But what seemed to be coming at us were twice as many men as we had been led to expect.

"How could this be?" I wondered.

"Someone said there's two armies joined against us," Lang offered. Surveying the field in front of me, I couldn't help but think him right.

"How are they going to flank so massive a group with any effect?" I wondered.

"If they charge through the tress, they'll cut us down like flowers in a field at harvest time," Whiley observed. "The Lord's will be done!"

"Amen," said Heigeland. "But we can try and help the Lord in his efforts!"

"Amen!" Everyone but Whiley agreed.

"Don't you be blaspheming," Whiley started.

"It's not blaspheming to suggest the Lord gave us brains for a reason!" Heigeland hissed. "I'm sick and tired of your ranting!"

"Oh, it's ranting now, is it," Whiley retorted. "Just you wait. The Day of Judgement ..."

"Look out!" Lang shouted. And not a moment too soon. From somewhere in the trees behind us came a whooping and a yelling. Men seemed to be rushing towards us and bullets started flying. I felt a stinging in my right leg as I dove to the ground, and the screams of men to my right and left convinced me we were under attack. We had no time to man the gun, or even point our muskets, before they were upon us, yelling, and thrusting their bayonets. With a blood-curdling cry, Lang took a mortal wound to the chest, tripped on me where I lay and fell prone on top of me. I struggled to free myself of him, while all around me men were fighting and screaming and dying. It was a scene of total chaos. The moment I pushed the body off me, someone else fell dead, or tripped over me and I struggled to pull myself out again. When I rolled to the side, the battle had rushed past me, and I sat up and watched with a kind of stupefaction as the horror played out before my eyes. Amidst the curling smoke of the guns and the pop, pop, pop of muskets, I saw men gutted like pigs at the slaughter house, and blood and brains and other matter strewn about the field. There were all the sights and sounds of battle magnified twenty fold by the nearness of it all. A man ran toward me with a musket raised, and I looked up into the face of my murderer, as he raised the barrel and smashed it down into my face. As I watched him bring the death blow toward me, he seemed to slow down, as if my impending death had slowed all my senses. As he moved, a patch of red spread out across his chest in an ever- widening circle. And then the barrel made contact with my head and all was blackness.

I don't know for how many hours I lay there, scarcely alive; not yet dead. When I was conscious of my surroundings and of how I came to be there, I tried to sit up and found myself once against pinned. This time underneath the corpse of my would-be executioner, his chest shot through, his face frozen in the same blood- curdling expression of hatred with which he had tried to end my life. Instead, he was still and lifeless. I pushed him away, sat up, and a rush of nausea hit me so suddenly I was forced back down. When my nausea subsided somewhat, I tried it again, more slowly this time. I raised myself onto one elbow. Fighting back the dizziness and trying to focus, I could hear nothing around me but the wind blowing through the trees. Somewhere in the distance I thought I heard shooting, but it could have been the wind. I was struggling to see through my blood-crusted eyes. I wiped them off best as I could with my sleeve. Around me the snow was stained red, and covered with guts and corpses. A man hung suspended from a low branch to my left, his face peaceful, his stomach ripped open and his entrails poured clean onto the ground. I threw up then, but there were no tears. I had no grief left for any of us tortured and torturing souls.

"What have we done! What have we done!" was all I could think, over and over again.

My head was throbbing. I was afraid the man had smashed my face all to pieces, and I was still vain enough to care, even after all I had seen. Slowly I raised my hand towards my aching face. I was forced to stop. The pain in my right arm was pretty bad. I wondered if the recent wound had opened up again. Using my left hand now, I traced the outlines of my mouth, my cheeks, my eyes. There was blood encrusted on my cheeks and forehead but I felt no gaping wounds. My face seemed to have escaped the death blow he would have struck, had a bullet not pierced his heart before he could deliver it full force. By the throbbing in my head, I knew there was a bad head wound. I felt my hair and it was caked with blood, some of it sticky and viscous as if the wound were still oozing. The pain was severe and I had to have it cleaned and covered if I were to escape disease – or worse.

Noises in the woods alerted me to the fact I was not alone, but I was too dazed and weak to move. I just sat there, awaiting my fate. In my present circumstance there was little I could do to protect or defend myself. The gun at my side was near out of bullets and I had no stomach left for killing. Presently five men came into view. They were rebel infantry and by the looks of them they had been drinking, for they were falling almost as much as they were walking.

"Well, lookee here, Jake, what have we found ourselves," one of them said. He was a coarse- looking man with a sagging belly and eyes made mean with drink.

"Looks like a yellah- bellied yank to me, Jake," said his companion, a trimmer man wearing an improbable red cap.

"You know whats we do with Yanks, don't yer?" asked a third, drinking from a hip flask and offering it to his friends.

"We invites them to tea," said the fourth.

"Lave im alone," said the fifth man, who appeared to be sober.

"You know, Bryan, you're gittin to be a real bore," said the first man. "We're at war with these men, we should kill 'em afore they kill us." He bent down and tried dragging me to my feet. I struggled to get my footing.

"The battle's over and he's been wounded. Just leave him be, there's been killing enough," said the man they called Bryan. He pulled me away from the first man and pushed me gently forwards. "On your way, fellah. Peace be with you."

"Peace be with you my arse," Jake spat on the ground. "Eee can be peaceful in heaven along with all the good men im and his kind killed today."

"I say we hang him," the third man said.

Four of them seemed to think this was a fine idea, and I didn't think my chances of getting out of there were good. They dragged me towards the trees. My right arm was hurting so much, I was fading in and out of consciousness. I became vaguely aware of a horse galloping up and a commanding voice yelling, "What the hell are you men doing? Release that man at once!"

They released me and I collapsed onto the ground. Painfully, I pushed my way up to a sitting position.

"What unit are you with?" the man continued. "Seventh Missouri Light Infantry," Jake answered. He sounded a lot different now.

"Have you men been drinking?"

"Us? What? No sir!" someone answered.

"Hmm!" the officer answered. "I have no time to deal with you now. You're a disgrace to the South, the whole bunch of you! Where is your unit?"

"They are up yonder," one of the men answered. "We got separated in the skirmishing."

"Then be on your way and join them," he said. "And don't let me catch you dawdling again!"

"What about our prisoner?" Jake said. He had a clear hankering to kill me.

"Be on your way and leave this man to me!" the officer replied. A bullet to the head is the way to do it, not a hanging!"

"Right, sir! That's good sir!" Jake replied. He seemed much more cheerful at the thought of my imminent death.

The men slivered off through the forest.

The officer dismounted and walked towards me. His boots were well polished and made of the finest leather. He was wearing fine leather gloves. There was a pistol in his right hand. He reached my side and knelt. I braced myself for the shot. Smooth gloved fingers slid over my mouth. "Don't yell." He said. "Those men are a disgrace to the uniform!" He fired into the ground. The sound reverberated through the trees. A bird squawked, angry to have its rest disturbed again by the travails of man.

The man released his grip and turned my face towards him. And stared, wide-eyed.

"Captain Clydemore! Eli!" I gasped.

For a split second we stared at one another.

"Josef!" he said. "I can't believe it!"

"I thought I'd never see you again!"

"I hated to leave that way! I didn't know what else to do when they released me."

"I got the book!" I tried to pat my pocket, but it was too painful.

"You're hurt!" he cried. He removed his glove and felt in my hair. "The head wound's deep, but it'll mend if you get it seen to."

"Could have been worse,"

"You could have been killed!"

"One of you'rn almost did that!"

"I'm sorry."

There was an awkward silence. He gave me a look so tender, I felt I would melt into him. The face inches from my own was gentle, full of love and concern. And then he shook himself, aware all at once of our situation. Two men, from opposite sides, alone in a clearing, staring at one another like lovers. With an agonized sound, he pushed me roughly away. "God, no!" he cried, rising to his feet.

"Here!" striding over to his horse, he pulled off a blanket roll and thrust it at me "Take this and keep yourself warm!" he said.

"What's the matter? Why are you talking like that!"

"We're men, Josef, or haven't you noticed? We're not…you're not…This cannot be!" We cannot be this way!" He leaped to his feet and strode towards his horse.

"Wait! Eli!" I called. "You don't understand!"

"Oh yes I do!" he called over his shoulder. "I understand now what my parents were afraid of. They're afraid of me. Of what I might be!"

"No! No! Eli! It's not like that! Come back! I can explain!" I struggled to get up but he was climbing onto his horse.

"I can't see you again, Josef!" he said, matter of factly. "I can never see you again!"

With that, he wheeled his horse around and rode off, afraid of what he felt, of what we both felt.

"He loves me!" I realized. "But he thinks I'm a man!"

I sat down suddenly, overcome.

The world had gone mad. Men were slaughtering one another by the thousands. Every family in our wonderful, new country was sending its sons-and maybe also its daughters- to die at their brother's hand. And in the midst of this lunacy, I had fallen in love with a Southerner; a man who represented everything I said I despised! We were on opposite sides of a war that was tearing our country apart. And he, for his part, had feelings for a girl he thought to be a boy, and who, therefore, was repugnant to him.

Chapter Eighteen

A detachment of Northern soldiers found me about three hours later. According to the report, I was stumbling about in a clearing near the battlefield, mumbling about finding my haversack, which, I did not seem to know, was slung over my shouulder at the time. Apparently, I was pretty belligerent, insisting I could find my own way back to camp thank you. And then I started making rude remarks about poor strategy, and jack ass generals and the like. These latter remarks the men graciously omitted from the report. However, they repeated them verbatim to Ryan, who asked them to, "Go easy on the young corporal. He really is quite a nice fellah." Ryan had seen them drag me into camp and rushed over, full of concern. Thereafter, any time I gave him an order he disliked, which was pretty much every day, Ryan threatened to convey my remarks to the general concerned. For the time being, though, he assisted in lifting me onto the ambulance wagon. I was conveyed in style to the hospital tent, where a doctor saw to my head wound and treated my re-injured arm.

The tent was crowded and rank with the smells of blood and feces. Ten to twelve tables were covered with horribly injured men. Three doctors moved smoothly between the tables, sawing off limbs with what looked to be farm tools, and screaming at their aides to administer more chloroform so as to knock the poor injured soul out long enough to finish their hacking. Being raised on a farm, I was used to seeing hogs and hens slaughtered; but I had never seen men cut up this way, and my stomach churned at the sights and sounds of it. Nor was I used to chloroform. It was a foul-smelling substance, forced onto the nose and mouths of the injured, so as to render them senseless enough to lie still while their limbs were being forcibly removed. Once inside the tent, I had been dumped unceremoniously on an empty table. I was about to slide off and get myself out of there, when someone pushed me down again so the doctor could see to me.

He was a bearded, cigar- chomping gentleman, with a blood-stained apron and arms.

"Where're you injured corporal?" he puffed, all the while poking at my person. I was terrified, lest he discover then and there, that I was not the man he took me to be.

"It's my head and my arm!" I insisted pulling his hands away from my belly and up towards my head. I would take the pain of that exertion any day over the indignity of his pushing and probing.

I was eyeing the collection of bloodied instruments, resting on a small table to the side of us, and especially the knife he was wielding in his left hand. He must have smelt my fear for he laughed and his huge bloodied paw patted my arm reassuringly.

"Don't you worry son. I'm not going to be taking your arm by the looks of ye."

He had deftly slit my coat sleeve with the point of the bloodied knife and was peering at the wound with interest. "Looks like it was healing well," he said.

"Yes, it was my ma's practice to seal a wound with a hot knife." I bit my lip to stop from yelling out as he poked around with a sharp blade.

"Hrump!" he snorted. "Fancy that."

He dabbed at the wound on my head with a wet rag, that had seen better days, and pronounced me fit to return to duty. I stumbled thankfully out of the tent. The young man accompanying me then directed me to report to Captain Mallory's headquarters. It was a slow walk over to Mallory's tent. He, thankfully, was not there at the time. Instead, the man in charge was a Captain Sorenson- a tall, thin man with a reedy voice and a distinct lack of presence. I was puzzled that the man had risen to the rank of captain. For the first time, I wondered if the men hadn't been right when they suggested that sometimes factors other than competence accounted for promotions within the military. At any rate, this Captain Sorenson was a distinctly unimpressive fellow. He pinned on my sergeant's stripes, wished me Godspeed and sent me on my way. When I reported for duty, I found myself in charge of two guns under the command of my old friend, Lieutenant Billings. I don't know which of us was more surprised by the news, him or me. In any event, the situation became at once more pleasant when it was discovered that none other than Ryan and Tom were among the crew on the first gun.

"Wow! Look, Corporal Peterson! It's Sergeant Schmidt!" Ryan yelled clean across the camp as soon as he caught sight of me. "How yer feeling, *Sergeant?*" He made a point of emphasizing my new title. I gave him a withering look, which disturbed him not at all. A whole pile of men crowded around us as Ryan swiftly made introductions.

The men in my new command were as follows. Ryan, was at the front of the first gun, along with a small, quiet man whom Ryan called Bobbie. His full name, I learned afterwards, was Robert Palmer of Chicago. There was one Jakob Muller, a recent immigrant from Maine, with fervent anti- slavery views. Patrick O'Reilly from Deefield was a tall, thin man who was always hungry. Twin brothers, Luigi and Greggorio Savarino, young men from Naples, Italy, were the funniest men on the crew. They could always be relied upon to make me laugh. For one thing, they were always complaining about the cold weather and the miserable army rations. All they talked about was their mother's cooking- which Ryan wasted no time in suggesting they go back and enjoy. Rounding out the group were Tom Peterson, the corporal, and the Powder Monkey- a scared young boy who looked to be no more than twelve or thirteen, and who went by the name Mischa. His full name was Mikhail Ilanovitch Drassolovitch, which is why the rest of us took to calling him Mischa pretty fast. It was clear he came from Russia, or somewhere near there, but his English was poor and he didn't talk a great deal. He had clearly taken a liking to Ryan, though, and he followed the man around like a loyal puppy. Ryan made great show of hating the attention. But since the man got his own way more often than not, it seemed to me he could not have been that displeased.

The men on the second gun were a strange lot. They had been together since they mustered into the Union army at the start of the war and they all hailed from a small town in Scotland with an unpronounceable name. They didn't mix with the rest of us. They each carried a small flask of a foul-smelling liquid in their haversacks, which they drank with gusto, and which had the effect or making them sleepy or pugnacious. More than once, I had sent Ryan and Tom over to break up a campfire brawl, which threatened to disrupt the very Union. But by the morning, they always seemed none the worse for wear, and friends again with the men they had threatened to slit ear from ear the night before.

On the other hand, fighting with the Rebs was winding down now that winter was approaching, and plans were laid down to exchange our tent camp for a more permanent site over the winter. Accordingly, work crews were drawn up to go into the forest and cut down trees to make huts for a tent camp. For our part, the men were detailed to dig ramparts around the camp, with cut- outs every hundred yards or so where we would mount the guns. This work occupied us for the next three weeks. Although I could not join in the digging on account of my rank and my sore arm, still I enjoyed the opportunity to talk to the men as they worked. For their part, the men were generous in their praise and generally pleased to find me elevated to sergeant. For, as Tom put it, they found me, "even tempered, fair-minded and occasionally possessed of a good idea or two, unlike that idiot Billings, may he rot in hell!"

"It's insubordination to talk about an officer like that!" I warned him.

"Oh, God, serg, you know darn well I'm right!" Tom lamented. You gotta save us from that creature. He's balmier than ever!"

"Balmier?"

"Crazier. He's a stickler for all the minutiae when we're drillin', but as soon as the battle's joined, he goes kinda looney!"

"Tom, you just gotta start speaking English!" Ryan slapped him on the back. "I only git about half what yer sayin'!"

"You fellahs here are butcherin' the language!" Tom pushed him back.

"Yeah, it's every man for himself with Old Billings in charge!" Ryan continued. "Good job we never paid 'im no mind anyways. You gotta watch out for us, serg!"

"Indeed!" I laughed. "Course, you'll be paying mind to *me* won't yer!"

"You! Oh yes sir, Sergeant Schmidt! Ain't no problem following your orders any how. They make sense!"

I wasn't about to get into an argument with them about military matters. I knew darn well that anything they did with respect to the gun made maximum sense. And anything Billings said, was liable to be wrong, or ill- timed or both. I also knew I had my work cut out for me if I was to avoid charges of insubordination serving under him! It seemed as if army life took you out of one danger, only to thrust you into another every day.

The building of our winter camp proceed steadily, the men being well aware of the layout of a Union camp as proscribed by army regulations. The basic idea was to lay down two rows of tents for the men. Behind these were the officers' huts or tents and behind them, the field officers' quarters. It was all very predictable and orderly in accordance with the army way of doing things. I read somewhere that the plan was modeled after the Roman Legions' camps in days gone by. After three weeks, the perimeter of the camp was almost entirely surrounded by an earthen barricade. At regular intervals, the wall was interrupted by the stern thrust of a ten pounder aimed directly at any rebel unit foolish enough to consider attacking the enemy within. We were all anticipating a long, somewhat dull sojourn inside the walls of the camp, when I was abruptly summoned to Captain Mallory's tent and told to bring all my things with me. Pleased as I was at the thought of leaving Billings and even Mallory behind, I was distressed at the thought of a transfer away from my men.

When I got there, I found Captain Mallory pacing back and forth in his tent, which was empty save for his adjutant lurking inconspicuously in the background.

"Ah, Schmidt!" he said as I made my entrance. "Come in. We have an assignment for you of a somewhat delicate nature."

Expecting something dangerous and exciting, I was disappointed and more than a little perplexed to find myself assigned the task of baby sitting a visiting dignitary. Colonel Roger Braithwaite (retired), was described to me as being a former highly-decorated member of His Majesty's Royal …..regiment and a current writer for the *Daily*………., a well-known London paper. It was, apparently, "of utmost importance to the Union cause" that Braithwaite receive a favorable impression of our side. The British had to be persuaded, by all means necessary, to NOT enter the war on the side of the Southerners- with whom they had long established financial and familial ties.

"Then why give the assignment to me?" I wondered. "I am only a sergeant and that only recent! Wouldn't a captain be a more natural choice?"

Mallory seemed gratified. "Thank you for the vote of confidence," he beamed. "However, it has been decided to downplay our apparent interest in the affair, while all the while believing it to be of the utmost importance!"

"I see," I said, although it was far from clear to me why we should play such silly games.

"Which is why we are offering this assignment to *you*, Sergeant Schmidt! I am confident that your natural intelligence and good sense will put our cause in the best possible light," Captain Mallory concluded.

"But what exactly am I to do?" I wondered. "Where am I to take the colonel?"

"You will take him wherever he desires to go," Mallory answered, "but you will steer him gently towards places that will reveal our cause in the best light, and away from anything that reveals us less favorably."

I thought to myself this was an especially vague and difficult assignment, and one fraught with dangers to myself were I to make what my superiors considered poor judgments. But I was not in any position to reject or alter my assignment, this being the army and Mallory being a superior officer.

"Um, how long is this assignment supposed to last?" I inquired delicately. "I feel a certain loyalty to the men under my command."

"Which is what makes you such a fine soldier and recommends you highly for this task," Mallory beamed. "Have no fear it will outlast the winter. Indeed, it may be that you are back in camp by the end of the year."

"Huh," I thought to myself, "from what I've learned so far about army promises, that means for sure I will not be back before spring." Time was to prove me right, but I put a brave face on it and prepared to do my duty as best I could.

The men were angry and disappointed when they found I was not to be with them during the long winter months.

Although they wished me well with my new assignment, it was with an obvious lack of enthusiasm and good humor.

"Fact is, serg," Ryan confided, "you know as well as I do there's not many in command as have any common sense to speak of, and when one of yer own gets promoted and you have confidence in 'im, well, you don't want to lose him to some jackass assignment that some blue blood could just as well take on, do yer!"

I understood well how he was feeling, sharing some of his misapprehensions and misgivings myself. But the army has its ways and apparently its plans included the fact that I was to baby-sit this British colonel, turned newspaper man, for as long as it took him to discover the justice of our cause.

"Hope he's a quick learner, 'sall I can say," Tom muttered morosely as I took my leave of them.

"Ye'll come back drinkin' tea and speaking funny, no doubt," Ryan threw in for good measure.

"And I'll miss you too, "I said as bravely as I could. These men had become as dear to me as my own brothers. Indeed, in many ways they *were* now my brothers. As much as Eli and Nate might be related by blood, Ryan and Tom and I were bound by suffering and struggle and I would never ever forget them.

"Come back soon, now," Ryan called out as I walked away.

I looked back at where Tom and Ryan stood, Tom leaning against a tree stump chewing something and Ryan kicking at the snow under his feet. My heart gave a sudden lurch and, in defiance of army protocol, I found myself saluting smartly. Both of them saluted back. "Y'all stay safe now," I called, "and that's an order!" And with a heavy heart, I walked away.

I took an instant dislike to Braithwaite. He was nothing like I expected. I had pictured the former British officer as tall and thin with a moustache and a cruel face. The man I met was stout, of medium build and sported one or two double chins beneath beady eyes. He had a cold, withdrawn persona, spoke infrequently and laughed less. We interacted rarely. Most days we sat in silence in the carriage as the army ferried us between one encampment and another. Mealtimes were largely spent in silence, my attempts at conversation rebuffed at every turn. I soon abandoned my good-natured inquiries into his family's composition and well-being, and withdrew into the silence he so obviously preferred.

As for our freedom of movement, it was far more circumscribed than Mallory's introduction suggested. Indeed, I had the feeling our route had been planned down to the last centimeter; but, if this were the case, the adjutant and driver who accompanied us gave no such indication. Instead, I was amused to find certain roads "blocked" and certain others "under construction" ("In the winter, yet!" I mused silently). And if Braithwaite caught on to the subterfuge, he said nothing about it either way. Our days fell into monotonous regularity. The adjutant wakened us at dawn, brought breakfast to our respective tents, and advised us we would be breaking camp within the half hour. There followed several hours of riding by carriage across a snow-covered winter landscape until we reached this encampment or that battalion headquarters, where introductions and salutations were briefly exchanged. Where then followed a sweeping recap of: battles fought, lost or, less frequently, won, prisoners taken, wounded, cared for and dead disposed of. Then the officer in charge would ask questions of Colonel Braithwaite, which were swiftly and politely rebuffed.

Arrangements were made for our comfort, meals were cooked and eaten, and, thankfully, bedtime, inevitably, arrived. The next day, the adjutant would waken us and the whole monotonous series of events would start up again. I began to think myself better off sustaining a hail of enemy gunfire than facing the prospect of another day of such tedium!

The battalions and encampments along the way had been most carefully selected, I daresay. Any right-thinking person would have speedily deduced the nobility of the cause for which we were fighting, based on the evidence presented. Indeed, it was hard to fathom how anyone could deny that individual liberty and dignity were causes worth fighting for. Nor could I imagine arguments against the right to own one's one land and shape one's own future. Weren't these rights to which every sane person could aspire? I scare could imagine how anyone having the facts explained to him, could waste one moment of his time disagreeing with the North and siding with the South! Indeed, my own dear friend, Captain Clydemore, himself hinted he would surely not be fighting for the South at all, had he not been born and bred to their erroneous ways!

At the thought of Captain Clydemore, I was conscious of a certain elevation in my temperature and a pounding of my heart. I comforted myself with thoughts of his safety over the long winter months, and with hopes that this terrible war would soon be over. However, I was not at liberty to discuss these thoughts with the eminent Colonel Braithwaite (retired), because the good gentleman had not seen fit to have a civil conversation with me since we left camp these several weeks past. In truth, on account of his disagreeable reluctance to engage in any civilized conversation whatsoever, I had resolved to dislike the gentleman very much indeed.

We had been on the road fully two months when the severe weather made further travel impossible, and we received word we were to spend the foreseeable future at a charming inn in the town of …., some thirty miles west of our country's capital. This land being firmly in the hands of Northern patriots, and all troop movements and campaigns having ceased for the winter, I was in agreement with my superiors that we could remain comfortably ensconced at the inn for the duration without fear of harassment.

The inn was a fine, several storied wood and brick-faced structure sitting to one side of the village's main square. It had a wrap around porch out front, complete with cushioned benches and picnic tables, none of which appeared to be occupied on account of the inclement weather. Inside the inn was warm and comfortable, with an abundance of fireplaces and small rooms, thoughtfully appointed and lit by lamps and welcoming fires. My heart jumped at the sight of something so cozy and welcoming. After months of hard campaigning and sleeping in tents, over-crowded barracks, or on God's good earth, the thought of a real bed was intoxicating. The couple who ran the inn introduced themselves as Helmut and Hildegard Happ from Stuttgart in Southern Germany. They were a plump, pleasant-looking couple in their middle years, round faced and bespectacled. She wore her hair drawn back in a tight bun, and he had side whiskers and wore a striped, buttoned waistcoat that scarcely covered the encroaching stomach. We were greeted warmly and bade to make ourselves at home and comfortable in what they hoped would be our home away from home for the winter. I warmed to them both at once and was determined to be pleased with my fate, despite the encumbrance of my taciturn, but unavoidable companion.

Once we were settled in our rooms, the couple urged us to make our way to the dining room where a warm meal awaited us after our long journey. Our adjutant and driver were amply provided for in the kitchen, and our horses had been unhitched and cared for by the couple's dependable stable boy. When I entered the dining room in my traveled worn blue pants and a dismally white shirt, I found a brightly lit fire burning in the glare, and a plate of steaming vegetable soup waiting for my companion and me at a cloth-covered table by the window. Outside, the snow-covered trees lent a festive air to the brisk November scene. Had it not been for the unpleasantness of my traveling companion, I could have imagined myself the luckiest person on earth at that moment. After thanking our hosts profusely, I tucked into my soup with gusto, quite prepared to pass another evening in stony silence, broken only by the unavoidable sounds of two people breaking bread and chewing their dinners. Fortified perhaps by two generous glasses of brandy and an ample cigar, my hitherto silent charge suddenly leant forward across the table and solemnly pronounced himself, "Well satisfied!" with everything he had seen and heard concerning the Union cause. "And I wish to thank you particularly, young man, for the patience and fortitude with which you have endured these several weeks of silent companionship."

"And what causes you to break your silence now?" I demanded sullenly, at once suspicious of this apparent change of heart.

"I have finished my investigations and I see no further purpose in adhering to my previous policy," he replied pleasantly.

I stared at him with what I imagine was a scornful expression. "I see. So I have been ignored for weeks and subjected to silent treatment for strategic reasons?"

"There's a war on. Nothing personal."

"Begging your pardon, but it felt pretty personal to me!"

"You sound a bit like my wife when she's in a huff."

"Yeah…well, women aren't always wrong."

"Hrump."

And that was that. For the remainder of our stay, the newly companionable Colonel Braithwaite was, if not the life and soul of the party, at least a pleasant enough fellow. He even shared with me a photo of his wife, a plump little woman with bad teeth, and their three pleasant-looking children, two males and one female. For my part, I had no photos to share, and few stories to tell about life before the army. I alluded vaguely to a farm and a few siblings from whom I had grown "estranged" and quickly changed the subject. So many people had been displaced and disconnected by the war. Braithwaite seemed more than willing to believe me one of them.

The winter passed soon enough. We spent our time reading and playing cards. In the afternoons, Braithwaite wrote long dispatches for the newspaper, which he was unable to send on account of the weather, and I amused myself with the substantial library provided by our accommodating hosts. With the coming of spring, the snows began to melt and the roads became more passable. I longed to rejoin my unit. For his part, Braithwaite seemed more than ready to conclude his American sojourn and return to his family. Standing in the now familiar lobby of the inn, we were hugged several times by a tearful Frau Happ, who declared me "skin and bone" and suggested I needed a good woman to take care of me! The good burgher, her husband, stood off to the side, rolling his eyes. As we left, he pressed a loaf of bread and a chunk of cheese into my hand.

"She means well," he whispered confidentially, as I climbed into the carriage behind Braithwaite.

I watched them grow smaller as we drew away and wondered again how we would have survived the winter had it not been for the generosity of our hosts, and the abundance of their food cellar, which never seemed to lack for bread, cheese and milk.

"I wonder how they have so much food," I said, leaning back in my seat.

"You don't know?" Braithwaite peered at me over the top of his spectacles. He had pulled a stack of papers from a leather bag he carried and was already engrossed in reading them.

"Why would I?"

He gave a wry smile.

"You don't think we stopped there accidentally, do you?"

"I assumed someone picked the place."

"That's right."

"Because it was safe."

"Reasonably so."

"What do you mean, reasonably so?"

"I mean we were unlikely to be killed staying there."

"A plus."

"And they would be able to feed us."

"And we knew this? The able to feed us part?"

"Exactly."

"Okay! You clearly know something I don't. What is it?"

"The army knows they have a lot of food."

"They do?"

"Yes."

"Why would they?"

"Why would they have a lot of food?"

"Why would they know?"

"Because they've been watching."

"Watching the Happs' store food?"

"In a manner of speaking."

"This is getting annoying. Look, I'm clearly missing something. Why don't you just tell me?"

"The army has been watching them because they're smuggling weapons."

"The Happs?"

"Yes."

"For which side?"

"Both."

"*Both?*"

"Yes."

"We know this and we let them do it?"

"Yes."

"But which side do they support?"

"Both."

"Both?"

"Yes."

"You can't support both."

"Why not?"

"Because they- WE- are at war!"

"You won't always be."

"We are now."

"And one day you won't be."

"But we are now!"

"Yes."

"I don't understand! And what has this to do with food anyway?"

"The Happs smuggle weapons. People buy their weapons using currency or food—whichever they have more of."

"What! Why do we allow this? Why don't we arrest them? Why were we allowed to stay there? We could have been..."

"Killed?"

"Yes!"

"Highly unlikely."

"Oh! I feel better now!" I slumped back in my seat.

He put his papers down and thought for a moment. "It's like this…. in any war, there are soldiers and there are civilians." He paused. I said nothing. "Soldiers survive because they are armed and organized and there are lots of them. Civilians, on the other hand, are vulnerable. No one looks out for them, not on a daily basis. They stay on their farms – or run their inns- until an army comes through and their crops are trampled, their livestock is stolen or eaten and their stores are raided. Once the army passes through, life goes back to something like normal. Only now, they have no crops, or food or guns to protect themselves. The problem is especially bad in the border states like Virginia and Kentucky. Those places get trampled on a regular basis by BOTH armies."

"You're saying that people like the Happs are likely to be raided by the North, and the South, on account of where they live?"

"Right."

"And they have to keep both sides happy because they never know which army is coming through next?"

"Exactly."

"That explains why they might trade in food. But trading guns? Why don't we stop them?" I still had trouble picturing the smiling Frau Happ hauling guns around and haggling over price.

"People like that are useful. They can find out all sorts of things, and they are usually willing to sell that information for a price."

"Is that what you did?"

"What?"

"Buy information?"

"Somewhat."

"What else did you do that I missed entirely?"

"I ate a variety of vegetables."

"You don't have to be rude"

He shook his head. "By watching what they served, I had a good idea whom they have been trading with."

"Because…?"

"You come from near Wisconsin, you said?"

I was immediately on guard. "Yes."

"How many yams did you grow every year?"

"Oh I see!"

"Now you get it!"

"And once you know they have been trading with Southerners…you know what they have been trading with Southerners…and this is helpful because…"

"Because I can use that knowledge to help me find out more."

"How?"

"I know which armies have been seen in the area at which times. I know how long crops can be stored without losing flavor or moisture. I make enlightened guesses- and I dig for information."

"All those times you shared a beer with Herr Happ?"

He nodded.

"And the times you helped Frau Happ carry those heavy barrels?"

"Exactly!" He picked up his papers and continued reading.

My head was spinning. I stared out at the landscape and struggled to take in what I had heard. I kept shaking my head. I felt so stupid. I had missed everything!

"So you're a spy, then?"

"In a manner of speaking."

I chewed this over.

"For which side?"

He looked up, and for the first time since I met him, he grinned.

"Why,… yours, of course!"

Part Two

May 1863 - August 1868

Chapter Nineteen

The night sky was clear and the air balmy. It had been raining all day and the banks of the creek were muddy and slippery. But an area along the creek bank had been cleared of brush and laid with small stones. Here, I could enter the water without slipping. No doubt this was the spot where the local farmers herded their cattle across on the way to market or to greener pastures. It had been my habit to bathe at night, long after I hoped most of the men had retired to sleep. Slipping off my wool jacket and pants, I pulled nervously at my cotton undergarments, tempted again to peel them off and give my naked body a much-needed wash. But after the narrow escape I had endured last time I tried it, I decided that caution was the wiser path and I slipped reluctantly into the water wearing my sodden cotton clothes. Even so, the cool water felt good as I waded silently towards the middle of the creek bed and sank gratefully to my knees. The water barely grazed my chin, and I tipped my head backwards to let the cool water permeate every inch of my no doubt stinking scalp. The May weather had brought more than its share of hot days and everyone's clothes stank of sweat, dirt, and fear. I could not suppress my laughter, as I pictured our mother's horrified expression, were I ever to tell her I had not had a proper bath these two long years!

Beneath the dark water, I risked untying the string of my undergarment and washed myself as best I could with one free hand. Then I retied the string and scrubbed at my short hair with the point of my fingers, grinding into the scalp and massaging out the accumulated sweat and grime. Two years of marching and fighting had hardened my slender frame, leaving it taut and strong. I had been wounded several times and my body was covered with scars and bruises, none of which troubled me over much- though the loosened teeth acquired when the young soldier had tried to bludgeon me to death, hurt somewhat if I chewed too hard on that side.

I had safely negotiated the slippery creek bed and was availing myself of my pants once more, when the sound of someone approaching through the darkness caused me to reach for my pistol.

"Hold yer trousers, Lieutenant Schmidt! Tis only I, yer trusted sergeant, come to pay yer a visit."

"Jesus, Ryan! You had me nearly shooting you through the heart!" I snarled, hurriedly fastening my pants and pulling on my jacket.

"After all this time, I don't know why yer so fastidious about dressing in front of us, lieutenant," Ryan grumbled. After all, it's not like yer has anything the rest of us don't have...with all due respect," he added hastily.

"I'll pretend I didn't hear your insubordination," I snapped. "What is it you want? Or did you wander out here to chat?"

"Look whose gittin' snippy!" he countered, in his familiar way. We were always ragging on one another when away from a crowd. God knows, we had been through enough together these past two years, that familiarity between us was the least likely to offend me.

"Much as I would like to come out here and pass the time of night with yer, as opposed to lyin in me comfortable bed and thinking about that full bodied farm girl we passed earlier today…"

"Ryan!"

"….I was sent to find yer. Yer's needed in the main tent."

"What for?"

"Well, me and the Captain, we're like this" In the moonlight I could see him make a sign with his two fingers indicating closeness, "but he thought he'd rather discuss it with you personally, seeing as how you out rank me 'n all."

"Oh very well," I sighed. "I didn't need much sleep anyway."

"If yer did, yer wouldn't be washing yerself in the creek in the middle of the night now would yer?"

"Ryan!"

"Hrump!" He made a dismissive sound deep in his throat.

We walked side by side back towards camp. Ryan was now a sergeant and still as irascible and incorrigible as ever. He shared my disdain for some of the pettier rules of military life, and never hesitated to show it to whomever happened to be around. At the same time, he was the most trusted and more trustworthy soldier you could ever hope to find. He had the total respect of his men. Even though, he wasn't always as deferential towards the higher ups as he could be, he was still tolerated, and even grudgingly admired, by many of them due to his standing among the men.

We entered Captain Feyler's tent to find that the two other lieutenants, and five sergeants, had arrived ahead of us. Captain Feyler was standing with his back to us consulting a map tacked to a large board. Next to him were his adjutant and another Captain I didn't recognize.

Captain Feyler turned as he heard us enter and bade us all move around the map.

"Thank you, Sergeant Hager. Lieutenant Schmidt, please join us." I went over and we all stared at the map.

"As you know, General G… is now in command of the army. He has big plans to crush General L… and force an end to the war."

Stony silence greeted this optimistic announcement. "Yes, I know you men are weary from two years of fighting. But with the right man in charge, the end is now in sight."

"If he can stay sober long enough to remember what 'ees doing," someone behind us muttered. I had a feeling it was Ryan.

"The plan is outflank Lee here, here and here." Feyler drew three strong red lines on the map. "Our part is to support Major General S's corp at this point (the red line grew thicker) and push on to here (the red line became an angry gash that tore the paper). Any questions?" He looked around expecting none. "Good. We move out an hour before dawn. Prepare your men."

At first, no one moved. Then the group of men shifted and, with little conversation, we turned and left.

Ryan and I walked side by side back towards our tents. Neither of us spoke until we were out of range of the others.

"Yer reckon this is gonna work?"

"It's a good enough plan…on paper," I suggested. "Trouble is, Lee is such a wily fighter, he probably anticipated every move and is *already* planning to outflank us."

"The plan is to outflank 'im."

I made a face. "So far, none of these grand plans has produced any grand results. We're two years into this war and the South is basically where it started and the North is getting nowhere."

"Blockade's beginning to work," Ryan offered hopefully.

"Was that a question or a statement?"

"Don't go gittin' morose on me now, lieutenant," Ryan hit my arm playfully. "Yer the one as is supposed to keep ME cheerful."

"I know that Ryan." I stopped in my tracks and looked at him. The dawn light was just beginning to break and the face looking back to me was as dear and familiar to me as any in my past. "I'm sure I'm just tired and I'll feel better after a few hours of sleep. It's just that nothing seems to be goin' right. I mean, we were *supposed* to sweep through the South and whip them into sense. This war was *supposed* to be over after three months. Instead, it's been two long years of fighting and dying, and what do we have to show for it?"

"If yer mean, are we winning, hell no!" Ryan laughed bitterly. Judging by the support in the streets, I would say the Rebs have us beat fair and square. Our sides lost all hope in a swift end to this thing. You ask me, we *ain't* gonna win. But it's treason to say so, an I won't repeat it fer the lads."

"Is it all for nothing then?"

"Yer know what, lieutenant? It's like my blessed mother always used to say, may she rest in peace," he spat unceremoniously on the ground, "Powerful men make war and powerful men sign peace treaties. An the likes of us, we just fight and die. But in between, we live our lives."

"Is this supposed to make me feel better?"

"Well, the point is, we made some good friends as a result of this war, didn't we?"

I couldn't help laughing. "Well, present company excepted, I would say that's true."

"And it sure beats farmin' for a living."

"I like farming!"

"I hate it. If I ever make it out of here alive, I'm moving into the city."

"And what will you do there?"

"Find myself a fat, rich woman, make lots of babies and drink meself silly."

"More of the same then!"

"If yer weren't my superior, I'd have to 'it yer."

"Good job I am then."

"Goodnight, lieutenant."

"Goodnight, sergeant."

I got back to my tent and once inside, threw myself onto the blanket. It was still dark and there was a slight chill in the air. The ground here was as soft as ground usually is, but it didn't bother me any, at least, no more than usual. I reached inside my shirt to feel the locket ma had left me. I pried open the catch. It was stiff now, the dirt and sweat of battle and fatigue had seeped under the hinges and, in the gathering light, I could just make out the faces of ma, my brothers and I, taken so long ago. I ran my thumb across the faded images and wondered whether either of my brothers was still alive. It was almost impossible to know for sure. Daily papers were getting scare in camp now. We were deep into enemy territory and the long lists of soldiers killed or missing were known to be incomplete or inaccurate. Many a widow had wept for the loss of a husband, only to discover him shivering on her doorstep, tired, hungry and escaped from the war. Many a man faded away in the heat of battle, never to return to unit or family. He simply went away and started a new life. The army had no choice but to list him among the missing or killed in action, and his suffering family had no choice but to believe it. Who was going to say different?

I sighed deeply, closed the locket and slipped it back inside my shirt. Outside the tent, I heard the first stirrings of life. Someone was stoking the fire and fixing the kettle for what passed as coffee. Some mornings, we got hot water mixed with whatever local plant the cook decided to throw in there. Other times, we got a shipment of beans and the stuff was so thick, you could clean your boots with it. Ryan liked to say the coffee was so bad it prepared you for battle. Most times, I was glad just to get something into my stomach.

I must have drifted off, for the next thing I knew, Ryan was waking me. I stepped out in the warm haze of a summer day. The mist was thick on the ground and you couldn't see but a few yards in any direction. The sun was already warm on my shoulders and I could tell by the smell in the air that the day was going to be a scorcher.

Off in the distance, I heard a bird calling its companions, and in a clearing beyond the officers' tents, a deer raised its head from eating the grass. We stared one another down for a while until it reckoned I was harmless and went back to eating.

Gratefully, I sipped the coffee Ryan had handed me and breathed in the warm summer air.

"Almost makes yer fergit the war, don't it?" Ryan muttered behind me. I hadn't known he was still there and I nodded my agreement. It didn't strike me as odd that he knew what I was thinking. He knew me better than a brother would by now, and strange to say, my woman's nature seemed scarcely part of who I was at that time in that place.

"All right now! Sergeants, call your men!"

A frenzy of bugles and shouting erupted throughout the camp. I felt, rather than saw the men running from their tents, pulling on boots, if they were lucky enough to have them, and shoes if they were not. A few men had neither, and their feet sometimes left marks in the ground where wounds had reopened and blood seeped through again. I played my part, walking to position, nodding my approval, shouting the commands. I could do it in my sleep by now. Indeed, at times it felt as if I were asleep, and it was all one very long, intense dream that I never thought to wake from.

As the sun rose higher, I could see a line of trees about a mile away, across which the enemy was marching. We were lying low, under a small rise, and the guns were set back far enough that the rebels hadn't seen them. When we opened fire, we hit them suddenly with a barrage of fire. The sudden onslaught sent panic screaming through their ranks. Men were running in all directions, screaming and falling down. Some had the presence of mind to draw their sabers and charge us, but the distance between gave us plenty of time to fire and they fell in the fields between us, their faces frozen for eternity in the snarl of battle. When the fighting started, my world narrowed again to the guns:

guns loading, guns firing. The guns were all that stood between us and eternity. I directed the men to keep firing, throwing death into the side of the rebel line. As their officers fought to maintain control, some of the rebels broke rank and turned and ran back the way they had come. This, of course, kept them straight in the line of fire. Others tried to run forward, with the same deadly result. Our guns tore into them before they were halfway across. So many men fell, their companions were forced to climb over them to keep going, making them in turn an easy target for my men. We killed them by the dozen. "Reload! Fire! Reload! Fire!" I screamed into the air. The men had no need of orders. They all knew what to do. We loaded and fired and loaded and fired. Again and again, I directed the gun towards the thick of the fighting. So many bullets ripped through the air around me, I could reach out my hand and see it ripped apart had I a mind to. I entered a place where death or life were as one. If I lived, if I died, it was all the same. I could control neither. I was no longer afraid. Death, if it came, was but a part of war. War was all I now knew of life.

At last, there were no more rebels to shoot. One by one, the guns fell silent. I looked up at the sun. It seemed to be around four o'clock. I realized my face hurt. Touching my forehead, I realized I was bleeding. A bullet must have grazed me. It didn't feel like much. I looked around for my men. I couldn't see Ryan.

"Sergeant Hager!"

"Eees over there, lieutenant!"

For a moment I feared the worse. But "over there" turned out to be a clump of trees to the south of the field. I could see Ryan standing with two or three other sergeants. They seemed to be looking at something. I turned back to the men.

"Are any of you hurt?"

"No, lieutenant. Nothing to complain about."

It was Georg who had spoken. He was a small, thin man with pale yellow hair and only a wisp of a moustache. He was teased unmercifully by the others. The men looked pretty battered but mercifully unharmed. I walked towards Ryan, angered that he had lingered so long on the other side of the field. The ground here was even and, just as we had had placed our guns below a rise, these guns too were strategically placed beneath the rise. As I approached the group of men, they looked up. I was about to reprimand him when something stopped me. Ryan's face wore a strange expression, something I had never seen before.

"What's going on?" I snapped, more forcefully than I'd intended.

"You gotta see this," he answered.

I followed him to the top of the rise. We were looking down on a flat piece of land, a small valley between hills to the north and south. The Confederate forces had been advancing to the west. Their guns had been situated to the east of our position, and their infantry had marched forward with the evident intention of attacking the Union army before it joined forces with General J. But we had moved up under cover of night and the rebel scouts had failed to discover our guns. Their force had been attacked on three sides by strong Union fire. The heavy assault forced their troops towards our infantry, which mowed them down as quickly as they fled. The results were stupefying. There in the valley before us lay the bodies of thousands of dead Confederates, stretching to the horizon as far as the eye could see. I had seen plenty of dead and dying since the start of the war, but this terrible sight was more than a soul could bear. I stared blankly at the piles of bodies, each fallen on top of the other like a grotesque pile of wood stacked up for winter. Beside me, I heard Ryan struggling for breath. My stomach heaved, but I could not look away. Everywhere I looked, faces were frozen in the agony of death. Eyes pleaded for pity where there was none. The closest dead man looked to me to be no more than twelve; his straggly brown hair had fallen across his face. Had it not been for the wicked gash across his throat, he would have seemed to be a choir boy, serenading his mother one Sunday morning in church. That one so young and innocent should die, I could bear no more! Even my tough-minded sergeant was fighting back tears. A sob erupted from deep inside me. I had been holding in so many tears: tears for my mother, for my lost brothers, for the Southern captain I would most likely not see again, for my lost childhood, for my struggling country, and finally, finally for myself. When the tears stopped, I was exhausted. My energy was gone and I felt the weight of the world pressing down on my shoulders. I wiped my face with my sleeve, gulped some fresh air and looked over to Ryan, who was waiting for me, his back to the valley.

"Ought to get the guns cleaned," I said.

"Yes, sir."

We walked back together. I could see the men had already started clean up.

"I cried like a woman," I said tersely.

"Ain't no shame in it," Ryan sniffed. "Ain't no shame in it at all."

Chapter Twenty

The sun was pretty strong that time of year and by daybreak the stench of decaying flesh was more than a soul could bear. Work details were set up at once to bury the dead Northern soldiers and parleys were arranged between Northern and Southern commanders to see when and how the Southerners could claim the same privilege.

"I wish to God they'd get their parleys over with, so the Rebs could git some of these people in the ground, where they belong," Ryan said to no one in particular.

"It's not right!" Jakob said. "Those men had mothers too!"

Of all my men, Jakob had perhaps the gentlest disposition. The loss of so many lives at one time was hurting us all pretty bad, but Jakob seemed to have the least defense against it. His eyes were red-rimmed and his face had a gray, drawn look about it.

"They'll decide soon enough," I laid my hand on his shoulder.

"You ain't like the others, lieutenant. You gotta heart!"

I nodded and continued my inspection. If only he knew how unlike the other officers I truly was. But it wasn't my woman's heart that made me different. I had seen plenty of the males wipe away tears since the fighting began. The difference was, they never spoke of it.

At noon the decision came down. The rebels would be allowed onto the field that afternoon to claim and bury their dead. They would be unarmed and under a white flag. No harm was to come to them so long as they followed the rules. Accordingly, around two o'clock, a line of Southern soldiers filed past our guard directed by their officers. Thirty men wearing an assortment of gray and blue woolens walked onto the field carrying picks and large gray sacks.

"What are them sacks for?" I heard Luigi ask.

"So's they can take a man's letters or photos with them to pass on to the family," Ryan answered.

"What if they don't got family?" Luigi persisted.

Ryan was silent.

I had never taken time to look at rebel soldiers before. In a battle, you don't study the look of a man when he is rushing to kill you. It struck me that the clothing the men were wearing was in a very poor state of repair. More than one of them was dressed in Northern blue, sporting a shirt here or a pair of pants there. I wondered if they had taken the clothes off some poor fallen soldier, or had bought them at a store in a border town. In any case, it was clear the men had less food and provisions than we had. As hungry as we were, our men looked more robust. The Southern men were scrawny and they looked hungry. No man who has been without food will fail to recognize the signs of hunger in another's face.

The Rebs paid us no mind as they walked in formation past the Northern line. There were about a hundred of us lining the path leading to the field, and we starred at them more with curiosity than anger as they shuffled past. We were all pretty much worn out with fighting. Exhaustion and hunger seemed like worse enemies than this sorry bunch of fellahs.

Suddenly, I gasped. The officer passing in front of me was Captain Clydemore! He must have heard me, because he turned and saw me and the look on his face was surprise, and …yes, delight! His face lit up in a smile of greeting, a smile he quickly suppressed as he realized the circumstances of our meeting. He inclined his head in a greeting and continued walking.

"Friend of yours?" Ryan asked, dryly.

"I know him, yes," I replied with as much dignity as I could muster.

"Hrump," he answered. Whether this indicated displeasure at my knowing a Southerner or recognition that I had friendships outside army regulations, I had no idea. Certainly I was not alone in knowing people on the other side. I knew men whose own *brothers* were in opposing armies. Indeed, I had lost count of the stories of cousins and in laws and brothers and fathers and nephews and friends, whom this war had torn asunder.

"Slavery's the work of the devil!" Muller muttered, seemingly to himself.

I looked to see to whom the remark was directed, but Jakob seemed to be addressing the air above the Rebs' heads. In any case, none of them paid him any mind. They kept on walking forward towards their grim and gruesome task.

On the elevated ground above the body-littered field, Northern soldiers kept their eyes- and their weapons fixed on the men in gray and blue. But a strange thing happened as the hot afternoon worn on. Before long, the details of Southern and Northern men digging and burying their dead blended all in together until you could hardly see where the Northern digging began and the Southern digging ended. The dead went into the ground and the living put them there. Wasn't much else you could say about it. The afternoon sun sank lower in the sky and evening drew closer. The savage heat of the midday sun yielded to the more bearable heat of early evening. Still the men sweated and drooped over their back- beating task. In spite of myself, my eyes sought out a certain Southerner, scanning the rows and rows of Southerners in search of officers, in search of a *certain* Southern officer. As if sensing my gaze, Eli stood up, stretched his back and looked over. Then he took a few steps away from his men and stood, gazing into the distance. Slowly I walked onto the field towards him, stopping far enough away that our sentries would not be unduly alarmed.

"Don't let your men see you talking to a Southerner," Eli said, half in jest, as I drew alongside him.

"Reckon it's all right if I check on your progress a little."

We both looked over at the straining men.

"I didn't think we would meet again." I said. For a long time, Eli didn't answer. Silence hung between us.

"I'm sorry." I made to leave.

"I always wish you well," he said suddenly.

I paused. "That's not what you said when we parted."

"I'm sorry. I was confused."

"You were cruel."

"Yes, I was."

I stared at him. His face was turned towards his men, his profile towards me. I noticed his chin was very angular. His black hair was damp with perspiration, and there was a black smudge on his cheek. It might have been a bruise.

He turned toward me. His piercing blue eyes were boring into me. I could hardly breathe.

"I'm not what I seem," I blurted out.

"I don't understand," he answered. I was staring at his mouth.

"...I..."

"Don't..." he said, raising a gloved hand. "We may both be killed."

"I know."

"The chances of us both making it through this war..."

I shrugged.

He bit his lip. The color in his face mounted. I felt his eyes boring into my soul. "If I live, I'll come and find you."

A gentle laugh erupted from somewhere deep inside me. "You don't even know my name!"

He looked confused.

"Runningbrook" I said.

"Your name?"

"My village. Runningbrook. North of Chicago. If I live, I'll go there."

"If I live, I'll find you."

"Your side might win."

"So might yours."

We stared at one another some more.

"I'll find you," he said simply.

"But..."

He shook his head miserably. "It doesn't matter. I have to find you."

He looked at me for what seemed an eternity. An understanding sprang between us in that moment. I felt as if he could see into my soul. My heart leapt. I wanted so badly to tell him the truth! I opened my mouth just as he turned. The words stuck in my throat. I couldn't speak.

I watched as he walked back to his men. Despite the heat and all he must have been through, his gait was still upright and his back was strong above his long, lean legs. I blushed to find myself thinking so, but I couldn't help myself. Heat from some hidden part of myself rushed through me. I swallowed and struggled mightily to shake myself loose from the magical reveries that had captured my spirit and transported me away from these killing fields. For the first time since ma died, I allowed myself to look into the future and see there hope and family. Why could I not tell him? Why could I not share with him that what he felt was love for a *woman*, not for a man; once again, I had allowed the man I loved to go away fearing his feelings were unnatural, and that I was something other than I was! Was it fear? Fear of what he would say? Fear of what the army would do? Fear of everything? No matter my feelings for the man, I found I could not speak. I could no more explain to Eli who I was, than explain to Ryan, or the others. To do so would mean shame-or worse. The army would not tolerate a woman, let alone one masquerading as an officer! I was as trapped in this man's uniform, as we all were in the war.

"If I live, I'll find you," he had said. "If I live, I'll find you."

"Say, lieutenant! Did you read about our latest glorious victory?"

I was dragged out of my reverie by the excited voice of our Powder Monkey. He was sitting with a bunch of men, holding out a well read scrap of newspaper and balancing his dinner bowl on his knees.

"Watch out, Mischa! You'll dip that paper in yer supper!" I managed to say, forced away from thoughts of Eli by Mischa's insistent tone.

"No, really lieutenant. You have to read this!"

The slaughter of so many rebels at one time was proclaimed a glorious victory in the Northern papers, which, on account of so much glory, were once more widely available in the camp. Parades had been held in several Northern cities, declaring this a turning point in the war. Predictions had been made about the conclusion of hostilities, as if skirmishes and battles were not continuing every day in some Southern theatre or another.

Mischa was now fifteen, a fact he had confided to Ryan and myself, with great solemnity after a particularly bloody skirmish a few weeks back. He was especially keen to prove to Ryan –and to me- how very mature and well read he now was. I walked over to where the men had set up camp around a miserable-looking camp fire.

"That's a sorry excuse for a fire!"

"Yes, well, if you can do better, we'll be happy to watch yer! With all due respect, lieutenant!" Ryan added cheerfully.

"One of these days, sergeant!"

"Ah, go on now! Yer know yer love me!"

There were days I thought Ryan was my only salvation in this miserable war, and this was one of them. Thank God for his cheerful loyalty, I thought gloomily. How could I bear another minute of it! Especially knowing that *he...*

"So what do yer think, lieutenant?" Mischa interrupted my reverie for the second time.

I looked down at the crumbled newspaper and scanned the article. "North Wins Another Glorious Victory!" I read aloud. There were several very vulgar comments from the men, then someone passed gas very loudly. That did it! We all started laughing. By this point in the war, the men and I were pretty scathing about the papers and the politicians. Most of us revered the President, but we had no more time for talk about glory. The only truths that mattered to a soldier were conducting himself with honor, staying alive and eating a good meal. We had more chance of the former than the latter. As for staying alive, that was in God's hands.

"Sit yerself down, lieutenant," Ryan offered good-naturedly.

"I think I will, sergeant," I said, availing myself at once of the offer.

Chapter Twenty-One

The years passed. Battle followed glorious battle. At least, that's what the newspapers suggested. We passed around these, "First-hand Dispatches from the Front," as our after-dinner entertainment, officers and men alike taking turns reading aloud of our valiant efforts in this or that skirmish.

"Gee, listen to this!" one man read with what I had come to recognize as a strong Kentucky twang to his voice. "General X comported himself with such distinction on the field, that at the height of the fighting, his men stood and cheered him on as he single-handedly raised the colors over the erstwhile Confederate stronghold."

"Well, I know every word of *that* to be true!" another laughed in what could only be a Chicago accent. "The good general certainly did raise the colors himself, but the "stronghold" in question was the officers' tent where I hear they kept the maps and the liquor. The closest he came to the fighting, was when one of his men was carried to the rear on a stretcher!"

The speech was greeted with gales of laughter. I caught Ryan's eye and was greeted with a surreptitious wink. I paid no mind to what some would consider insubordination. In my eyes, too, these press accounts were fictitious nonsense. They were mindless pulp, created to keep up the spirits of the good folks back home. What made me mad, were the continuous references to the bravery of generals and other high ranking officers. In my mind, it was the sustained efforts of Billy Yank that kept us winning battles, not the self-satisfied smirks of a few over-privileged political appointees.

"Now people, people," Ryan declared. "To be fair, there are a good few officers out there who are brave, resourceful and deserving of their rank."

"Is that so, sergeant?'

"Indeed, it is, my mistrustful corporal. There are indeed a good few officers. Trouble is, they aren't really that good and there are so damn few of them!"

The men fell about laughing. I found myself laughing too.

Ryan came and sat down next to me, cheerfully offering his pipe. I declined.

"You ain't got many vices, lieutenant," he said, taking a long, satisfied pull on his pipe.

"Oh, I got plenty," I smiled. "I just don't show 'em as much."

"Reckon we'll get out of here soon?"

"I darn sure hope so."

We sat and stared into the fire in satisfied companionship. All around us men were playing cards, whittling on pieces of wood or writing letters home, aided by the flickering fires that were doted over camp. Ryan and I were fond of coffee, in my case, and tobacco, in his. Whenever we could, we would sit together after diner, savoring our vices and chewing over the events of the day. Over the past few months it had become clear the war was winding down. The South was getting squeezed into a tighter and tighter corner. Grant had Lee on the run, and it was widely thought by the Northern command that the end was almost in view.

"Will you miss it at all?" Ryan asked absent-mindedly staring into the fire.

"You know it," I answered without hesitation.

Ryan puffed on, with no sign of emotion.

"So will I," he said tersely.

No sane man would have missed the war, and no one but a soldier could have known what he meant by "missing," nor by my answering that I would. But there was a closeness developed by men under fire. It was the camaraderie born of fear and courage and close escapes and wounds and death all around you. Nothing in civilian life could ever match it. No amount of friendship or family could ever duplicate the exhilaration of survival, nor the gratitude felt after placing your life in the hands of your comrade and finding him true to the task, and yourself still alive to acknowledge it. Then too, for me there was another aspect. Back home I was girl, a woman always having to prove herself and find a space in which to act without being told, "you cannot." Out here I was a man. No one ever questioned whether I *could,* or *should,* do a task before me. It was assumed that I *would* and suggested that I *could.* And when I proved that I could, I was promoted. No such chance would ever be afforded my female self. And why? Simply because. To me it made no sense. I knew myself to be as tough, as smart, even as strong as many men. Indeed, having lived in both worlds, I could not say I found the average man any different than the average woman. He was ruder perhaps, a little unkempt in some cases and preoccupied with bodily functions in others. But his morals, his virtue, his doubts and his fears were no different from a woman's. I was at home in both worlds, but preferred the male's, where society seemed to me to be more forgiving and a lot more accepting.

"Yer don't want to go back, do yer?" Ryan said suddenly. I blushed a little, fearing he had read my mind.

He patted my hand. "'s okay fellah, yer secret's safe with me."

"My secret?"

"That you like it here."

"Oh yes, I see."

"There's lots of us do," he went on kindly. "It's the companionship, ain't it…that and the steady food."

"I've gotten fatter," I smiled, patting my stomach, which admittedly was smaller than his.

"A lot of us has," he laughed, sticking out his. "Don't get used to it, lad. We'll all be thinner once we're back on the farm. No one eats like a soldier on the winning side."

"D'you reckon we'll ever meet again?" I asked suddenly, starring off into the distance.

"I reckon we never will," he replied.

For a long time, we sat side by side looking into the fire.

Chapter Twenty-Two

And then, as suddenly as it had begun, the war ended. Word came down that General Lee had surrendered to Grant at Appomattox. Improbable as it seemed, the war was over! We had won!

We greeted the news with stunned disbelief. Inside me was overflowing joy, mixed in equal amount, with nostalgic disbelief. I was at once ecstatic at the thought of going home and buying back the farm, and devastated at the prospect of losing my men. I wanted to go home, but I wanted the rights and privileges of being in command, as I was during the war. I couldn't wait to see Eli and Nate but I couldn't bear to lose my men and especially Ryan.

The day before we were shipped back North, the officers were summoned into the captain's tent. What he told us stunned us into wide- mouthed disbelief.

"Any chance the report is wrong, sir?" someone spluttered.

The captain shook his head. "None whatsoever. I delayed passing on the news until it was verified at the highest levels. The President has been shot!"

"And we're sure he's dead?"

"Yes, son. I'm afraid we are." The captain's voice was smooth and understanding. His eyes were misted over. No one trusted themselves to speak. We left the tent in silence and stumbled back to the men.

"What is it? What's wrong?" Ryan asked, sure hostilities had broken out again.

"They killed Lincoln," I managed in a broken voice. "The miserable curs assassinated Lincoln!"

"We're sure he's dead?" Ryan whispered.

"No doubt about it," I whispered back. Doctor's tried to save him, but they couldn't." Fiercely I drew my sleeve across my eyes. "The bullet entered his brain."

"Oh God, no!" Ryan paled and sat down abruptly.

It was left to individual officers to break the news. Men stood around in shocked disbelief. Tears flowed freely amid wild cries for vengeance. Among the negro volunteers, grief was especially strong. "He was our defender!" one man cried. "Who will fight for us now!"

Grief, anger, disbelief and above all, profound sorrow was our lot for the next several weeks. A pall descended upon our spirits that no success on the battlefield could dispel. We were a country without a leader; a body without a head. We had lost the dearest, truest friend in Washington.

After the mournful train ride across country, the massive crowds, the ceremony, the speeches and the laying to rest, life for the troops took on a monotonous sameness. Day followed dreary day, with nothing ahead to lighten our load. Alongside the sorrow of losing my friends, my companions these five long years, came the realization that the country and, indeed that life, would never be the same. Pulled apart by war, we were now to be pulled apart during peace. Everything was uncertain. Nothing was secure. The ground beneath our feet had been shaken forever.

No sooner had this blow been struck, than I received orders to return home. There was no time to consider the news or decide how to feel about it, it was time to leave! As the train pulled out of the station, I pushed through a swath of my fellow officers and thrust my head out of the window, straining to see Ryan and the others one last time. They had all come to the depot to see me off. As the train started moving, I could see Ryan, scanning the windows, trying to find me. When our eyes locked, he snapped into a smart salute. I did the same. I stood watching his round, familiar figure until it faded and then disappeared entirely out of view.

I stood at the window a very long time, trying to come to terms with what was happening. I was going home. The war was over. I should have been overjoyed. Instead, I was miserable and wracked by doubts. I was traveling back to the life I had left, but I was no longer the same. I was Josef now, not Rebekkah. Rebekkah was forever changed. My life, my self, everything I once had been was strange and unfamiliar to me. I had lived all these years as a man in the company of men. Was I now to forgo all that I had learned and all that I had been, to be a woman, a mere woman, once again? I wasn't sure I could do it. I wasn't even sure I wanted to try. And what would I do without my friends? What of Ryan and Tom and Ernst and all the others? We could never meet again, not if I were Rebekkah, a being unknown to any of them! How would I begin to explain that I was not the man they thought they knew, but another being altogether? How could they ever forgive or accept me?

The train passed through the countryside, carrying me back, mile by awful mile, towards the world of my past, a world that had grown strange to me. Time alone would tell whether I would sink back into the life I had left, or fail miserably in the attempt.

Chapter Twenty-Three

I was able to ride a wagon from Washington to Chicago. There a farmer with an empty wagon and an urge to talk gave me a ride as far north as Midway. I assured the kindly soul I was well used to walking, which is what I did for the remaining twelve miles. It occurred to me I was still dressed as a man. While it seemed normal to me, I realized it might seem strange to those, like my brothers, who had known me as a woman.

The village of Runningbrook hadn't changed much in the years I been gone and seemed to have escaped the worse ravages of war. The village store needed a coat of new paint and the inn was a little worse for wear, but the smithy was larger than when I'd last seen it and there was a grocery store on the town square where one of the town's several beer halls used to be. I stood on the corner and took in my surroundings. Across the way, a few of the town's people were staring, as if trying to place me. None of them seemed quite sure who the young stranger in their midst could be. Finally a gruff older gentleman I recognized as Mr. Lenz came over to me and doffed his hat very politely.

"Well, young gentleman, you look like you're newly returned from the war."

"Yes, sir. That would be right," I said evenly, watching his puzzled expression as he peered into my face.

"You excuse my saying, but you look like one of the Reinhardt boys what went off to fight."

"I do?" I said." I was not going to make this easy for the old man, nor for anyone else for that matter.

"Master Eli and Master Nate volunteered to fight early on," he continued, adding in a quieter voice, "They were very brave."

"Indeed, it sounds that way," I responded seriously. "Are they…?"

"And they had a sister," he continued. Ignoring me. "Purty young thing she was too."

"Oh," I said, continuing the conversation reluctantly. "As for her brothers…"

"Took off shortly after they did," he continued, seemingly oblivious to my side of the conversation. There was nothing for it but to play along.

"What happened to her?" I said impatiently..

"Darned if I know," the old man said glumly. "They say she went west to see her pa, but no one knows fer sure. Just upped and disappeared."

"Fancy that."

I waited for him to continue, but it seemed he had tired himself out. He stood there, head down and hat in hand, seemingly lost in thought.

"And her brothers?" I tried again.

"Beg your pardon?"

"Her brothers?" I insisted, growing more impatient. "What news of them?"

"The farm was took before they left, you know."

"Yes I know." The astute listener would have detected my mistake here but the old man, being lost in a world of his own, gave no hint he had caught on.

"There was no place to come back to, you see."

"Yes, I know," I repeated, louder now. "But what news of the brothers?"

"One of them is living at the old Wessling place."

"Wessling Farm?"

"That's the one," he said, brightening now. "….Say, where are you running off to, young fellah? You haven't said your name!"

If I wasn't exactly running, I sure was walking quickly. Heck, I'd been doing this for five years now. Why would today be different? Besides, this time I was running toward something good. I marched briskly away from that well- remembered village towards the Wessling Farm. Not six miles from the place I had been born and raised, the Wessling Farm was an older building than the house I was raised in by about ten years. The Wesslings and the Reinhardts had been neighbors- friends- for the longest time. Ma said the Wesslings, the Kiests and the Reinhardts came from the same part of Germany. In fact, the Reinhardts and the Kiests were kinfolk. Their great grandfather married our great grandmother's sister, back in the old country. I wondered if my brother had claimed kinship when he came back, so he could stay a while until his siblings returned. I wondered which of my brothers had gotten home first, Eli or Nate?

It was late afternoon when I got there, but the light had not yet faded. The old place looked a little worse for wear, this was not uncommon at the end of the war, as I was soon to discover. Many of the younger, fitter men had gone off to fight and left the women and the weak and infirm to run the farms. It takes a lot of muscle to run a farm, and the women had their hands full raising the children and tending to the crops and animals. In the struggle to stay alive, routine tasks like fixing the roof and putting on a new barn door were low priority.

When I saw the familiar roof peeking through the trees, I straightened my coat and walked down the road towards the little farmhouse, wondering which of my brothers was home and whether he would even recognize me. As I drew closer, old Mrs. Wessling came shuffling into view, her basket filled to overflowing with large white eggs.

"Frau Wessling?" I called out in my woman's voice.

She looked up, saw my man's clothing and gave a start.

"It's me, Frau Wessling. It's Rebekkah!"

"Rebekkah? Rebekkah Reinhardt! Is that you?" She peered at my uniform with interest, then shrugged and yelled for my brother. "Praise be! Praise be! Nate! Nate you come here now! Nate, it's your sister!"

From inside the house I heard a yell of surprise and delight. I expected the door to fly open and lovable Nate to come crashing through. Instead I heard the steady thump, thump, thump of a cane. *Then* the door crashed open and through it my brother Nate came clip-clopping through the door. He was leaning pretty hard on a pair of walking sticks and his right pant leg flapped uselessly where his leg should have been. Then too, his face was all smashed up. His right eye stared off into the distance and his left eye found me, but blinked too rapidly in the setting sun.

"Rebekkah?"

A cry of pain escaped my lips as I stared at the shattered hull of my once handsome brother.

"That bad?" he cried.

"God no, "I lied. "You're alive! Thank God, you're alive!" I ran forward and grabbed him in a bear hug that plain risked knocking him off balance.

"Take it easy there, little sister," he said, clearly embarrassed. "Where have you been? What are you doing dressed like this? Are you home? For good?" His grip was as tight as ever as we clung to one another. I heard the door close quietly behind us as Frau Wessling slipped inside the farmhouse, leaving us be.

Nate pushed me back and stared at me a while, running his fingers across my scar and searching my face for other signs of wear. Apparently satisfied, he nodded towards the porch where a couple of chairs sat waiting for us. I gave him time to propel himself over then took my place at the edge of the seat next to him. I could not take my eyes or my hands from his person, I was that glad to see him.

"What's this all about then?" he asked simply.

"What's what?"

He made a face.

"The clothes?"

"The uniform. Them's lieutenant's stripes."

"I joined the army!"

"You did what!"

"I got myself promoted."

"Pro…But how? You're a…"

"A woman?"

"Yep!" He leaned forward and ran his hand up my leg.
"You're not …you're not a…"

"Git off me!" I yelled. "One more feel and I'm gonna run
you through!"

"I'm your brother, goddamn it! And I wanna see if you're
fit."

"I'm fit! And whatever happened to asking?"

"You ain't exactly bin forthcoming," he snarled.

"You ain't exactly bin around to inform," I snapped back.

We stared one another down a moment, then his shoulders
slumped.

"Whatcha wanna join up fer anyway?"

"Same as you. Earn the money to buy back our farm."

"When d'ya do it?"

"Right after you and Eli left. Bin looking fer you ever since.
You heard from Eli?"

His face twitched and a heavy silence came from him that
chilled my soul.

"Oh God! Not Eli! When? How?"

"Summer of '63 around Washington."

"Oh Nate!" A wave of such intense sorrow came over me
then. I tried to hold it back, but it came upon me in wave after
wave. How long he sat and let me grieve, I cannot say. Finally, I
wiped my face with the back of my sleeve.

"Yer plain wore yourself out," he said after a while.

I was too spent to answer.

"Come inside and lay down for the night. We've got all the time we need to catch up with one another's news. All the time in the world."

Slowly he stood up and motioned me to join him. I slipped my arm under his and with his weight leaning against me, we walked into the house. I turned aside all offers of food and drink. Whatever her thoughts, Frau Wessling never mentioned the uniform. She just fussed around me a bit, directing me to a straw mattress in the corner and covering me with a home-made quilt. I was too spent to thank her. I nodded and mumbled and closed my eyes. I felt myself sinking deeper and deeper into an exhausted rest. I awoke late the following day. Frau Wessling was out with her hens again and Nate was sitting at the kitchen table, reading through some papers.

"You awake now sleeping beauty?" he asked in the tone I remembered from before the war.

"Awake enough to whip you," I replied, "no matter that you've lost a leg."

"Yer all heart, sister of mine. Or are you my brother now?"

"Sister. And I can still whip you!"

All that day and the next we sat at the kitchen table, talking of the war and of campaigns and battles lost and won. All three of us had been in light artillery units and our experiences of the war had been remarkably alike, albeit I had been an officer and my brothers not.

"Did you get to see Eli?" I asked with some hesitation.

"We were in the same company, sis," he answered sadly. "I saw the shot that killed him. And the man that killed him die."

"By your hand?" I couldn't help asking.

"By another's sword," he answered quietly. "It all happened so fast."

"Did he…?"

"There wasn't time. One minute he was there. The next minute he was gone."

"How…?"

"Shot through with shrapnel. Dropped like a stone. Never even cried out."

"You were there?"

Nate was silent. I looked up to see him struggling for composure. As I reached out to put my hand over his, he looked up. "It was me he died saving," Nate said miserably. "He pushed me aside and it got him instead!"

"Oh, Nate!"

"Now ye hate me!"

"Hate you? You're my brother. You're both my brothers!"

"He died saving me!"

"You'd have done the same for him. And I for you. That's our way and you know it, Nate. It wasn't your fault!"

"It's those Southern ditch hunters!" Nate wiped his face with the back of his sleeve and sniffed. "All this time in the goddamn army and you still don't cuss!"

I laughed at that. "Ma could forgive me the clothing, but never the cussing! I guess I just daren't!"

"How d'yer git away with it then? Being a woman 'n all?"

He blushed a little at the thought of it, and I fought back a smile.

"Some day when you're old enough, I might tell you!" I whispered conspiratorially.

"Old enough!" he spluttered. "I'm darn well older 'n you!"

"And I outrank you, don't forget!"

"Yer not likely to let me!"

"Darn right I'm not!"

In the days that followed, a new pattern of living came about. The first time I removed my soldier's uniform, it was taken and washed and mysteriously disappeared. In its place were a bunch of dresses and a couple of dozen pinafores. I found the clothing tedious and took to wearing Nate's old clothing every chance I got. Nate and the old woman were clearly disturbed by my distain for woman's dress. But I found the restrictions of women's clothing unbearable after the freedom of striding the world in pants and shirts. I wasn't going to argue. I just wouldn't comply. Finally, they tired of fighting me and we compromised. I agreed to dress like a woman in town and they agreed to stop harassing me. I was used to being in charge and I guess they knew it. I would wear what I pleased around the farm.

In time, my brother's haggard face took on a softer hue. Good food and the lack of danger allowed him to settle down and eat proper meals. He filled out a bit and even his bad eye seemed to work better. We discussed the war a little less. One day, we were sitting on the porch after a morning's work and I caught him starring.

"What are you looking at, brother?" I smiled, catching hold of his hand.

"I was wondering how you did it, all those days living among men?"

I thought a while. And then I said, "It wasn't all that different from living on the farm."

271

"How so?"

I let go his hand and settled back in my chair. "Well, for one thing, I grew up with brothers. I was always fighting to get my share of everything: attention, respect…food! You and Eli were always taking the last chicken leg, or the best bit of meat."

"We did not!"

"You did so!"

"Then too, you were always telling me you were better than me. Better shots, better farmers, better hunters…I had to prove you were wrong."

"You were always the best shot among us. You could drop a rabbit half a mile away," Nate said ruefully. "You made me feel stupid. A man's 'sposed to be better at that sort of thing."

"Why?"

"What d'you mean, why? Just is, that's all."

I leaned forward. "That's what I mean! It's stupid! Why's it gotta be that way?"

He shook his head. "You sure are peculiar!"

"Because I ask questions?"

"Because you wanna stir things up!"

"Maybe some things *ought* to be stirred!"

He made a face and gave a low laugh. "Go on. How d'you get yourself promoted?"

"Nothing much, I guess. Just doing my job."

"Doing your job! What dyer mean? Following orders?"

"Well, yes. But seeing what needed doin' too."

"How d'dyer do that?"

272

I thought about it for a minute. "It's hard to say. You just see what needs to be done."

"In a battle you mean?"

"Yes."

He sniffed. "I don't like having a man fer a sister…"

"Well that's …"

He held up his hand…."but I want you to know I'm right proud of yer."

"Thank you, Nate!"

"I hope you killed a lot of that Southern scum!"

"Nate!"

"That's what the army's for, ain't it?"

"That's not what you said when you and Eli joined up!"

"That's what I say now that I've been in it!"

"Killing's only part of it!"

"What else is there? Southern scum!" He spat on the ground.

"They're men just like us!"

"The hell they are! Wish we'd killed every one of them!"

"They were doin' what they thought right. Just like we were!"

"The hell they were!" He stood up, trembling, and his face grew a wild shade of red. "They killed your brother. They did this to me! They scarred your face! They took everything from us! And you say they were just like us!"

I tried to take his hand. He snatched it violently away. "They…they killed our brother…they….hurt you …and me… but Nate, that's what happens in war. We killed their brothers too! We took their fathers and their husbands. We took their pride. We won, Nate! They lost the war!"

"They started it!" he snared. "They started it! I hope they rot in hell for what they done!"

He turned and swung away as fast as his leg and his cane would take him. I watched as he made his away towards the road, moving awkwardly, his stride made uneven by haste and temper. His pain was unnerving. There was nothing I could say. I let him be.

I sat back down. I thought of Ryan, and Petersen, and the Southern captain with the crinkly eyes…"It's about the men," I thought. "It's about the men you fight with, and the truths you believe in enough to die for." My brother's words came back to me. They had taken my brother. They had taken Eli's leg. And Virgil! They had killed Virgil in front of me! I remembered the look on his face as he breathed his last. I remembered the screams and the stench of fear and death all around us on the battlefield. I thought of all the killing and dying and the countless acts of courage and bravery. And I couldn't hate them. None of them! Not the Southerners who tried to kill me. Not the Southerners I tried to kill. Not any of it. To my dying breath, I couldn't explain it. But I couldn't hate. Not any more.

"Hate led to this war," I said to no one. "Hatred and anger and different ideas about things…."

"So what's to be done?" the trees seemed to ask me. "What's to be done when men disagree?"

"We talk, then we argue, then we fight," I concluded. "We always have…and we always will."

"And then…?"

"And then the living come home."

An image of Captain Clydemore flooded my mind.

"They're people, just like us," I said with certainty, "people just like us!"

"So, why'd we fight them?" the trees asked.

"Because we had to."

Chapter Twenty-Four

Nothing more was said about the South that day, and I felt it best to let the subject be. My feelings on the subject were as intense as Nate's, and I saw from his demeanor that my brother had no patience for my opinions. I resolved never to bring the subject up, but the next day after dinner, my brother raised it again. We were sitting side by side on the porch, watching the sun sink lower in the sky, when he suddenly asked, "What was it like, killing men, you being a girl 'n all?"

"I didn't think about it, Nate. I was doing my job."

The light in the fields was slowly changing from bright to dusk. Night was creeping in, but the air was still balmy. A feeling of contentment washed through me.

"Your job?"

I tried to remain even- tempered. I didn't want to fight. "I was a soldier. An officer. I had my orders. And my men to think about."

"Your men!"

"Yes, my men. I had to keep them safe. And I had to do my job. You ask me what it's like to do things as a woman. I can't tell you. I've always been one!"

"Except…"

"Come on, Nate! I've always been a better shot than you and Eli. And I handle a plough just as well as you do! I loved every part of being on a farm! The only part I didn't like was what you all called 'woman's work.' I didn't like *that*!"

"Why not, sis? You're not…"

"I like men, Nate! I don't want to *be* one! I just want …"

"To act like one!" He shook his head again. "I don't get it!"

"That's not it! I don't want to *act* like one!"

"What then?"

I tried once more to explain. "Men get to do things!"

"Such as…?"

"Going to war!"

"And that's so good?"

"It's better than sitting at home waiting!"

"You think so?"

"I know so!"

"You're my sister, Beck, but you sure are peculiar!"

"I want something more than sitting at home and waiting."

"Hmm. My sister, the rebel killer!"

"Don't call me that!"

"That's what you were."

"They're people …just like us!"

"There you go again!"

"You brought it up!"

"Maybe I did!"

"I don't hate them, Nate."

"Well, I do! I hate the whole miserable lot of them and I wished we had pursued them to their homes and killed every last one of them! I would go down there now and do it myself if I… if this…."

"Oh Nate!" I reached out my hand. He pushed it away.

"Don't you feel sorry for me! Don't you dare feel sorry for me!"

"I don't have to! You feel sorry enough for yourself!" The words were out before I could stop them. He gave me a look of utter fury.

"Easy for you to say with your lieutenant's stripes and your two good legs and your fancy opinions!"

"Nate!"

"Get off me!"

"I don't want to see you this way!"

"What, the one legged freak?"

"No! It's not your lost leg that bothers me. It's your lost…."

"What?"

"Innocence!"

"Innocence? Are you out of your mind? They butchered us. They killed our brother! They took my leg! And you talk of innocence?"

"They suffered as much as we. Maybe more! They're… we're …they're our brothers…"

"Don't you *dare* say that to me. Don't you *dare*! *My* brother's lyin' in the ground near Washington and my sister's gone out of her mind and those bastards will never, NEVER be brothers to me…" he spat. "Do you hear me?"

His face was so distorted it hurt me to look at it. I knew that nothing…nothing I said would change his mind. His heart was as hardened against the South as many on their side were surely hardened against us in the North. Our country was as torn after the war as it had been during it.

"What's to be? What's to become of us? I stared out as the trees slowly darkened and darkness settled upon the land once more.

Things were not the same between Nate and I after this. We never spoke of the war again, but it hung between us like an unseen wall dividing our hearts as surely as if we argued every day. Frau Wessling tried to patch things up, not understanding the source of our grievance or the reason for our growing silences. But despite her cheerful efforts, and her attempts to make life comfortable and pleasant in our new home, the two of us kept an obvious distance from one another.

I began to wonder about our long term future. Frau Wessling was clearly happy with our presence. With no remaining family of her own and in her advancing years, she was glad enough of two strong backs around the farm. And despite the loss of one good leg, Nate was a strong and skilful handler of the horse and plough. There was no chance of regaining our old farm, no matter that we had enough money between us now for the down payment. Georg Kessler had sold it outright to a settler from the east, a Russian man with an unpronounceable name and a brood of hungry mouths to feed. He told us he had no intention of selling the homestead, and wished us well since we were now neighbors. Our future, if it were to be in these parts, clearly rested with the Wessling property. Since Nate had gotten here first, it fell to me to move on. It became clear to me, that was what I would have to do. But it seems fate had other plans for me.

Life on the farm settled into routine. Despite our differences and my growing conviction that I had to move on, my brother and I made a pretty impressive team and the farm began to blossom and grow. We made it a point never again to discuss the war. Nate's heart was bitter; his America was forever divided between the brave Northern soldiers and the treacherous Southern rebels. Meanwhile, my country was united again, firm in the belief that while slavery was wrong, we were all just Americans, doing our duty. Some of our neighbors tried to find out where I'd been for the duration of the war, and how I came to return in a borrowed officer's uniform. We never answered their questions, and never spoke of the war, and in time their questions died away. Whatever they thought and however they felt, they kept it to themselves, and that was fine by us. Visitors to the farm got accustomed to my wearing pants, and working boots in the fields. As long as I turned up in church wearing dresses and smiling pretty smiles, they kept their thoughts to themselves, and so did I.

For her part, in return for help around the farm, Frau Wessling forgave us rent and made Nate and I equal partners in the holding. Her brother and her only son had died at the start of the war. Being a widow, she was well pleased of the company, and of the chance to live out the rest of her years with the comfort of family around her. On a visit to the market town of Granger, we all stopped by at the lawyer's office and she signed over the farm to Nate and me, her only request being, to live out her days in her own home with us. We were overcome by the generosity and love shown us by this dear old woman. As long as I was there, I labored alongside Nate to make her remaining years as comfortable and pleasant as they could possibly be.

Some of the money we had earned as soldiers went to very good use. We bought a plough, several horses and a brood of pigs so special, that in time they won all sorts of prizes and earned us quite a name for ourselves. Only one thing marred our happiness then, and that was the fact we lived together as man and sister. It was not exactly the life we had pictured for ourselves, as we moved towards the end of youth. Nate solved that problem when he started consoling Eli's fiancée, the lonely and distraught Miss Kaltenbach. In time, Lena learned to love the younger brother maybe as dearly as she had loved the older, so I came to know her as sister-in-law after all. She and Nate inherited her father's farm, and when Frau Wessling joined her husband beneath the elm in the garden, the Wessling farm fell to me. I became as much a land and pig farmer as any man in the county!

As months passed into years, thoughts of Captain Clydemore faded into the past, along with the war. He was but a memory now, a long lost hope of something I would perhaps never have. Several men came a courting, and were duly dismissed with polite but firm indifference. I had no need of a man to keep me, for the farm was long since successful. I had company enough with Nate and his family living close by. And though there were things Nate and I could not and would not discuss, the love of a wife and children softened his heart enough that it made room once more for me. Between Nate's growing family and my pigs and the farm, I had work enough to occupy me. Why then did I sometimes wish for more? I had never known a man's love, and besides Captain Clydemore, had never yearned for it. He alone had wakened something within me. He alone had captured my heart.

After the war ended, I had made many inquiries of the captain, his unit and his plantation, all to no avail. Army records were scattered and incomplete and those in power had no wish to share what they had with a mere woman, let alone with a woman with no obvious connection to the officer in question.

"Why, madam, would you wish to know the whereabouts of a Southern slaveholder?" That was the common response to repeated inquiries. Short of traveling through the South to find him, I had no hope of further contact. And my wish to find my Southern captain had to be measured against the odds of never finding him, and of losing my livelihood trying.

Three years went by. I was now a mature woman of twenty-five with a thriving farm and respect in the community. Those who had known of my days in the army were silent on my behalf. I packed away my uniform and memories along with mama's locket. From time to time, I took it out, dreaming of the day I might pass it down to a daughter of my own. But my daydreams faded. Gradually I took it out less and less until, at last, I didn't take it out at all. As for my "eccentric" preference for men's attire, it was accepted by most, along with the weather and the price of grain.

One warm Saturday morning in May, I drove the horse and buggy into Runningbrook to buy some brushes for the sow and her litter. A group of townsfolk were gathered on the corner, sounding agitated. As I parked the wagon and walked across the square, I heard raised voices and I sensed the agitation and unrest even before I could make out the words.

"…think you can come up here and cause trouble, you are much mistaken."

"….how do you have the nerve to show your face around here?"

I could not make out the individual to whom the words were addressed, but whatever was said in response seemed to placate some in the crowd. Amidst the grumbling and shouting there were cries of, "Well said!" and, "Let the fellah be!"

"I'll be damned if my son died fightin' his kind, so he can come up here and make a mockery of us all!" someone cried in an agitated state.

"I assure you, sir, I mean no disrespect. I am looking for a friend. That's all!" I thought my heart would stop beating when I heard that voice. Pushing my way through the crowd, I came upon Eli, standing hat in hand before the crowd. Mr. Pearson's face was pressed almost as close to his, as mine would wish to be.

"Mr. Pearson, stop!" I heard myself cry out, "That gentleman is my friend!"

All eyes turned towards me, including Eli's. The crowd murmured. Some evil stares were shot in my direction, but I paid them no mind. My eyes were seeking out a different face. The crowd broke into smaller groups and slowly drifted away, Pearson spitting an ugly wad onto the ground as he passed by. One by one they walked away, until no one was left standing outside the store save Eli and me.

With a beating heart, I swept the bonnet off my head and let it fall behind me. My hair, long since grown back, tumbled down. I looked at Eli. Thinner now and paler too, he was dressed in once fine civilian clothes, a size or two large for his slender frame. He stood rigidly, his eyes wider than saucers. Finally, he spoke.

"Jo…Josef?"

I bit my lip and nodded miserably.

"You're a woman?"

"Uh huh"

"You were always a woman?"

"Uh huh"

He stared at me without speaking. His chest was moving violently up and down. Then he spun on his heel without a word.

"Eli, please! Let me explain!" I cried, grasping his arm as I ran after him.

He wrenched his arm away and kept walking.

I watched him go, my own heart pounding uncontrollably.

Abruptly he turned and marched back to me, his face a dark mask of fury.

"You were in the army?" He shook his head violently as if trying to shake it all into making sense. "I don't understand!"

"I tried...I wanted to tell you!"

"All that time...All that time!!! You let me think you were a man!"

"*Everyone* thought I was a man!"

"You couldn't have told *me*?"

"I tried...I wanted...When...*how* could I have told you?"

His face darkened. "You let me believe that I ...that I..."

I reached for his arm. "Eli..."

He snatched it away. "Don't even *think* of touching me! All this time, I struggled against...because I thought..." Finally he exploded. "You lied! You lied to me!"

"How could I not!" I cried miserably. "I never meant to lie...not to *you*! It was an accident! A twist of fate!"

"I'm getting out of here!" Eli said angrily.

He started down the street. Shamelessly, I called after him, "Eli! Eli!"

But he kept walking. Miserably, I turned to walk back across the square. He caught up with me halfway across. I was spun around by strong arms, then swept against his chest, his arms tight around me and his mouth pressing down onto mine. His mouth felt hard and soft all at the same time. It was the strangest, most wonderful sensation I have ever felt! Then I was clinging onto him and kissing him back and laughing and talking and touching his face and murmuring things and hearing him murmur them in return. I thought I should burst from pure happiness.

"Are you a woman now?" he murmured against me.

"What do you think?" I answered.

He kissed me some more. "I think I'll marry you before you change your mind again!"

"You're a Southerner!" I said hotly.

"That doesn't seem to bother you." he said simply. "Besides, I'm moving North!"

"What if I won't have you?" I demanded.

"Are you saying you won't?" he held me from him and stared into my eyes.

"The neighbors won't like you!"

"I'm not marrying *them*!"

"It won't be easy, winning them over!"

"So far, this has been easy?"

"And your family?" I murmured, "What will they say?"

"I'm here," he answered. "They're not."

"Oh."

"Maybe they'll like the grandchildren!"

I felt myself blushing.

"That's one thing you can't manage as a man!"

"Yes, well…." I was not anxious to discuss such matters! "I won't obey you," I declared, recovering my dignity. "I'll obey no man!"

"I'm sure you won't… Mrs. Clydemore!"

His look was enough to make me blush. I wasn't sure where to direct my eyes.

"I can't believe… all that time…you were a woman!" he exclaimed. He grasped my hand and impulsively kissed it!

Perhaps being a woman isn't so bad after all! I mused. I had no idea what had come over me that morning, dressing as a female for a trip into town. And now look what it had brought me! "Eli?"

"Yes, dear?" he murmured, looking up from my hand.

"I hope you like pigs!"

About the Author

S. J. Schinleber is a full-time teacher and writer living in the Chicago area. Born in England, she is a lover of history, whose work includes, most recently, the story of a suburban Chicago fire department, focusing on the lives and experiences of the men who fight fire and rescue those in need. She is working on a second novel about the Civil War an extract of which begins on page 293.

A Promise of
Redemption

Prologue

It was around noon on a hot, July day in the 1840s, the exact date escapes me at this point in my story because my eyes are focused entirely on the face of the young woman which is, at this moment, contorted in agony. Indeed, as she holds fast to the reins and fixes her eyes on the distant forest, her head is thrown violently backward, as if jabs of pain were coursing through her body. The horse swerves abruptly with the jerk of the reins, but, being well-versed in the ways of man-and woman- he moves back to the center of the road and races forwards in the direction they are traveling. The woman recovers and fixes her eyes on the road, her arms and body rigid with purpose. A fine sheen of perspiration covers her face and neck and the collar of her dress droops where the damp has seeped into it. She wipes her glistening face with the arm of her sleeve, grips the reins tightly and urges the straining beast to work even harder in pursuit of the approaching goal. It seems to be her intention to reach the forest and to find shelter in its cool embrace and hidden spaces.

Her body contorts again and she cries aloud, doubling over on the wagon bench and leaving the reins to droop limply at her sides. Confused, the horse slows, but the dear creature continues forwards. They are close to the woods now and the woman can barely remain in place, so relentless are the pains.

Reaching the cover of the first trees, she shivers uncontrollably and directs the horse off the path towards a copse of trees barely out of sight of the road. There she half tumbles, half climbs from the wagon, falling the last few feet onto the ground. Coughing and gasping, she lays upon her back on the grassy floor barely aware of the fallen branches that claw at her beneath the sodden dress. Her legs are splayed open, forced apart by the pressure of the life that will escape her now. The pain and the pressure force her to cry out and the sound echoes through the trees.

Her head is thrust back on the forest floor and her eyes squeezed shut against the brightness of the summer sky that peeps through the branches as if wanting to share in the glorious arrival of innocent human life. No such joy informs the heart of the young woman, alone, in her agony and fear, save for the faithful pony, sweating in his traces. Convulsed by the rhythmic pains of young life determined to be born, the woman screams and twists away from the agony that hammers through her and will not be denied. No midwife attends to her terrified needs; no mother's hand soothes the sweat-covered brow; no cloths await the blood-covered baby. In the lonely and silent forest, hidden creatures listen to the noisy arrival, but no human voice cries out and no human hand stays hers when she wraps the wriggling mass of flesh into the bundle of her torn and stained clothing and thrusts the painful mess under a nearby bush.

Staggering to her feet, naked beneath the leaf-covered garment, the woman fixes her hair, smooths her dress and climbs back onto the wagon, her head filled with the story she will tell of an overhanging branch and a vicious fall from the safety of the wagon. As she lifts the reins, she seems to hesitate, as if some divine messenger pleads with her to reconsider. But the moment passes. The woman lifts the reins and, without a backward glance, turns the wagon around and directs the horse to retread the path over which they have lately traveled. Whether anyone else will soon ride into that shaded clearing, she cannot say. But as she drives away, a man steps out of the shadows where he has been hiding and stares after the woman, his face contorted with grim fury.